best of

APEX MAGAZINE

v.1

WWW.APEX-MAGAZINE.COM

Best of

APEX MAGAZINE

Edited By
Jason Sizemore & Lesley Conner

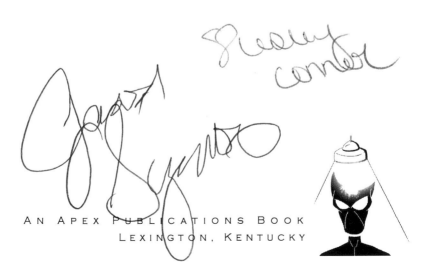

An Apex Publications Book
Lexington, Kentucky

This anthology is a work of fiction. All the characters and events portrayed in these stories are either fictitious or are used fictitiously.

Best of Apex Magazine: Volume One © 2016 by Jason Sizemore & Lesley Conner

ISBN: 978-1-937009-37-3
Cover Art "Life is a Dance in the Rain" © Adrian Borda
Title Design by Justin Stewart

Published by Apex Publications, LLC
PO Box 24323
Lexington, K.Y. 40524

Visit us at www.apexbookcompany.com.

(Lesley)

For Brian, Bradley, and Quinn, who support me no matter what challenge I undertake.

(Jason)

For Susan, Lindsey, and Ryan, who deal with my obsessions like champs.

CONTENTS

FOREWORD

Lesley Conner
Apex Magazine, Managing Editor

WHEN JASON AND I DECIDED to publish *Best of Apex Magazine: Volume 1*, I knew that I wanted to include the stories that made me feel, the ones that made me cry or laugh out loud. The ones that left me gasping for breath as I read the final words. Those are the stories that stay with me no matter how much slush I read or how many issues of *Apex Magazine* we publish.

But what if my favorite stories—the ones that I want to drag out in front of my friends and shout "Look! Read this! It is amazing!"—weren't Jason's? For a few days this thought nagged me. We hadn't discussed *how* we would select the stories and I fretted that it would be a battle of editorial wills.

I shouldn't have let this thought worry me; Jason and I have been reading and discussing slush together for well over a year now and most of the time we get excited about the same stories. But still I worried. For one thing, Jason is much more familiar with the stories published in Apex's early days than I am. He accepted and published them while I was still unaware of the amazingness that is Apex. So my first order of business was to go back and reread all of the fiction from before I was directly involved with the magazine. This quickly became overwhelming because 1) there is so much of it, and 2) the quality is all phenomenal.

Then I started making a list of all the stories that really stood out to me. The ones that I could read over and over again and they would continue to be magical with each reading. I knew Jason was making a similar list and that we would eventually compare them.

When we finally sat down to hash out the final table of contents, our vision for the anthology matched up really well. After adding all the stories we both had on our lists, those that were award winning and nominated, and the ones selected by our readers as Story of the Year, there were only four spots left to discuss. Despite my fears, filling those spots was easy. For the sake of excitement, I wish I could say there was struggle, one of us threatening or offering the other something in exchange for getting in a story the other didn't like, but that just isn't so. The conversation went something like this:

"What about this story?"

"Oh, yes! I've always wanted to give that story more attention. What about this one?"

"I love that story. Of course!"

We're so boring.

But boring or not, I am damn proud of the anthology we have put together. We have a good mix of established authors who are being nominated for and winning awards, and newer authors whose names may not be well known, but whose writing blew us away. The stories are beautiful, emotional, and often dark; in my opinion, they encapsulate the essence of what *Apex Magazine* is.

So there you have it. The *Best of Apex Magazine*. With a lineup this remarkable, I can't wait to see what the next six years brings.

December 1st, 2015
Smithsburg, Maryland

JACKALOPE WIVES

Ursula Vernon

Nebula Award Winner
WSFA Small Press Award Winner
Cóyotl Award Winner
World Fantasy Award Nominee

THE MOON CAME UP AND the sun went down. The moonbeams went shattering down to the ground and the jackalope wives took off their skins and danced.

They danced like young deer pawing the ground, they danced like devils let out of hell for the evening. They swung their hips and pranced and drank their fill of cactus-fruit wine.

They were shy creatures, the jackalope wives, though there was nothing shy about the way they danced. You could go your whole life and see no more of them than the flash of a tail vanishing around the backside of a boulder. If you were lucky, you might catch a whole line of them outlined against the sky, on the top of a bluff, the shadow of horns rising off their brows.

And on the half-moon, when new and full were balanced across the saguaro's thorns, they'd come down to the desert and dance.

The young men used to get together and whisper, saying they were gonna catch them a jackalope wife. They'd lay belly down at the edge of the bluff and look down on the fire and the dancing shapes—and they'd go away aching, for all the good it did them.

For the jackalope wives were shy of humans. Their lovers were jackrabbits and antelope bucks, not human men. You couldn't even get too close or they'd take fright and run away. One minute you'd see them kicking their heels up and hear them laugh, then the music would freeze and they'd all look at you with their eyes wide and their ears up-swept.

The next second, they'd snatch up their skins and there'd be nothing left but a dozen skinny she-rabbits running off in all directions, and a campfire left that wouldn't burn out 'til morning.

It was uncanny, sure, but they never did anybody any harm. Grandma Harken, who lived down past the well, said that the jacka-lopes were the daughters of the rain and driving them off would bring on the drought. People said they didn't believe a word of it, but when you live in a desert, you don't take chances.

When the wild music came through town, a couple of notes skittering on the sand, then people knew the jackalope wives were out. They kept the dogs tied up and their brash sons occupied. The town got into the habit of having a dance that night, to keep the boys firmly fixed on human girls and to drown out the notes of the wild music.

Now, it happened there was a young man in town who had a touch of magic on him. It had come down to him on his mother's side, as happens now and again, and it was worse than useless.

A little magic is worse than none, for it draws the wrong sort of attention. It gave this young man feverish eyes and made him sullen. His grandmother used to tell him that it was a miracle he hadn't been drowned as a child, and for her he'd laugh, but not for anyone else.

He was tall and slim and had dark hair and young women found him fascinating.

This sort of thing happens often enough, even with boys as mortal as dirt. There's always one who learned how to brood early and often, and always girls who think they can heal him.

Eventually the girls learn better. Either the hurts are petty little things and they get tired of whining or the hurt's so deep and wide that they drown in it. The smart ones heave themselves back to shore and the slower ones wake up married with a husband who lies around and suffers in their direction. It's part of a dance as old as the jackalopes themselves.

But in this town at this time, the girls hadn't learned and the boy hadn't yet worn out his interest. At the dances, he leaned on the wall with his hands in his pockets and his eyes glittering. Other young men eyed him with dislike. He would slip away early, before the dance was ended, and never marked the eyes that followed him and wished that he would stay.

He himself had one thought and one thought only—to catch a jackalope wife.

They were beautiful creatures, with their long brown legs and their bodies splashed orange by the firelight. They had faces like no mortal woman and they moved like quicksilver and they played music that got down into your bones and thrummed like a sickness.

And there was one—he'd seen her. She danced farther out from the others and her horns were short and sharp as sickles. She was the last one to put on her rabbit skin when the sun came up. Long after the music had stopped, she danced to the rhythm of her own long feet on the sand.

(And now you will ask me about the musicians that played for the jackalope wives. Well, if you can find a place where they've been dancing, you might see something like sidewinder tracks in the dust, and more than that I cannot tell you. The desert chews its secrets right down to the bone.)

So the young man with the touch of magic watched the jackalope wife dancing and you know as well as I do what young men dream about. We will be charitable. She danced a little apart from her fellows, as he walked a little apart from his.

Perhaps he thought she might understand him. Perhaps he found her as interesting as the girls found him.

Perhaps we shouldn't always get what we think we want.

And the jackalope wife danced, out past the circle of the music and the firelight, in the light of the fierce desert stars.

Grandma Harken had settled in for the evening with a shawl on her shoulders and a cat on her lap when somebody started hammering on the door.

"Grandma! Grandma! Come quick—open the door—oh god, Grandma, you have to help me —"

She knew that voice just fine. It was her own grandson, her daughter Eva's boy. Pretty and useless and charming when he set out to be.

She dumped the cat off her lap and stomped to the door. What trouble had the young fool gotten himself into?

"Sweet Saint Anthony," she muttered, "let him not have gotten some fool girl in a family way. That's just what we need."

She flung the door open and there was Eva's son and there was a girl and for a moment her worst fears were realized.

Then she saw what was huddled in the circle of her grandson's arms, and her worst fears were stomped flat and replaced by far greater ones.

"Oh Mary," she said. "Oh, Jesus, Mary, and Joseph. Oh blessed Saint Anthony, you've caught a jackalope wife."

Her first impulse was to slam the door and lock the sight away.

Her grandson caught the edge of the door and hauled it open. His knuckles were raw and blistered. "Let me in," he said. He'd been crying and there was dust on his face, stuck to the tracks of tears. "Let me in, let me in, oh god, Grandma, you have to help me, it's all gone wrong —"

Grandma took two steps back, while he half-dragged the jackalope into the house. He dropped her down in front of the hearth and grabbed for his grandmother's hands. "Grandma —"

She ignored him and dropped to her knees. The thing across her hearth was hardly human. "What have you done?" she said. "What did you do to her?"

"Nothing!" he said, recoiling.

"Don't look at that and tell me 'Nothing!' What in the name of our lord did you do to that girl?"

He stared down at his blistered hands. "Her skin," he mumbled. "The rabbit skin. You know."

"I do indeed," she said grimly. "Oh yes, I do. What did you do, you damned young fool? Caught up her skin and hid it from her to keep her changing?"

The jackalope wife stirred on the hearth and made a sound between a whimper and a sob.

"She was waiting for me!" he said. "She knew I was there! I'd been—we'd—I watched her, and she knew I was out there, and she let me get up close—I thought we could talk —"

Grandma Harken clenched one hand into a fist and rested her forehead on it.

"I grabbed the skin—I mean—it was right there—she was watching—I thought she *wanted* me to have it —"

She turned and looked at him. He sank down in her chair, all his grace gone.

"You have to burn it," mumbled her grandson. He slid down a little further in her chair. "You're supposed to burn it. Everybody knows. To keep them from changing."

"Yes," said Grandma Harken, curling her lip. "Yes, that's the way of it, right enough." She took the jackalope wife's shoulders and turned her toward the lamp light.

She was a horror. Her hands were human enough, but she had a jackrabbit's feet and a jackrabbit's eyes. They were set too wide apart in a human face, with a cleft lip and long rabbit ears. Her horns were short, sharp spikes on her brow.

The jackalope wife let out another sob and tried to curl back into a ball. There were burnt patches on her arms and legs, a long red weal down her face. The fur across her breasts and belly was singed. She stank of urine and burning hair.

"What did you do?"

"I threw it in the fire," he said. "You're supposed to. But she screamed—she wasn't supposed to scream—nobody said they screamed—and I thought she was dying, and I didn't want to *hurt* her—I pulled it back out —"

He looked up at her with his feverish eyes, that useless, beautiful boy, and said "I didn't *want* to hurt her. I thought I was supposed to—I gave her the skin back, she put it on, but then she fell down—it wasn't supposed to work like that!"

Grandma Harken sat back. She exhaled very slowly. She was calm. She was going to be calm, because otherwise she was going to pick up the fire poker and club her own flesh and blood over the head with it.

And even that might not knock some sense into him. Oh, Eva, Eva, my dear, what a useless son you've raised. Who would have thought he had so much ambition in him, to catch a jackalope wife?

"You goddamn stupid fool," she said. Every word slammed like a shutter in the wind. "Oh, you goddamn stupid fool. If you're going to catch a jackalope wife, you burn the hide down to ashes and never mind how she screams."

"But it sounded like it was hurting her!" he shot back. "You weren't there! She screamed like a dying rabbit!"

"Of course it hurts her!" yelled Grandma. "You think you can have your skin and your freedom burned away in front of you and not scream? Sweet mother Mary, boy, think about what you're doing! Be cruel or be kind, but don't be both, because now you've made a mess you can't clean up in a hurry."

She stood up, breathing hard, and looked down at the wreck on her hearth. She could see it now, as clear as if she'd been standing there. The fool boy had been so shocked he'd yanked the burning skin back out. And the jackalope wife had one thought only and pulled on the burning hide —

Oh yes, she could see it clear.

Half gone, at least, if she was any judge. There couldn't have been more than few scraps of fur left unburnt. He'd waited through at least one scream—or no, that was unkind.

More likely he'd dithered and looked for a stick and didn't want to grab for it with his bare hands. Though by the look of his hands, he'd done just that in the end.

And the others were long gone by then and couldn't stop her. There ought to have been one, at least, smart enough to know that you didn't put on a half-burnt rabbit skin.

"Why does she look like that?" whispered her grandson, huddled into his chair.

"Because she's trapped betwixt and between. You did that, with your goddamn pity. You should have let it burn. Or better yet, left her alone and never gone out in the desert at all."

"She was beautiful," he said. As if it were a reason.

As if it mattered.

As if it had ever mattered.

"Get out," said Grandma wearily. "Tell your mother to make up a poultice for your hands. You did right at the end, bringing her here, even if you made a mess of the rest, from first to last."

He scrambled to his feet and ran for the door.

On the threshold, he paused, and looked back. "You—you can fix her, right?"

Grandma let out a high bark, like a bitch-fox, barely a laugh at all. "No. No one can fix this, you stupid boy. This is broken past mending. All I can do is pick up the pieces."

He ran. The door slammed shut, and left her alone with the wreckage of the jackalope wife.

She treated the burns and they healed. But there was nothing to be done for the shape of the jackalope's face, or the too-wide eyes, or the horns shaped like a sickle moon.

At first, Grandma worried that the townspeople would see her, and lord knew what would happen then. But the jackalope wife was the color of dust and she still had a wild animal's stillness. When somebody called, she lay flat in the garden, down among the beans, and nobody saw her at all.

The only person she didn't hide from was Eva, Grandma's daughter. There was no chance that she mistook them for each other—Eva was round and plump and comfortable, the way Grandma's second husband, Eva's father, had been round and plump and comfortable.

Maybe we smell alike, thought Grandma. *It would make sense, I suppose.*

Eva's son didn't come around at all.

"He thinks you're mad at him," said Eva mildly.

"He thinks correctly," said Grandma.

She and Eva sat on the porch together, shelling beans, while the jackalope wife limped around the garden. The hairless places weren't so obvious now, and the faint stripes across her legs might have been dust. If you didn't look directly at her, she might almost have been human.

"She's gotten good with the crutch," said Eva. "I suppose she can't walk?"

"Not well," said Grandma. "Her feet weren't made to stand up like that. She can do it, but it's a terrible strain."

"And talk?"

"No," said Grandma shortly. The jackalope wife had tried, once, and the noises she'd made were so terrible that it had reduced them both to weeping. She hadn't tried again. "She understands well enough, I suppose."

The jackalope wife sat down, slowly, in the shadow of the scarlet runner beans. A hummingbird zipped inches from her head, dabbing its bill into the flowers, and the jackalope's face turned, unsmiling, to follow it.

"He's not a bad boy, you know," said Eva, not looking at her mother. "He didn't mean to do her harm."

Grandma let out an explosive snort. "Jesus, Mary, and Joseph! It doesn't matter what he *meant* to do. He should have left well enough alone, and if he couldn't do that, he should have finished what he started." She scowled down at the beans. They were striped red and white and the pods came apart easily in her gnarled hands. "Better all the way human than this. Better he'd bashed her head in with a rock than *this.*"

"Better for her, or better for you?" asked Eva, who was only a fool about her son and knew her mother well.

Grandma snorted again. The hummingbird buzzed away. The jackalope wife lay still in the shadows, with only her thin ribs going up and down.

"You could have finished it, too," said Eva softly. "I've seen you kill chickens. She'd probably lay her head on the chopping block if you asked."

"She probably would," said Grandma. She looked away from Eva's weak, wise eyes. "But I'm a damn fool, as well."

Her daughter smiled. "Maybe it runs in families."

Grandma Harken got up before dawn the next morning and went rummaging around the house.

"Well," she said. She pulled a dead mouse out of a mousetrap and took a half-dozen cigarettes down from behind the clock. She filled three water bottles and strapped them around her waist. "Well. I suppose we've done as much as humans can do, and now it's up to somebody else."

She went out into the garden and found the jackalope wife asleep under the stairs. "Come on," she said. "Wake up."

The air was cool and gray. The jackalope wife looked at her with doe-dark eyes and didn't move, and if she were a human, Grandma Harken would have itched to slap her.

Pay attention! Get mad! Do something!

But she wasn't human and rabbits freeze when they're scared past running. So Grandma gritted her teeth and reached down a hand and pulled the jackalope wife up into the pre-dawn dark.

They moved slow, the two of them. Grandma was old and carrying water for two, and the girl was on a crutch. The sun came up and the cicadas burnt the air with their wings.

A coyote watched them from up on the hillside. The jackalope wife looked up at him, recoiled, and Grandma laid a hand on her arm.

"Don't worry," she said. "I ain't got the patience for coyotes.

They'd maybe fix you up but we'd both be stuck in a tale past telling, and I'm too old for that. Come on."

They went a little further on, past a wash and a watering hole. There were palo verde trees spreading thin green shade over the water. A javelina looked up at them from the edge and stamped her hooved feet. Her children scraped their tusks together and grunted.

Grandma slid and slithered down the slope to the far side of the water and refilled the water bottles. "Not them, either," she said to the jackalope wife. "They'll talk the legs off a wooden sheep. We'd both be dead of old age before they'd figured out what time to start."

The javelina dropped their heads and ignored them as they left the wash behind.

The sun was overhead and the sky turned turquoise, a color so hard you could bash your knuckles on it. A raven croaked overhead and another one snickered somewhere off to the east.

The jackalope wife paused, leaning on her crutch, and looked up at the wings with longing.

"Oh no," said Grandma. "I've got no patience for riddle games, and in the end they always eat someone's eyes. Relax, child. We're nearly there."

The last stretch was cruelly hard, up the side of a bluff. The sand was soft underfoot and miserably hard for a girl walking with a crutch. Grandma had to half-carry the jackalope wife at the end. She weighed no more than a child, but children are heavy and it took them both a long time.

At the top was a high fractured stone that cast a finger of shadow like the wedge of a sundial. Sand and sky and shadow and stone. Grandma Harken nodded, content.

"It'll do," she said. "It'll do." She laid the jackalope wife down in the shadow and laid her tools out on the stone. Cigarettes and dead mouse and a scrap of burnt fur from the jackalope's breast. "It'll do."

Then she sat down in the shadow herself and arranged her skirts. She waited.

The sun went overhead and the level in the water bottle went down. The sun started to sink and the wind hissed and the jackalope wife was asleep or dead.

The ravens croaked a conversation to each other from the branches of a palo verde tree, and whatever one said made the other one laugh.

"Well," said a voice behind Grandma's right ear, "lookee what we have here."

"Jesus, Mary, and Joseph!"

"Don't see them out here often," he said. "Not the right sort of place." He considered. "Your Saint Anthony, now…him I think I've seen. He understood about deserts."

Grandma's lips twisted. "Father of Rabbits," she said sourly. "Wasn't trying to call *you* up."

"Oh, I know." The Father of Rabbits grinned. "But you know I've always had a soft spot for you, Maggie Harken."

He sat down beside her on his heels. He looked like an old Mexican man, wearing a button-down shirt without any buttons. His hair was silver gray as a rabbit's fur. Grandma wasn't fooled for a minute.

"Get lonely down there in your town, Maggie?" he asked. "Did you come out here for a little wild company?"

Grandma Harken leaned over to the jackalope wife and smoothed one long ear back from her face. She looked up at them both with wide, uncomprehending eyes.

"Shit," said the Father of Rabbits. "Never seen that before." He lit a cigarette and blew the smoke into the air. "What did you do to her, Maggie?"

"I didn't do a damn thing, except not let her die when I should have."

"There's those would say that was more than enough." He exhaled another lungful of smoke.

"She put on a half-burnt skin. Don't suppose you can fix her up?" It cost Grandma a lot of pride to say that, and the Father of Rabbits tipped his chin in acknowledgment.

"Ha! No. If it was loose I could fix it up, maybe, but I couldn't get it off her now with a knife." He took another drag on the cigarette. "Now I see why you wanted one of the Patterned People."

Grandma nodded stiffly.

The Father of Rabbits shook his head. "He might want a life, you know. Piddly little dead mouse might not be enough."

"Then he can have mine."

"Ah, Maggie, Maggie… You'd have made a fine rabbit, once. Too many stones in your belly now." He shook his head regretfully. "Besides, it's not *your* life he's owed."

"It's my life he'd be getting. My kin did it, it's up to me to put it right." It occurred to her that she should have left Eva a note, telling her to send the fool boy back East, away from the desert.

Well. Too late now. Either she'd raised a fool for a daughter or not, and likely she wouldn't be around to tell.

"Suppose we'll find out," said the Father of Rabbits, and nodded.

A man came around the edge of the standing stone. He moved quick, then slow, and his eyes didn't blink. He was naked and his skin was covered in painted diamonds.

Grandma Harken bowed to him, because the Patterned People can't hear speech.

He looked at her and the Father of Rabbits and the jackalope wife. He looked down at the stone in front of him.

The cigarettes he ignored. The mouse he scooped up in two fingers and dropped into his mouth.

Then he crouched there, for a long time. He was so still that it made Grandma's eyes water, and she had to look away.

"Suppose he does it," said the Father of Rabbits. "Suppose he sheds that skin right off her. Then what? You've got a human left over, not a jackalope wife."

Grandma stared down at her bony hands. "It's not so bad, being a human," she said. "You make do. And it's got to be better than *that*."

She jerked her chin in the direction of the jackalope wife.

"Still meddling, Maggie?" said the Father of Rabbits.

"And what do you call what you're doing?"

He grinned.

The Patterned Man stood up and nodded to the jackalope wife.

She looked at Grandma, who met her too-wide eyes. "He'll kill you," the old woman said. "Or cure you. Or maybe both. You don't have to do it. This is the bit where you get a choice. But when it's over, you'll be all the way something, even if it's just all the way dead."

The jackalope wife nodded.

She left the crutch lying on the stones and stood up. Rabbit legs weren't meant for it, but she walked three steps and the Patterned Man opened his arms and caught her.

He bit her on the forearm, where the thick veins run, and sank his teeth in up to the gums. Grandma cursed.

"Easy now," said the Father of Rabbits, putting a hand on her shoulder. "He's one of the Patterned People, and they only know the one way."

The jackalope wife's eyes rolled back in her head, and she sagged down onto the stone.

He set her down gently and picked up one of the cigarettes.

Grandma Harken stepped forward. She rolled both her sleeves up to the elbow and offered him her wrists.

The Patterned Man stared at her, unblinking. The ravens laughed to themselves at the bottom of the wash. Then he dipped his head and bowed to Grandma Harken and a rattlesnake as long as a man slithered away into the evening.

She let out a breath she didn't know she'd been holding. "He didn't ask for a life."

The Father of Rabbits grinned. "Ah, you know. Maybe he wasn't hungry. Maybe it was enough you made the offer."

"Maybe I'm too old and stringy," she said.

"Could be that, too."

The jackalope wife was breathing. Her pulse went fast, then slow. Grandma sat down beside her and held her wrist between her own callused palms.

"How long you going to wait?" asked the Father of Rabbits.

"As long as it takes," she snapped back.

The sun went down while they were waiting. The coyotes sang up the moon. It was half-full, half-new, halfway between one thing and the other.

"She doesn't have to stay human, you know," said the Father of Rabbits. He picked up the cigarettes that the Patterned Man had left behind and offered one to Grandma.

"She doesn't have a jackalope skin anymore."

He grinned. She could just see his teeth flash white in the dark. "Give her yours."

"I burned it," said Grandma Harken, sitting up ramrod straight. "I found where he hid it after he died and I burned it myself. Because I had a new husband and a little bitty baby girl and all I could think about was leaving them both behind to go dance."

The Father of Rabbits exhaled slowly in the dark.

"It was easier that way," she said. "You get over what you *can't* have faster that you get over what you *could*. And we shouldn't always get what we think we want."

They sat in silence at the top of the bluff. Between Grandma's hands, the pulse beat steady and strong.

"I never did like your first husband much," said the Father of Rabbits.

"Well," she said. She lit her cigarette off his. "He taught me how to swear. And the second one was better."

The jackalope wife stirred and stretched. Something flaked off her in long strands, like burnt scraps of paper, like a snake's skin shedding away. The wind tugged at them and sent them spinning off the side of the bluff.

From down in the desert, they heard the first notes of a sudden wild music.

"It happens I might have a spare skin," said the Father of Rabbits. He reached into his pack and pulled out a long gray roll of rabbit skin. The jackalope wife's eyes went wide and her body shook with longing, but it was human longing and a human body shaking.

"Where'd you get that?" asked Grandma Harken, suspicious.

"Oh, well, you know." He waved a hand. "Pulled it out of a fire once—must have been forty years ago now. Took some doing to fix it up again, but some people owed me favors. Suppose she might as well have it… Unless you want it?"

He held it out to Grandma Harken.

She took it in her hands and stroked it. It was as soft as it had been fifty years ago. The small sickle horns were hard weights in her hands.

"You were a hell of a dancer," said the Father of Rabbits.

"Still am," said Grandma Harken, and she flung the jackalope skin over the shoulders of the human jackalope wife.

It went on like it had been made for her, like it was her own. There was a jagged scar down one foreleg where the rattlesnake had bit her. She leapt up and darted away, circled back once and bumped Grandma's hand with her nose—and then she was bounding down the path from the top of the bluff.

The Father of Rabbits let out a long sigh. "Still are," he agreed.

"It's different when you got a choice," said Grandma Harken.

They shared another cigarette under the standing stone.

Down in the desert, the music played and the jackalope wives danced. And one scarred jackalope went leaping into the circle of fire-light and danced like a demon, while the moon lay down across the saguaro's thorns.

GOING ENDO

Rich Larson

THEY SAY THE REASON IT'S MOSTLY fems who go endo is because of the whole penetration thing, like us sirs can't handle the wet interface, but once on leave I got my face pulped in a blood-brawl at Decker's Draughts & Dopamine, and since the autosurgeon took five whole hours putting my jaw back together I woke up with a supersize catheter stuffed up my cock. Going endo can't be worse than that, I don't think.

Though I guess it might depend on the exo. Some of them, when they get old and the neurals start to break down, they get tetchy, like. Their movements get jerky and their endos come out with nosebleeds and the skin around their dockets all inflamed. I lay that on the techs, mostly, and I'm saying that as a tech. I mean, Puck is as old as any exo in the squad, but you'd never guess it from the gleamy bluish black of her hide, decalcified daily by yours truly, or the way she swims the vacuum, slicing through it like a seven-foot scalpel.

Ye, Puck's the slickest, quickest, baddest exo in the squad, I brain. Her and her endo, tough old fem by name of Cena, have 73 confirmed ghosts, but everyone knows the actual kill count's well over a hundred since not all corpses are retrievable, especially in space.

Cena's old, as said, but hard and wiry, not flabbed out like some other endos, and she keeps her silver hair buzzed down to stubble around her brain docket. When she's climbing into Puck, with the nerve dockets notched all up her spine whirring open, unpeeling like little electric blooms, sometimes I imagine Puck's vanes going in, and think how who's to say, really, who's the exo and who's the endo.

Off to my shift, though. A tech's work is never

Ha, see what I did?

There's still a few pirates holed up in the Oort cloud with smart-mines and camouflage, and cleaning them out is dirty vicious work—exo work. It's been ongoing for a month now; some people say we're dragging it out purposefully because the Company wants our contract extended. So yeah, the whole squad's getting a little edged, but still no cause for what happened today.

One tick all was grand, all the endos slithering out with dark rings under their eyes but still laughing, joking, and then one of Puck's tendrils was clinging hard to one of Cena's spinal dockets, as they want to do after ten, twelve hours bonded, and instead of prying it nice and gentle or letting me handle it, she slipped a flicker out of her arm, one of those little blades in the subcutaneous sheath that everyone thinks makes them a fucking ninja, and lopped it clean off.

Puck jerked back and shivered, and I must have winced or something because Cena gave me this look, like 'Where's your testicles at, jellyfish?' and went right on ungearing. I've seen other endos pull that flicker trick, since the vanes do grow back and all, but Cena's an old hand and she should know better.

So when the endos all staggered off to their Dozr tabs and hash, I took a little extra time getting Puck into her nutrient bath, fiddling the growth hormone levels just a bit, and was real careful around her fresh stump with the rubdown. Grody-odd thing happened, then: right before she sank down into the tank, she gripped my hand with one of her intact tendrils and gave it a little squeeze, like a thank-you squeeze, almost.

Gods and AIs know I don't get one from Cena.

They say all exos look the same, but of course that's people who've never seen them up close, or only seen the faked-up digital kind in net-games and such. I've been stale-streaming old combat footage from the Company's archive—it's lock-and-key shit, they pricked my thumb to get my gene signature and everything—and I can differentiate most of the exos on our squad, even with motion blur.

Puck's easy to spot. She's not the brawniest exo out there, but she's quicksilver smooth, languid almost, long slender grapplers ribboning out behind her as she swims. Vacuum combat's a vicious ballet, and she's the prima, which is what they called the slickest, quickest, baddest dancer, sawing through pirate hullsuits, dodging thermal seekers, slinging her hooks and pinballing from surface to surface in a way gravity-bound brains can't wrap around.

Cena deserves the felicitations, of course, as she's the one controlling. But when you see the two of them side by side in the vestibule, back after a raid, Cena all small and sweat-drenched and Puck this big tower of graceful muscle and carbon tubing, it's hard to remember who pulls the strings. I bet it feels like being God, going endo. Especially with Puck.

❂

Right so, I had to stay late cleaning filters the other night and got back to my bunk with my hands all smelling like ammonia and yeast even after I scrubbed them. Fumes gave me a crippler headache, too. All in all, it felt like a real shitty evening, so I dropped some Dozr and got myself bunked to sleep and wake with better stars.

But then Feris sends me a spike out of nowhere. Feris is this fem I dock up with every so often when I'm on gravityside leave, and I did meet her at Decker's but it wasn't her who smithereened my jaw, and anyway, now she pops up all brainfucked on dust and really horny, saying all this sexy dreggy shit like, come on, soldier, let's burn some virch, I want you deep in me, my bod's the exo your cock's the endo.

I'm like, I just took Dozr, I'm off to the sandman, and she's like, just get into virch and we'll dial back the time perception. Usually I don't do that, because it razzes my REM cycle, but I was having a shitty evening and Feris, even on dust, is better than a lot of pay-to-play pros, so I plugged in. We dialed perception to 1/13, which would stretch my five realtime minutes before the Dozr kicked in to just over an hour.

She was skinned with a pretty standard Pretty, the kind that plumps up the lips and more so the breasts, shops out the belly fat and the body hair and any moles it deems disturbing. Her extended eyelashes loaded as solid black chunks and for some reason her naked skin had this annoying coat of glitter on it, like graphite, and by the time I got inside her I realized Pretty just wasn't doing it for me.

Maybe it was the Dozr, but her dreggy talk from before had given me an idea, so while I was quarter-heartedly thrusting away I scanned through a bunch of skins until I found this one I'd tagged drunk one night, more as a joke than anything, and reskinned her with it.

It wasn't perfect, but it was a solid effort. The vanes curled and flexed the right way, and the hide was smooth and dark as pitch, none of this glitter stuff. Feris's base skelly was still human-size, of course, but that worked out better, almost, since I was halfway enveloped in slip -slidey flesh every time I pushed into the space the program estimated her quinny to be at.

On my end, my prong was burying in a warm amorphous gelatin, probably meant to look like insulator, and the way it gripped me, accurate or no, had me throbbing harder than I'd ever, and if it weren't for the virch's help I'd already be erupting. Feris could tell I was getting really into it; panting and grunting she asked what I'd swapped skins to.

I told her to just concentrate, like, but I felt her tug the info up like a stitch—should've masked it, I know. She booms in my ear: what the fuck, are you fucking serious, an exo? And that rankles, so I'm like: so what, I know you skinned me your dad one time, that old man had the exact same teeth as you.

That razzes her bad, and she says I'm a real grody-odd fucking perv, and the second she gets her climax she pops right out of virch. Hypocrite.

❤

They say smartmine's a misnomer, since most of those things are dumb as the space rocks they burrow in, but today one of them lived up to its name and the unbrainable happened: Puck took a big hit. She came back to the vestibule in a pod pushed by medics, all ready with oxygen for Cena in case she'd depressurized, but when she peeled open, Cena was cocooned real well, just pale and shaking a little from the bio-feedback.

But Puck was fucked. Half her vanes had been ripped right off by the detonation, and her hide was cratered by shrapnel, wounds raw and weeping in the spots she'd tried to tug it out. Seeing her like that, the way she was shuddering, I couldn't hardly breathe, like it was my ribs that had been bombed out. I put my hands on her and the medics were barking, like, get her out, get her out, and I realized they meant Cena.

I was slow and careful, but mostly the tendrils came free easy, spilled limp out her dockets like dead things. Only one stuck, and I thought I saw a tear slide out from Cena's eyelid when I jiggered it loose, and another tear when she stood up, trembly, and saw Puck so massacred. But it was probably just the biofeedback.

The medics took Cena away, and then I set to helping Puck into the nutrient bath. Her hide was trying to seal up around the shrapnel, which causes all kinds of problems, so I had to work quick. I zippered into a wetsuit and slipped down into the tank with her, dialing up the aqueous content so I could tread in place.

She shivered every time I dug a piece out with my pliers and fingers, but I patted her and talked to her low and soothing-like after each, while I sprinkled the cell-knitters. When it was all done she traced the little wounds with one tendril, then wrapped my hand again, like she's done a few times now, and squeezed. Under the treacly surface, I think I felt another tendril brush the inside of my leg, but maybe it was my imagination, and I then felt sort of guilty for imagining that with Puck all smithereened.

But I also felt sure, even though I know it's dumb, that I would've spotted that fucking smartmine.

Puck's out of vacuum at least ten days, out of combat maybe double that. I'm getting her healthy, though. Extra cell-knitters, extra growth hormone, and when I can swing it I bring some dopamine boosters that make her flex and then slack, like a stretch and a sigh, and set her tendrils wriggling happy-like.

Some of the endos are actually getting razzed, if you can believe. Say I'm not taking as much time getting their exos decalcified and prepped and such. But Puck's priority right now—she's the best exo in the squad, and don't they want her back full strength, slick quick bad as ever? Wouldn't guess that, of course, from how Cena's been acting.

She's only been through to check up once, crouching by the tank and stroking Puck's vanes a little, but talking to someone in half-virch the whole time. Then she comes over to me at another exo and says, are you balancing the hormones, are you kneading those left-side stumps, all this check-list shit as if she knows better than me. Swaggers off already in half-virch again, blathering to some Company man, probably looking for hurtpay.

When I went back to Puck's tank, all her right-side vanes, the healthy ones, poked out and waved to me. She recognizes my voice lately, I brain.

They say dreams are from alien satellites, at least they say it where I'm from, beaming the news reels from other multiverses and splicing them all together. Don't know if I believe it now I'm grown, but I can't sleep either way because I keep having this one particular dream that wakes me up and then vanishes before I can get my hooks in.

So when it happened in the deep of last night, I figured I might as well get to the vestibule early, do some scrubwork on the filters long before my shift well and truly started. The corridors were all chilly and quiet on my way, biolights grown on the ceiling ushering me through the dark with a sickly-blue glow. So quiet I could almost hear the gravity humming.

The door pricked my thumb and gave the old DNA a taste, then slid right open. I'd forgotten the lights in the vestibule are timed, so I had to fumble at the equipment locker in the dark, which is why I dropped my clampjack. It clanged real loud on the floor and I swore, and as I crouched down to get it a vane slucked out of Puck's tank. It curled in tight, which is what she does when she wants something, and I thought maybe that one scar was itching her again.

I went over and peered down into her bath. The tanks are lit from the bottom with a soft grainy orange, and when the ceiling lights are off it has this surreal thing to it, like peering down into an alchemist's cauldron, especially with Puck's flesh dark and slick and gleaming, with her drifting at the surface of the tank, vanes all swirling around her, spinning one way and then the other like a dancer. Beautiful.

She was still wriggling her one tendril around, razzed about something. I didn't have my wetsuit, since I was only planning on doing filters, but I didn't want her hurting all night, so I leaned one way, then the other, then thought, who's watching, and shucked off my thermal and my boots and the rest of it and hopped down into the tank.

It was thick with proteins, like sliding into a warm pudding, and the smell filled my nostrils and made me a little heady. I couldn't spot any irritation on Puck's hide; all was smooth and slick, but since I was in there I started to do her a bit of a rubdown. And then it happened.

Puck opened, sliding apart like a blossoming vine, exposing the raw scarlet of her internals, the sparking blue cords of her neurals. That dream I'd been having came back all at once. But this was real, and scarifying, mad, electric. Her tendrils grasped at me, and I realized, gods and AIs, she wanted me to go endo.

Tranced-like, I climbed inside, letting the tendrils push and pull, and Puck sealed up around me. The yeasty smell got stronger, and in the dark I could feel her insulation fluid seeping in all around me, gritty and warm, and I could feel her inner vanes wrapping my limbs, searching for dockets, but of course I only had the brain docket, for virch and such, and even as I thought that I felt a tendril creep up my neck. Bone-deep rasp and meaty squelch, and suddenly, I could see.

Our tank was a red blotch, one of a dozen in the grayscale plane of the vestibule, and above us the electrical wiring pulsed like delicate pink veins. Heat, electricity, motion. Then Puck's implants kicked in, and targeting reticles started dancing over my retinas, then scrolls of trajectories, angles, vectors, all the things an endo would know to interpret.

I could feel her in my gray matter like a soft ghost. I could feel her vanes caressing my skin, slipping down the notches of my spine, still searching. It was like no virch I'd ever tried, like no dust I'd snorted or spiked ganja I'd smoked. Puck's tendrils slipped down, and down, and finally one slipped between the cheeks of my ass and my prong stuck up hotter and harder than ever and I was throbby, achey, nearly—

And that was when Puck peeled open and a tough old hand dragged me sputtering up and out, seeing sparks as the vane in my brain docket tugged free with a wet pop and the vane down under did likewise. Then it was me crouching there shivering on the slicked deck, cock still bobbing half-mast, and Cena looming over me foaming mad, saying she knew it, she fucking knew it.

I was getting iced, I knew that much, out of the squad and out of the Company, and I felt so gutsick, not just with getting caught, but knowing I'd never see Puck swim vacuum again, or wriggle into a nutrient bath, or wave at me on my way past. But then I thought, why is Cena here without gear, why is she only wearing a bodywrap, and then I realized.

"You came here for some freestyle," I said. "Came to hop in the tank just like I did. Go endo."

Her face went flushed, which I'd never seen before, and she said she would slice my fucking eyeballs out, but then she said, ye, well, when you go solo for a whole week you get to missing her. She looked down at Puck, all tender and such, and it made me fucking furious.

"That's goof and you know it," I told her. "You're the one who got her mauled, and you haven't even tapped on her tank since. I'm the one who actually gives a fuck about her."

Then it was her turn to be furious again, and she told me I didn't know shit, said how the Company was growing a new batch of exos and she'd been begging up and down all fucking week to keep Puck active, how they'd wanted to cut costs and recycle her after the smartmine, and since she spent all day in virch she'd started to come at night.

"Recycle," I echoed back, feeling like the hollow sort of thing that echoes, and I swear Puck squirmed at the word. Just thinking it made me shudder myself. "That's utterly fucked," I said. "Puck's the slickest, quickest, baddest…"

"She is, but she'll get lazy if you keep being so soft on her, tech," Cena cut me off. "Slicing a vane now and again just keeps her fresh, is all."

I wanted to argue that, but right then I said, "Alright, alright, so this stays between us, ye?"

Cena nodded her stubbly head, and I realized I'd never really talked to her before, not for this long, and she didn't seem so shitshow. In the shadows she even looked sort of mysterious, sort of sexy. Then Puck reached her vane out of the bath and draped it over my bare foot, and when I looked over I saw she'd done the same to Cena's.

She squeezed.

"Is there room for two in there?" I said, because I thought it was worth an effort. To my surprise, Cena grinned at me, teeth bright white in the gloom, and glanced at my cock getting thick again against my thigh.

"Never tried," she said, "but first shift's not for another few hours."

Puck's tendrils curled more than I'd ever seen before as Cena stripped down and we slipped down into the warm tank, three grody-odd cogs in a wet interface.

CANDY GIRL
Chikodili Emelumadu

Shirley Jackson Award Nominee

THE TROUBLE STARTS WHEN I pick up my umbrella, and it pricks my finger.

"Ouch!" I examine the wound. It is not bleeding, but when I squeeze it a thick, brown substance very like foundation starts to come out.

"What's that?" asks my cousin Ginika watching the liquid.

"Dunno. Pricked my finger. This came out." I squeeze some more. Suddenly the neat little prick rips along its length like a ladder in tights.

"Hmmm. That doesn't look right. We should see someone."

We get on her Vespa, me holding my index finger out, umbrella in the other hand. It's slow going before we hit the main road; up and down, around potholes brimming with rainwater, beside gutters teeming with rubbish. Children scuttle out of our way leaving rubber balls, tyres, and hastily drawn 'Swell' games on earthen streets, only to come back to their play when we pass. People wave. I recognise some of them as my father's guests at my traditional wedding a few days before and wave back. The rip has reached the first joint on the finger. The brown trails out shiny and thick to coat my nail, blown backwards by the wind.

At the village hospital the doctor sees us as soon as he hears Ginika's imperious British accent.

"Harrumph," says the doctor. He is shaped like a cockroach, head smaller than his body. It doesn't help that glasses cover more than half his face; thick, powerful lenses giving him bug eyes.

"Harrumph," he says again and probes the wound. It tears some more.

"It keeps doing that," says Ginika.

"Does it hurt?" the doctor asks.

"No. I feel a bit like a zombie, actually."

"Zombie?" says the doctor. He scratches the top of his sparse dome. Flakes of dandruff rain down like manna onto the shoulders of his dusty brown coat.

"Yes, zombie. You know, like in *The Mummy*. Grrrrrr brains." I gesture with my arms straight out, doing the penguin paddle of a typical zombie.

"Ah, Fela," says the doctor brightening. He is thrilled. "Zombee o, Zombee." He executes a small dance. His tie flaps about, a big band of faded blue pointing to his talking shoes. Ginika eyes him. She clears her throat.

"So can you do anything?"

"No," he says. When we leave he is still dancing in his oversized coat, wiggling his bottom.

Ginika spits at the clinic. "Stupid people. I know where we can go." She starts up her motorcycle again. *Of course she does*, I think. Ginika knows all the nine villages of our hometown like the back of her hand courtesy of annual holidays to Nigeria. Unlike me.

Another bumpy ride. Lots of foliage slapping my face, loose sand slowing the wheels so that Ginika has to push off in places with her feet. We weave around women with baskets on their heads and babies on their backs. The occasional dog dashing across. Stupid sheep standing in the middle of the road as if wool has suddenly become vehicle-proof. It gets cooler the deeper we ride. The light is dappled green from all the tall, tall trees. Ginika pulls up in front of a concrete bungalow in the middle of a clearing, still swirly from broom marks. She claps and says kpoi-kpoi.

A woman steps out of nowhere. She is in green and brown Ankara print like she is pretending to be a tree. Her hair is all tied up in a scarf of the same material, elongating her head.

"Ozulu, we have a problem," says Ginika.

"Let me see," Ozulu says. She takes one look at the wound. "What did this?" I hand the umbrella to her. "Hmmm. Follow me. Take off your shoes." Ginika already has hers off.

Inside, I see the concrete is in fact greyish clay. It is cold against my feet. Spacious. There are patterns drawn into the walls and a fireplace filled with dry wood.

"Sit," says Ozulu. Everything is made from clay or mud or wood; raffia mats on the floors, mud benches line the walls, there is a mud bed piled with cloth and pillows and what looks like a deckchair with padded cushions. I take the deckchair.

Ozulu reaches into a fired clay pot. Her arm disappears up to her armpit. When she pulls it out again she has scooped a big cup of water. The tips of her short butterfly sleeves flutter in the breeze coming from the open doorway. She dumps the water into a cream enamel basin and peers into it.

"Ah. Come and see," she says to me.

I go to her and look over her shoulder. It's like watching TV in HD. A man is clutching my umbrella and swaying. A ripple on the water and the scene changes. Now he is bending low, going through the small doorway of a brown mud hut covered in white chalk squiggles. The thatched roof brushes his back. The water ripples again.

"Paul? What does he have to do with anything?"

"You know him?" Ozulu asks. Ginika joins us over Ozulu's other shoulder.

"Yes. He's my ex, Paul."

"Where is this?"

"I reckon that's his hotel room. He leaves for the airport soon. He wanted to stay back after the wedding to take in some of the local sights…"

"He is here now? In this village?"

I nod.

"Ngwa, call him now. Tell him to come here."

"I told you that Whiteboy was trouble." Ginika casts me a disparaging look.

"Gini," I warn her with my eyes. My eyeballs feel as though they are rolling through sludge. The liquid on my finger has turned to paste. It has bits of white along the seams of the wound.

"He bewitched the umbrella," says Ozulu. She gets up to throw the water on the soil outside.

"Bewitched?" I can hear the flies in the clearing, sluggish from the humidity. They echo the buzz of the many load-bearing motorcycles on the road, far away from the clearing, strangely soothing. Everything is magnified; the sounds of leaves swishing in the breeze are wind chimes, birds flitting from branch to branch conduct mini-operas.

"No. Not Paul," I say. "He couldn't hurt a fly." I start to close my eyes.

"Don't sleep o," says Ozulu. She doesn't raise her voice but I can tell when a warning is a warning and not a suggestion.

"Do you want me to make the call?" Ginika doesn't even wait for me to answer her before she starts dialling which is a good thing because I can't move my neck to nod. I feel a tickle on my hand. The skin has split down to the web of skin between my fingers.

Paul arrives in a fluster. He jumps out of the vehicle before his hired driver stops. Immediately the air changes. It becomes hot and suffocating and the trees' leaves clack-clack endlessly like wooden planks smacking out a secret code.

"Darling, I came as fast as I could." He sprints towards me. "Are you alright?"

Ginika grabs him by the front of his kaftan. "What the hell are you playing at, Whiteboy?"

"Nothing." Paul flinches under the onslaught even though she comes up to just under his chest. His forehead is dotted with perspiration. "That's a bit tight."

Ginika tightens the hold some more. He starts to cough.

"Enough," says Ozulu, and even the trees quieten down. "You. Come here."

Paul stumbles towards her, iron filing to magnet. He brushes the embroidery at his neckline to straighten it. It is white thread against butterscotch linen. His sandals are brown; his toes look like cooked potato chips, long and golden. If my mouth didn't feel full of toffee itself, I might have told him he looked good. *On second thoughts, perhaps not*, I think. Paul had a way of holding on to things forever. Which explains why I invited him for my traditional wedding in my village.

"There will be mosquitoes," I said. "It's the rainy season." He threatened to jump into the Thames if I didn't. Ginika still thinks I should have let him.

"Tell me," says Ozulu. Paul looks at Ginika glowering behind him at the doorway. She flexes her huge thighs as if she is considering Famke Janssening him between them.

"Erm…" Paul tugs on his neckline. He pops the single button.

"I'll start you off. You went to see that fool Agwoturumbe for a potion. Don't lie. I've seen it."

"What kind of potion?" Ginika's shadow moves closer. Paul flinches but he can't move forward away from Ginika because Ozulu isn't letting him. My armpits squelch with oiliness.

"A love potion," says Paul. Ginika slaps him on the back, hard. My hearing is a bit woolly but the cords on her neck don't lie so I know she's put her back into it. She hits him and he contorts his body, sinking onto the hard ground, trying to burrow.

"Ginika, ozugo," says Ozulu. Ginika obeys. "Now tell me what that vagabond Agwoturumbe did."

"He… I… he made me say a spell we wrote. You know with an object that belonged to my beloved…"

"I am not your beloved," I say but apparently nobody hears me. They are still turned towards Paul.

"I chose the umbrella because…well, you know how I love the fairy tales Muna." He gestures to me. "I chose the umbrella because…"

"…Sleeping Beauty…"

"…pricks her hand on a spindle, quite clever actually. You see, since umbrella spokes can be described as spindles or in the very least, *spindly* and in the absence of a real one…" Paul is standing almost straight again, buoyed by pride. Typical. It is just like Paul to make a shambles of things and expect to be praised nonetheless. This is why I broke up with him. Well, one of many.

"Idiot."

They all turn to me. So I say 'Idiot, idiot, idiot,' glad that my tongue seems to be working again. The veil of lethargy lifts for a moment and I give what I hope is my most fearsome look. Paul blanches. Ginika smirks. Ozulu looks indifferent.

"Do you have it?"

"Eh?" asks Paul like an idiot. I slump back into my deckchair. It's not the firmest and I seem to be slipping down the side but beggars can't be choosers especially when they can no longer hold themselves upright.

"The spell. Do you have it on you? I want to see it."

"You can't. I have it in here." Paul taps his head with one long finger. He looks around as if he is waiting for someone to pat him on the back again but Ozulu's stare makes his smile falter.

"Yes. Right. How does it go? 'Eke, Nkwo, Orie, Afo…' "

Paul's Igbo is not the greatest but considering that he learnt it within three months of meeting me it is quite impressive. That was another reason I dumped him, this need to ingratiate by intently subscribing to all aspects of Igbo culture. Suddenly, it was a crime to eat foods other than Onugbu soup and breadfruit and Ji Awai at our house. Or to speak English. It was too bizarre. At first I was proud; what person wouldn't be? Then I realised it wasn't *me* me he wanted. He wanted to belong and it didn't matter whom he needed to fixate on to get in.

Ozulu is listening hard. I see her inhale sharply. The hollow at the base of her throat stays concave. She is holding her breath. Ginika too looks like a dog about to bite. I rummage in my brain. What was Paul saying? I cannot concentrate. My mind keeps wandering and all I want to do is…

"Don't sleep," says Ozulu without turning around. "Did you say 'Ihe'?" she asks Paul.

"Sorry?" Paul is distracted. He had continued reciting, happy at a chance to show off his skills. He never could pick up on non-verbal cues.

"That last line. Did you say 'Ihe m bu n'obi'?"

"Yes. 'What I love the most' I believe." Paul looks as if he is about to launch into recitation again. Ozulu raises her hand.

"You stupid nincompoop," growls Ginika.

"That foolish man," Ozulu says. "Does he not know the gods are tricky?"

"What?" Paul looks distressed. He hates to be on the outside of anything. "What am I missing?"

"All these Efulefu relocate to the village and think they can suddenly all become dibia to reconnect with their roots. No cleansing, no training, nothing. No mastery of the language either by the looks of things. And yet that poser Agwoturumbe grew up in Enugu city, a few hours that way." Ozulu points with her chin.

Ginika looks pained. "It's like giving a child a gun to play with."

"Will someone tell me what is going on?" Paul's lower lip sticks out as if he wants to cry.

I pull myself up and wipe the sweat on my forehead with the back of one hand. *Is it me or is my sweat brown?* I think.

"You said 'Ihe.' "

"That's right!" Paul looks indignant.

The deckchair is slippery on the back of my thighs and my dress is riding up and suddenly it all makes sense. "Ihe. Thing. Not 'onye,' person. You asked to be given the thing you love the most and then you bewitched my umbrella to prick me and transfer your spell to my blood."

Paul thinks for a moment. His mouth drops open. "But…but…"

"Please tell me I can kill him now," says Ginika, pulling a pocket knife from the back pocket of her jeans. "Please, somebody just say the word."

People often forget that Ginika grew up in roughest Peckham because she speaks posh on account of her scholarship-bestowed accent. Paul seems adequately frightened.

"You love chocolate. That's the thing you love the most. Oh Christ, I'm turning into bloody chocolate, aren't I?"

"But…but…" says Paul again. Now I really want to slap him but my body feels like a boulder is on it and I really *really* have to close my eyes now. I hear a thump.

"Why do you have to be so violent, Ginika?" he wails.

"Because I don't like you."

"But I like you. You're a fierce Igbo goddess."

Ginika thumps him again. "Shut up, goat. I am not a goddess. Don't bring their wrath down on me."

"I can fix it! Let me call 'Turumbe…" Paul pulls out a phone from his breast pocket and dials quickly.

"Too late," Ozulu sing-songs, peering in another basin of water. "Looks like he's getting punished already. He's in no shape to help anyone." A small smile curls round her mouth. She throws the water outside again.

"Is she going to die?" Tears stream down Paul's face. "Please, please, Muna, I don't want you to die." He crawls on his hands and knees to me. "I love you. I love you so much, I wanted you to stay with me forever, that's all. Like we are supposed to."

"But we aren't meant to be together," I say. Breathing feels like sucking in corn pap through a straw. I am getting restless because there is something which I am forgetting to remember. Paul takes my hand. I don't have the strength to pull it back. Something warm slides from inside my ear to drip on my shoulder.

"Please say you forgive me," Paul blubbers. He kisses my hand many, many times. He pauses, licks his lips. "You taste like Bounty."

"Figures. You know I hate Bounty. Couldn't you make me some nice dark chocolate instead?"

"I like it," says Paul with lips that seem to have been dipped in excrement.

"So should I kill him or what?" asks Ginika. "We can make it look like militants kidnapped him or something. This is Nigeria, after all."

"No. Your cousin will be dead by nightfall anyway. Let me consult the Oracle." Ozulu disappears behind a doorway hidden by a raffia mat.

Paul has given up on crying. He is now licking my arm unashamedly. It tickles and seems to stop my arm feeling too heavy so I let him. He closes his eyes, licking, licking, head tilted like a cat. Ginika taps the knife against her teeth.

"Kill him, kill him," she mutters like a demented person. Paul scuttles to the other side of the deckchair away from her, picks up my other arm and starts to lick again.

"Mmmm…Mars Bar," he says.

Ugh. All the ones I hate.

"I see you already have the right idea," says Ozulu, coming out of her inner sanctum right behind him.

"How do you mean?" asks Ginika.

"Turns out he has to eat her," she says.

"Right…right here?" Paul raises his head from my arm. When he speaks strings of caramel criss-cross his teeth. "In public?"

"Idiot. Not like that," barks Ginika.

"You have to consume her. Energy doesn't die, it simply changes state. But if you eat her, at least we will be able to control where she goes. She will be on this plane and…"

"Inside Paul?" It is a cruel cosmic joke. Paul wishes for us to belong together and he gets his wish. All this while I have been mellow, could barely hear my own heart beating but suddenly it speeds up. The chocolate gushes out of my ears and streams down my eyes, blinding me.

"What's happening? Muna!" Ginika drops the knife and runs towards me.

I cannot bear the thought of being in Paul for one minute. To be with him forever? Hellish. The more I think about it the more the chocolate gushes. There is a crumbling sound. Paul looks sheepish, my finger in his hand.

"Sorry," he says, stuffing it into his mouth. Ginika slaps him hard and it flies out.

"Ow!" says the man I will be bound to for the rest of this lifetime.

"Try to calm down," Ozulu says to me. "I will make you something to drink. It will slow your heart rate so that you don't melt so quickly."

"You hate me because you're racist!" screams Paul. "You can't stand that I, an outsider, know as much as you about your culture."

Ginika scoffs. "Please. I hate you because you're *you*. I like Tom alright."

"Tom," we say in unison. I forgot to call my new husband. My phone starts ringing. My handbag shakes where I dropped it by the door.

"That'll be him now. Gini please—"

"Got it."

"He knows," says Ozulu. "He knows you're going."

"I know." All along I had been calm. Too calm. But now my distress must have alerted Tom to the fact that all was not well. It's been like that since we met.

"Puh," scoffs Paul. "I'm her true soul mate."

I do not favour him with a glance. All that is within me is reaching for the phone in Ginika's hand, but she places it to my gloopy ear.

"Something is wrong," says Tom, cutting to the chase as he always does. His voice washes over me like a blast of cold air from a freezer. The runny chocolate slows to a trickle.

"Yes. I'm melting."

A pause.

"Tell me."

And this is part of the reason I married him. There is no problem too big for Tom. I can picture him in his shirt and tie, sleeves rolled up to bare veiny forearms, hardhat firmly on his head. I wish he didn't have to return to work immediately, that I didn't let nostalgia keep me back. I keep stopping to breathe, to swallow. When I finish, Tom exhales.

"I'll kill that sonofabitch."

"No don't! I'll die, too. Then I might be stuck with him forever."

Tom pauses a long time. "Tell me what to do."

But I do not know. I do know the exact moment he takes the hard-hat off to run his fingers through his hair though.

"Muna, you fight. Fight. You hear me? You understand?" His voice is low-low.

"I hear you."

"We have this life to live. Our life. Ours," says Tom.

I don't know what to say. Talking seems to have drained me further. The sound of drills punctuate the empty spaces of our conversation.

He grinds his teeth. "I'll handle everything, you hear? Don't worry."

I hand the phone to Ginika. I don't want to talk about my own funeral arrangements or obituary fake though they might be. Ginika nods a few times and hangs up.

"Ngwa," she points to Paul. "Eat."

With a rapturous look, Paul dives in.

Curious thing, being eaten. There is not really pain, more of a discomfort, like having spiders crawl all over your skin or walking with small, smooth pebbles in your shoes. After I speak to Tom it is easy letting my mind drift. Here is Paul, chomping on my cheek, his face bulging, chocolate leaking through his teeth as if he is in the throes of a nasty strain of something. He takes a bite out of my neck, breaks off a shoulder, and crunches a nougat wrist. When he reaches for my breasts Ginika wallops him but Ozulu puts a hand out to stop her.

"He must eat all of her to keep all of her. You don't want some of her faculties gone, do you?"

Paul smiles the smile of a triumphant child that doesn't realise it is in trouble. He suckles on a breast which stretches high, high, high before breaking off. It wobbles in his mouth, gleaming a dull red.

"Turkish delight!" Paul claps. He attacks the other one with gusto. By the time he gets to my belly button he looks peaky.

"Can I rest for a while?"

"I am sure you can but you *may* not. Finish up! This is your fault, stupid!"

Paul eats and eats and eats. It amazing how long I remain conscious, but with each bite the strings which tether me to my body break off one by one.

"Gini," I croak. I think 'Take care of Tom' but I can no longer find the right words. Ozulu peers into my face.

"She's going," she says.

"Gini—" I try again.

"I know," says Ginika. She wipes away her tears before they drop. "I will."

I let go and float away.

I bet you're wondering how I wrote this. I took Tom's advice. Testicular fortitude, my friend. There's a lot to be said for this life. After he went back to London, I settled in Paul's balls—them being unoccupied and all. It was easy to spread, take over his whole self, easy to push him out. He tried to get the doctors to take his balls when he realised what was happening, of course. He told them he felt a lump. They found nothing. He tried to cut his balls off himself, and I caused him to twitch all over and faint. After the third time, passing out and gashing his head open on the sink with a knife in his hand, he was put on suicide watch and medication. I slipped in then. Tom signed my release forms a few days ago. Nowadays, all that is left of Paul is somewhere in the toes of my right foot, misshapen as a result; corns and calluses and weepy, yellowing nails.

I put a sock on it.

If You Were a Dinosaur, My Love

Rachel Swirsky

Nebula Award Winner
Hugo Award Nominee

IF YOU WERE A DINOSAUR, my love, then you would be a T-Rex. You'd be a small one, only five feet, ten inches, the same height as human-you. You'd be fragile-boned and you'd walk with as delicate and polite a gait as you could manage on massive talons. Your eyes would gaze gently from beneath your bony brow-ridge.

If you were a T-Rex, then I would become a zookeeper so that I could spend all my time with you. I'd bring you raw chickens and live goats. I'd watch the gore shining on your teeth. I'd make my bed on the floor of your cage, in the moist dirt, cushioned by leaves. When you couldn't sleep, I'd sing you lullabies.

If I sang you lullabies, I'd soon notice how quickly you picked up music. You'd harmonize with me, your rough, vibrating voice a strange counterpoint to mine. When you thought I was asleep, you'd cry unrequited love songs into the night.

If you sang unrequited love songs, I'd take you on tour. We'd go to Broadway. You'd stand onstage, talons digging into the floorboards. Audiences would weep at the melancholic beauty of your singing.

If audiences wept at the melancholic beauty of your singing, they'd rally to fund new research into reviving extinct species. Money would flood into scientific institutions. Biologists would reverse engineer chickens until they could discover how to give them jaws with teeth. Paleontologists would mine ancient fossils for traces of collagen. Geneticists would figure out how to build a dinosaur from nothing by discovering exactly what DNA sequences code everything about a creature, from the size of its pupils to what enables a brain to contemplate a sunset. They'd work until they'd built you a mate.

If they built you a mate, I'd stand as the best woman at your wedding. I'd watch awkwardly in green chiffon that made me look sallow, as I listened to your vows. I'd be jealous, of course, and also sad, because I want to marry you. Still, I'd know that it was for the best that you marry another creature like yourself, one that shares your body and bone and genetic template. I'd stare at the two of you standing together by the altar and I'd love you even more than I do now. My soul would feel light because I'd know that you and I had made something new in the world and at the same time revived something very old. I would be borrowed, too, because I'd be borrowing your happiness. All I'd need would be something blue.

If all I needed was something blue, I'd run across the church, heels clicking on the marble, until I reached a vase by the front pew. I'd pull out a hydrangea the shade of the sky and press it against my heart and my heart would beat like a flower. I'd bloom. My happiness would become petals. Green chiffon would turn into leaves. My legs would be pale stems, my hair delicate pistils. From my throat, bees would drink exotic nectars. I would astonish everyone assembled, the biologists and the paleontologists and the geneticists, the reporters and the rubber-neckers and the music aficionados, all those people who—deceived by the helix-and-fossil trappings of cloned dinosaurs-- believed that they lived in a science fictional world when really they lived in a world of magic where anything was possible.

If we lived in a world of magic where anything was possible, then you would be a dinosaur, my love. You'd be a creature of courage and strength but also gentleness. Your claws and fangs would intimi-date your foes effortlessly. Whereas you—fragile, lovely, human you—must rely on wits and charm.

A T-Rex, even a small one, would never have to stand against five blustering men soaked in gin and malice. A T-Rex would bare its fangs and they would cower. They'd hide beneath the tables instead of knocking them over. They'd grasp each other for comfort instead of seizing the pool cues with which they beat you, calling you a fag, a towel-head, a shemale, a sissy, a spic, every epithet they could think of, regardless of whether it had anything to do with you or not, shouting and shouting as you slid to the floor in the slick of your own blood.

If you were a dinosaur, my love, I'd teach you the scents of those men. I'd lead you to them quietly, oh so quietly. Still, they would see you. They'd run. Your nostrils would flare as you inhaled the night and then, with the suddenness of a predator, you'd strike. I'd watch as you decanted their lives—the flood of red; the spill of glistening, coiled things—and I'd laugh, laugh, laugh.

If I laughed, laughed, laughed, I'd eventually feel guilty. I'd promise never to do something like that again. I'd avert my eyes from the newspapers when they showed photographs of the men's tearful widows and fatherless children, just as they must avert their eyes from the newspapers that show my face. How reporters adore my face, the face of the paleontologist's fiancée with her half-planned wedding, bouquets of hydrangeas already ordered, green chiffon bridesmaid dresses already picked out. The paleontologist's fiancée who waits by the bedside of a man who will probably never wake.

If you were a dinosaur, my love, then nothing could break you, and if nothing could break you, then nothing could break me. I would bloom into the most beautiful flower. I would stretch joyfully toward the sun. I'd trust in your teeth and talons to keep you/me/us safe now and forever from the scratch of chalk on pool cues, and the scuff of the nurses' shoes in the hospital corridor, and the stuttering of my broken heart.

ADVERTISING AT THE END OF THE WORLD

Keffy R.M. Kehrli

FIVE YEARS AFTER HER HUSBAND died, two years after she moved to a cabin in Montana, and six months after the world ended, Marie opened her curtains to discover her front garden overrun with roving, stumbling advertisements. Marie hadn't seen one since she'd sold her condo and moved out to her isolated cabin. She shuddered.

There were at least twenty of the ads, and for all it seemed they were doing their damndest to step lightly, her red and yellow tulips were completely trampled. Marie had stubbornly continued to cultivate those flowers despite the certainty that she ought to be using the gardening space and the captured rainwater to grow food. Not that it mattered what she'd been growing there. It was all mud now.

The ad nearest her window looked quite a bit like a tall, lanky teenager. It moved like one as well and might have fooled her except that its forehead was stuck in price scrolling mode. Faintly glowing red letters crawled across its forehead from right to left.

TOILET PAPER… 2 FOR 1 SALE… RECYCLED…

Marie could only recognize the daffodil bed by memory. She snapped the curtains shut.

She wrapped a floral print terrycloth robe around herself and hustled from her sparsely furnished bedroom into the kitchen. She was relieved to see the fences she'd put up to keep the deer out of her vegetable garden, while never quite successful, had at least managed to keep her vegetables safe from the ads.

That, of course, would not bring back her flowers.

She glowered at the ads through her kitchen window and filled a glass from the pitcher of well water she kept by the sink. She fumbled open the Tuesday box on her medication canister. Like most mornings, she was thankful that she had filled her prescriptions prior to the end; otherwise she would have none by now.

She would have to go to the garden, and although the advertisements were designed to be perfectly harmless, Marie found she was frightened by the way they lurched over the ground. She suspected this was due to the uncomfortable way their silent progress reminded her of zombie films.

Robert would have been fascinated. A year or so before his death, an advertisement had come up to their door. In those days, the ads had acted more like people than those that now plagued her gardens, and it had stood obediently on the front step until they'd opened the door.

Marie had argued that it was better to leave the door shut, because if an advertisement left without delivering its pitch, it would learn not to come back to the house. The way she figured it, and the way several of her favorite independent video bloggers figured it, listening to the ads was like feeding a stray cat.

Robert did not seem to be overly concerned that they would never get rid of the ads. "Don't be ridiculous," he said. "They'll last maybe another few years at the most, and then the companies will all move onto something that costs less. Right now, they're cheaper than sending employees door-to-door." He opened the door despite Marie's protestations.

"Hello," the advertisement said, hands clasped before it. "I was wondering if you had a few moments to talk about your retirement?"

Marie shook her head and turned back into the house. She busied herself with embroidery, although she still kept an eye on Robert to be sure he wasn't buying anything. No matter how clever her Robert thought the ads were, she did not want to encourage the companies to make more of them.

After a few minutes of animated conversation, the ad left and Robert came into the dining room. He asked, "Have you ever wondered how sentient they are?"

Marie shook her head. She didn't like the ads, and the best emotion she could muster toward them was similar to the way she felt about mosquitoes. Other people thought they served a purpose; she didn't, and it was not worth the argument.

It became apparent that Robert was actually waiting for her answer, and he sat down heavily in one of the other dining room chairs. Marie finished a particularly difficult stitch. "They aren't. They just recognize patterns."

"Yes, but so do we," Robert said. He put both hands on the table and sat up straighter. "How close are they to sentience? They're so much more sophisticated than a recorded ad. They're art."

A few more stitches. Marie laughed. "Art? They're advertisements not art. It can't be art if it's just meant to sell things."

Robert had looked thoughtful. He'd leaned over the table slowly, put his chin in his hands and looked at her. "And yet you like Mucha prints, and those were all selling something," He'd said.

If Robert was still alive, and the world had not ended, Marie supposed he would have gone out the front door and immersed himself in a sea of advertising conversation. As it was, she faced the corporate-orphaned menace alone with an old broom and her largest hammer.

She *had* hoped they would simply wander off on their own, but after watching through the window for a few hours, she determined they knew where she was. Marie suspected her RF chip was still broadcasting her ID number. She and Robert had bought them before they truly understood how much advertising money had subsidized the price.

She stood on the threshold of the home she'd purchased with her retirement and the last of Robert's life insurance payoff, ready to defend it against even the most pernicious of sales pitches.

Marie hefted the hammer over her head and held the broom out like a lance. At least thirty ads were in the front garden now and more stumbled up the gravel road to her home.

"Get *off* my property!" Her voice only shook a little.

The ads turned to face her. They were designed to understand when they were told to leave. This was meant to limit the annoyance factor. Even in the best of times, the command had rarely worked.

Forehead screens changed from flesh colors to scrolling text. The subtlety had gone out of advertising entirely. She wondered if that was a function of being away from human contact for months on end, or if she was just surrounded by a crowd of defectives.

"Go away!"

The ads crowded in closer, becoming an ocean of words and prices and markdowns, factory blowouts and email addresses for the next get-rich-quick scheme, male enhancement drug names, tag lines for movie sequels that shouldn't exist, and cash advance loan shark promises.

"Marie…it's been so long."

At the corner of her cabin, just behind her favorite rhododendron, she saw a figure she recognized immediately and might have known by voice alone.

Robert.

Robert as he'd looked when they'd first met, back in the twentieth century, when they had both been younger and he had been alive. He—it, the ad, wore a very simple black two-piece suit and held a hat under its arm. It looked like the suit Robert had worn to their wedding, but the shoes were different, as though the advertisement had not fully accessed the public files on their marriage.

Through the first three years after his death Marie had never grown used to the way the ads shifted to Robert's form. Now the image spread out like ripples on a pool, the skin of the ads universally deepening almost to a shade of olive, hair lengthening and straightening and taking on that blue-black sheen she'd fallen in love with.

The forward press of ads stopped just outside of her reach, processing the shift from advertising bot to facsimile of her husband. The ads stopped broadcasting on their foreheads, all except for the broken one, which was now fidgeting from one foot to the other in a way that would have tricked Marie into thinking it was actually human if the sale on toilet paper hadn't been scrolling from one temple to the other.

They were all malfunctioning.

"Have you been waiting?" one of the Ad-Roberts in front of Marie said. She poked it in the chest with her broom handle, and it didn't seem to mind.

Another ad said, "Have you missed me?"

"Lonely out here," said a third.

Marie picked up her hammer and slowly, careful to avoid tripping on the doorframe, backed into her house.

She shut the door.

The first time Marie had seen an ad take on the appearance of Robert had been only a few weeks after the funeral. She had opened the door one morning to find Robert standing outside. There was a split second when she found herself wondering if she'd imagined the past few weeks. Then she realized she was looking at an ad. Marie thought about Robert rotting in the ground, dead and alone.

The ads were not meant to use the likenesses of the deceased. What they could do was almost as bad, but far less illegal—taking those likenesses and shifting them ever so slightly until the ad looked familiar, but not sufficiently to be recognized.

Whether it was an act or not, the ad looked just as surprised as she was. Its eyes opened wide as it accessed her file and, for an instant, it looked like Robert had when he realized he'd said something he shouldn't have. The ad opened its mouth as if to speak, but Marie hadn't wanted to know what it was about to say. She'd slammed the door shut.

It turned out later that the malfunction had been semi-common. Marie could have gotten in on a class action lawsuit but, instead, she'd packed up and sold the condo. She'd moved to the cabin shortly afterward, wanting a place that wouldn't remind her of Robert, who had always loved cities.

All the ads except for one shifted back to their default appearances after Marie returned indoors, but they didn't go away. She kept her shades down and tried to ignore the tromp-tromp-tromping noises of footsteps outside her house.

The gardens had seen better days.

The *most* curious thing was that no matter how content she had been with her hermit's life before, now the ads were outside her door she missed the sound of Robert's voice. She wished she could hear it again, as long as it wasn't a haphazard lead-in to a sales pitch.

Marie sat alone on these mornings, extremely alone, now she had the rustling sounds of the ads to remind her.

That was why on one fine Wednesday afternoon in mid-April Marie invited an advertisement in the guise of her dead husband inside for lunch.

They sat together at a white table with a blue checkered tablecloth and a plate of tiny sandwiches inside Marie's small kitchen. Ad-Robert had attempted to pull her chair out for her, but she would not allow it. She had placed her hammer under her seat before letting the ad in. Even though she didn't think it was dangerous, Marie thought it best to be prepared. Once they were seated, she poured mint tea for them both.

Marie had cultivated the mint herself, of course.

The ad that looked like Robert smiled dumbly at Marie, and the sunlight that filtered into the room lanced brightly across faintly silvered hair. When it smiled, crow's feet spread from the crinkled skin around its eyes. Try as the ad might, however, the months without upkeep had so eroded its ability to keep up with its reference recordings of Robert's inimitable gestures that the resulting attempt looked like a badly choreographed farce.

Marie sipped her tea, watching the ad in silence. It had asked her a leading question, as they'd walked through the front room: something about stock options, which would never draw Marie's interest, even if stocks or money had meaning anymore. Ads were designed not to speak again until the thread of conversation was taken up by a human. She looked out the kitchen window. Ads still filled the backyard. She wondered if they were sharing her location, like bees dancing to show each other the path to fresh flowers. The ads wandered back and forth through what was left of the pansies.

Marie sighed, and Ad-Robert cocked its head.

Either the conversation lag had been too much for its memory banks, or it parsed the sigh as an answer.

The ad asked, "I mean, I don't mean to pry, dear…but you have thought about retirement, haven't you?"

The ad sounded like Robert and, at the same time, sounded like the ad that had spoken to Robert six years before. Marie thought of the hammer under her chair and had to wait to respond because of the sudden thickness in her throat. "Of course I have." It wasn't exactly a lie, but at the same time, the question was moot.

Ad-Robert looked down at its tea but did not drink. It held the cup a few inches above the table and let it steam out into the air. "You ought to be buying biotech. I can help you find the right companies."

Marie said, "I'm sure they're not in business anymore."

The ad tried to do one of Robert's dismissive hand waves, but its wrist motors jerked and the effect was lost. The ad didn't seem to notice. "Of course they're still in business!" Its eyes focused on the space above Marie's left shoulder, as it tried to connect to the Net. Marie was fairly certain that, with the exception of any identification chips she may have, there had never been a wireless connection in a twenty mile radius.

Marie finished her cup of tea and maneuvered the conversation into a realm she cared for a bit more than imaginary finances. She poured more tea and dumped a spoonful of honey into it. "I've been thinking about planting corn soon, but it's hard to get to a flat patch of ground that isn't constantly underfoot these days." She'd heard rumors that some of the ads were able to carry on regular conversations if prompted properly. A few companies had discovered their ads had been held hostage by lonely people for weeks or months on end.

Ad-Robert didn't move, frozen with what would have been confusion if it had been human.

Marie waited, but the hope she had for a decent conversationalist faded when Ad-Robert only asked, "So, about your retirement?"

Marie had tried to look for survivors a week after the satellite television signals had gone out. She'd loaded up her old pickup truck with water, emergency bandages, and even a few fall vegetables to share with her neighbors.

One eye on the road and the other on the gas gauge, she made her way down the mountain, looking for turnoffs to the isolated cabins of her neighbors. She hadn't known them well before everything went to shit, but she figured now was a good time to make an exception. It was a beautiful, quiet day. She pulled onto the highway, and no cars passed her in either direction. All the cabins were empty. This confused Marie, since she hadn't taken the people who lived in them to be the sort who would run for civilization at the first sign of trouble. She supposed she had been wrong about them, for whatever that mattered. Marie filled the back of her pickup truck with canned and dried food from their pantries and tried to ignore the smells that emanated from their closed refrigerators.

She only made it halfway down into the valley before the wind shifted to come up out of the south. She gagged, slammed on the brakes of her truck and pulled over onto the shoulder. Even a few miles away, the collective stench of several hundred thousand bodies rotting sour in the early September heat, was too much for her.

She couldn't imagine anyone living closer. Reluctantly, she had turned the truck around and headed back to her house.

Marie couldn't destroy the ads. She had trouble even thinking of it because, no matter how wrong their gestures, every ad looked too human.

The ad she kept indoors at least pretended to listen to her from time to time. She could almost ignore the outdoor ads, except for when she had to pass from her house to the well, from the well to the garden, or from the garden back to her house. She had given up on her makeshift pump system the second or third time the ads had trampled holes into the hose. She'd forgotten how hard it was to carry water from the well to the garden by hand, and it didn't help that the ads were always underfoot.

"Get out of the way," she said, exasperated, when the ads stumbled into her few well-worn paths. Even if the ads were not in her garden, it was hard to get enough water to the plants. Every trip with the bucket took twice as long as it should have.

In the evenings, she did not embroider as much as she used to. She was too tired, now, and too worried about whether or not she'd be able to keep her food crops alive and healthy enough to give her a harvest that would last the winter.

Marie grew accustomed to the indoor ad's, "Good morning, sweetheart." It said the same thing every morning, as she passed from her bedroom into the kitchen. The ad always sat in the same chair at the table, in the same position, waiting for her to wake.

When it became apparent that Marie wasn't interested in the ad's sales pitch, it was confused for a long time. It sat and listened, nodding absently to her words in the way Robert had done just before he'd died, when she hadn't been able to tell if he'd understood or not.

She remembered how her own grandparents had spoken exclusively about the past in their old age. She'd still been studying for her math degree, and she hadn't had any time for those stories.

Marie told the ad about other things, about how to know when it was time to pick a pear, about the earth-poison smell of tomato vines and the acid-sharp taste of the fruit.

She was trying to explain the particular crumbling feel of good soil and the moist smell of fresh potato when Ad-Robert interrupted.

It was the only time the ad interrupted her. At all other times, it had been perfectly behaved.

"Have you ever considered your death?" it asked.

Robert had once asked her that. They'd been young, and it had been more a joke than anything else. Marie couldn't look at Ad-Robert when she answered, so she stared out the window at orange-tinged clouds that hung over the forested mountains around her home.

"Yes," she said.

She had been planning to go grocery shopping the day the world ended, after she'd weeded the gardens and picked some zucchini. But she'd turned on the news that morning to pick up the one local channel available from her satellite dish.

Biological agents. Super bug. Nobody on the channel or in any of the borrowed clips could determine if they thought it was terrorism or just freak random chance. It was a virus then it was a bacterial infection that antibiotics couldn't touch. Masked and suited reporters questioned the sobbing, quarantined mothers of sick children. Scientists and doctors postulated that if the illness killed its victims so soon after infection, then it couldn't spread much farther.

The rebuttal was simple: there was no way to know how long it gestated, and how long it was contagious. The rebuttal sparked more panic, because the man giving it finished by pointing out that the entire human race could already be infected and not know it.

Marie had turned off the television and sat on her porch in the late summer sunlight for a few hours, and when she'd turned it back on, she hadn't gotten any reception.

A day later the electricity had been cut off.

One morning when she walked into the kitchen for her medication, the ad did not greet her as it had for the past month. Instead it sat, silent and dark, a life-sized doll made out of LCD and carbon. It no longer appeared to be anything like Robert. It was just a lifeless machine that had grown tired of masquerading as her husband.

She stared at it for a long time, expecting it to come to life with another skewed economics lecture. In case it had a sleep function, she prodded it with a wooden spoon, poking it resolutely in the stomach, the arm, the face. Nothing.

Marie sat down on the other side of the table, leaned far over it and stared at the ad. The face was not really human, but she traced the features with her fingertips, over the smooth hills and valleys that gave the ad a physical presence when it was on. The screen itself was cold to the touch, and she left little skin-oil smudges behind.

Down the neck and across the chest, she could see scratches and scrapes from tree branches and possibly animals. Places where she might have noticed pixels out if she'd looked at it closer.

Marie sat back in her chair. When she had finished crying, she was left with the problem of disposing of the body. She felt foolish, too… Hadn't she meant originally to kill the stupid things?

The ad was lighter than she'd thought it would be. For all it was nearly the size and build of Robert, it was made of far lighter materials than flesh and bone. Marie was able to drag it with one hand under its left shoulder. She carried her lightweight shovel with her other hand, prodding or swatting any of the outdoor ads that got in her way.

They were still as obnoxious as ever, hovering, surrounding, circling Marie and the dead advertisement like sharks around a sinking boat. The air filled with pitches, slogans, prices.

"We don't have to pay until 2045!"

"I really think you'd like these perfumes, honey."

"Come and visit, the alcohol's free!"

Marie trudged along the thin dirt path that led from her little house, until dry pine needles crackled under her clogs and under the feet of the ads that followed her in a herd. When the ground went flat for a bit, she dragged the ad through a few feet of sparse sword fern.

She dug a shallow grave under a tamarack and covered the ad with just enough dirt to hide it from view. She didn't think anything would dig it up, but she felt a little bad for not making the grave deeper when the other ads walked over the mound of dirt mixed with pine needles.

Marie wiped her face on the sleeve of her rosebud blouse, and then she took her sweet time walking back down the mountain, still ignoring the advertisements that seemed entirely unaware of the loss of one of their number.

Marie found the second dead advertisement a few days later top-pled over on the front walkway to her house, scuffed from the feet of the other ads, as motionless and empty as the one that had died in her kitchen.

She thought seriously about burying it with the other ad, but then she looked at the crowds of them that filled her yard and thought bet-ter of it. So Marie dragged the second advertisement out to her shed, and she propped it up between a rake and a hoe, leaving it to collect dust. She realized she could have left it out among the other ads, but she didn't like the idea of her home being surrounded by forgotten bodies.

Every few days she found another, sometimes only toppled over as though its batteries had simply quit, and sometimes sitting tucked against the side of her house as though it had powered down.

She filled her shed with them and started setting the others up as scarecrows, guarding her vegetables from the birds, though they did nothing to keep away the smaller animals and deer when they didn't move.

The month lengthens and becomes two months, then three, four, five. The ads still come, but there are fewer, and as time goes on, Marie finds that sometimes weeks pass between appearances. Now, when the ads arrive, they are little danger to her gardens, and she is able to har-vest what she needs without them getting in her way.

They come to her to die and sometimes, when it has been a long time between visits, she lets the ads inside, and she listens to them while she serves sandwiches and tea she has made from what she can grow on the plot of land behind her house. The ads that make it to her mountain are moving slower and slower, and Marie is not surprised. She is moving slower these days, too, though she is not sure if that is the weather, leaning in toward winter, working cold into the ragged edges of her joints, or what is left to her now the pills have run out.

Every so often, the ads look like Robert. Sometimes they look like her friends; sometimes they look like her mother. Sometimes they look like nobody she has ever known, and sometimes they look like she imagines her children would have if she and Robert had ever cared to try.

Maybe when the winter is done, she thinks, she will climb down from her mountain to see what is left. The smell of the dead in the city will have gone by then, and there may be other survivors on other hills, looking for her. She holds the slightest of hopes that there are fewer ads because they have found others and not just because they were never meant to last for so long, lost and alone in a dead world.

THE PERFORMANCE ARTIST

Lettie Prell

ON THE FIRST DAY, SHE SITS there wearing a black dress that is neither provocative nor sexless. Yet visitors who flock in from the cold January streets and ascend to the atrium on MoMA's second floor are mesmerized, for the entire space is awash in a video installation depicting various interactions between machines and flesh. The footage flashes across the walls and sweeps over the woman sitting in the chair. Some images are recognizable: beams of light illuminating eyes during exams, prostheses being fitted to amputees, a dental hygienist cleaning teeth, a kitchen cook working a meat grinder. Other clips are strange: a small device crawling up a person's spine, thumping sharply as it goes; people sprouting electrodes; a man strapped face-down and gripping handlebars while the lower half of the table slides back and forth, stretching his torso. The bizarre imagery quickly infects the ordinary scenes until everything "seems an invasion of humans by the things they have wrought." Or so writes the *Times* critic in an article that splashes across the Sunday *Arts & Leisure* section. The performance artist is the talented Anna Pashkin Bearfoot, the critic raptures, who charged onto the scene last year with a week-long piece where, while nude, she built a robot amid a jungle of potted plants. The current installation is slated to last a full month.

The second day the crowd swells, despite a nasty frozen mix that pelts Manhattan. Today, a real machine squats eight feet from Anna, and to her right. *What is that?* and *I don't know* are repeated many times before the crowd engages its collective intelligence:

"I think it's one of those downloading machines."

"Are you sure?"

"To transfer human consciousness into a computer?"

"I'm not sure."

"That would explain the shots of the meat grinder. Lose the meat."

"Yes, it is a downloading machine. I saw it in *Scientific American*."

"But she's not sick."

"We don't know that."

"They would never let her, surely, if she's healthy."

"No law against it."

"I bet she's going to."

"Why else would it be here?"

"She's going to use it."

"Omigod."

"She's going to download herself *here*? At MoMA?"

The art critic zips out a new article. On the third day, the line to get in stretches to Sixth Avenue. Today Anna is speaking, still dressed in plain New York black. Every fifteen minutes she says the same thing:

"By my words you will know me. I am my true self and no other. I shed the inessential. I shed woman. I shed race. I shed age. I shed status."

On the fourth day, Anna sits in the same spot wearing a hospital gown. The line to get in curls around West 54th. The drama outside the museum overshadows the exhibit itself. Police keep a careful eye on dozens of protestors lined up across West 53rd, shouting slogans like, "It's a lie. She will die." And, "Only God grants eternal life."

The daytime talk shows focus on ethics, rules and regulations. Can a medical procedure even be performed at an art museum? Would visitors be required to don surgical masks? All the guest medical experts condemn the Lazarus Project for creating such a circus. By the end of the day, a MoMA spokesperson assures the public that the actual procedure will not be part of the live performance. The statement only serves to inflame interest, since it constitutes official confirmation that the artist is indeed going to download her consciousness into a computer. The nighttime talk show hosts eagerly point out the careful wording of the statement leaves open the possibility of a video installation of the procedure.

No one is disappointed. On the fifth day visitors ascend to the atrium to find Anna Pashkin Bearfoot is not sitting in her place. The downloading machine has been rolled to the central position. The video shows a montage of the artist's life. There are home videos of her as a toddler on a tricycle, and again at a birthday party, taller than the other girls though she tries to compensate with a slouch. Then footage of her as an adolescent, dancing and singing in her mother's living room, long dark hair swinging across her face like a curtain in a breeze. This scene gives way to a young woman of about nineteen, playing keyboards in a band in a club, barely visible in the low light, yet her looming presence is unmistakable. Then a bright scene of her painting a huge canvas stretched across the floor in her studio, her arms swinging gracefully one moment, and then staccato the next, with a surprising intensity. Then at last, brief flashes of her now-famous performance piece with the robot. Her breasts sway as she fits a mechanical arm and tests it. Then Anna on her knees before the completed robot. It is only roughly human, like a toy. It works its mechanical jaw yet produces no sound, and pumps its arms ineffectually. Then Anna is on a talk show, saying, *The robot piece affected me personally, yet I cannot explain how. I only know I'm not done with this yet.*

Visitors wander thoughtfully from this installation to find one of the adjoining exhibition rooms is guarded by security. No one under twenty-one is admitted. Every half-hour a fresh crowd files in, excited and nervous, while the previous visitors, shaken and pale, exit from another door. The art critic from the *Times*, we learn in the paper, had witnessed the downloading live. Anna doesn't want to dwell too much on her private thoughts and motives for undergoing the procedure, the article states. Instead, she'd like viewers to contemplate their own mortality as flesh, and to invite an internal dialogue between reality, reason, and their own religious and cultural belief systems.

"Some people are convinced they are witnessing my death," she is quoted as saying. "It's a legitimate point of view, and perhaps the more beautiful image—a celebration of the ephemeral in the face of manipulation by technology. I'm sure it will be an unforgettable moment." It is. Nearly a hundred people have undergone this procedure, but hers is the one that catches and holds the world's attention. The prime time news analysts discuss the phenomenon. Why her? She is receiving three times the attention as the first one to download. An answer forms. She is not terminally ill, elderly, or oozing money. She is doing this as art, which is intriguing and distasteful all at the same time. We must find out what kind of a person she is, so we may analyze her and come to some understanding why she would do this.

After a week of record-breaking attendance, international attention and endless replays of all available footage of Anna Pashkin Bearfoot's life, the exhibit changes yet again. The multi-media show is completely gone, replaced by a single forty-two-inch video screen hooked up to a laptop computer on a stand in front of it. On the big screen is Anna Pashkin Bearfoot.

"By my words you will know me," she says to the crowded atrium. Her words are also broadcast to the street outside, and podcast around the world. "I am my true self and no other."

The crowd reacts in the ensuing silence. "This is fake."

"It's her."

"The Turing test results prove it's the same person."

"Not with her. This could be staged."

"Did you see the footage of the download? It's her."

The day-time talk show hosts throw out their regularly scheduled programming to make sure everyone understands the Turing test evaluates whether a human interviewer can tell the difference between a machine's answers and a human's answers to the same set of questions. Experts in artificial intelligence flood the channels to discuss the variations to the Turing methodology, and the extensive tests performed on downloaded consciousness to date. Arguments appear to erupt, but the stilted dialogue is obviously rehearsed.

"Turing tests measure intelligence. A key component we have not tested is whether the downloaded mind is capable of *unintelligent* human behavior. That would be essential to its humanity."

"No, the crucial thing is whether the downloaded mind exhibits intelligent behavior that is *not* human. If it does, then it's not really human."

"But what if it is *more* intelligent than us? That's not a failure of the procedure, but a sign of evolution to the transhuman."

"Yet studies done to date find the downloaded person interacts as he or she would when they were in a body. Nothing more nor less. Study after study."

In the meantime, the Anna Pashkin Bearfoot on the video screen invites viewers of the exhibit to type questions to her, which she answers verbally. The transcription of these conversations begins to accumulate on the wall of a nearby exhibit room. People come to watch or participate in the live interrogation, and then go to read prior conversations in the exhibit room. She never refuses to answer a question, no matter how personal.

Q: When did you experience the most sadness in your life?

A: When I was twenty, and broke up with my boyfriend at the time. Funny, I should have said it was when my mother died, but she had been in a great deal of pain for so long that her death was a relief. It was the boyfriend. I was so young and unsure of myself. Things had turned bad between us. We were never happy anymore when we were together. I was the one who broke it off, but it really hurt, and I felt so sad for months.

The questions and answers quickly mount into the hundreds. The conversations win over the populace. Former skeptics embrace downloading, and make provisions for it in their wills. Church attendance, which had been on the decline for more than a decade, plummets.

❤

It is the end of the second week, with still two weeks to go. The game changes. Rather, the game begins.

"By my words you will know me," she says from the screen, her face aglow. "I lay myself bare and offer my memories. I invite you in turn to manipulate these. Change anything. Change my choices. Change my life events. Simulation software will project how that change would have altered me as a person."

The crowd, which has been expecting to participate in the now-famous conversations, falls silent. For a long time, no one moves. Then a young man, stylishly scruffy in the manner of a New School intellectual, approaches the keypad and begins browsing the menu on the little screen. Others edge forward to read over his shoulder. By this time, thanks to the media, the crowd is familiar with the highlights of Anna Pashkin Bearfoot's life: born of a single mother, taken to art early, first in the form of music, then painting, then performance. She had three significant relationships but never married. Her mother died several months prior to Anna's recognition for her robot-building performance.

"Look at this," says the young man, scanning the options. "She was beaten by her mother's live-in boyfriend."

The crowd drinks this in, even as memory sequences ripple across the screen. Some flinch and turn away.

The young man clears his throat. "One of the options for choice is to have her sexually abused."

The crowd murmurs, a mixture of condemnation, puzzlement and interest.

The young man makes his selection. The crowd flows forward. The rape sequences are blurred, and show little since they are from Anna's point of view. The projection software leaps forward at a rapid pace, showing a more deeply traumatized child producing even more intense music and art, and then following a bout of drug abuse and rehab—

"She's incredible," the crowd concludes in one longing breath. Even the people who didn't usually come to art museums—and Anna Pashkin Bearfoot's performance had drawn many of those—could detect the difference. The art critic nearly falls flat on the floor in his excitement.

"Let me try," says an older woman standing three-deep in the crowd. The game fever has begun. Anna is abused more, much more, given various disabilities. Others treat her kindly, erase past traumas, boost her intelligence. The effects are sometimes at odds with prior results. Similar traumas applied at slightly different time periods produce genius, or early suicide, or a career as a florist. One change results in her studying engineering for two years, although she does not graduate but follows a lover to Mumbai and becomes a dressmaker. Often she becomes an artist of varying degrees, sometimes staying with music as her chosen career, sometimes remaining a painter, sometimes taking up glass blowing, photography or sculpture. The art critic opines that "the heart of the artist remains constant in the face of circumstance."

As with the questions, each alteration in Anna Pashkin Bearfoot's life is posted in the adjoining exhibit hall, along with a brief summary of the projected life resulting from each change, and samples of any artwork these alternate selves produced. The exhibit is "a study of how small changes can propel a person onto a different life path, as if countless parallel universes are a probability away, waiting to be activated," writes the critic. The alternative lives accumulate through the remainder of the week, and into the next. The performance piece has been a smash success.

On the last day of the installation, visitors gather in the atrium to find the interactive game removed. There is Anna on the large screen, and in front of the screen, the crude robot she made in her performance piece last year. The Anna on the large screen is a frozen frame. She regards her audience, her mouth hinting at amusement. Then the screen winks off.

The robot suddenly works its jaw, but it is a crude robot and cannot speak. It holds up an arm, containing a thick charcoal pencil in its clamp of a hand. The robot spins to the left and rolls on its skates-for-feet toward an easel where a pad of paper is mounted. It writes slowly in a child

-like scrawl: *I AM ANNA. BY MY WORDS*. The rest is left unwritten.

The crowd, after an initial stunned silence, murmurs to itself, seeking understanding:

"Is that really her?"

"It could be a stunt."

"It's her."

"She wants us to believe it's her."

"It can't speak. She can't speak."

"She can only show us it's her."

Meanwhile, the robot has traded the charcoal stick for a cordless electric hacksaw suitable for cutting metal or bones. The robot tries to sit down but falls over backward instead. Laboriously, it uses its arms to right itself into a sitting position on the floor, legs straight out in front. The saw whizzes to life. The robot applies the vibrating blade to its left upper leg.

"Isn't anybody going to stop her?" The voice has to strain over the noise.

No one bothers to answer. Everyone watches as the saw makes its progress, its whir commanding attention, so sharp that some cushion their teeth with their tongues. Several minutes later the leg rolls away with a clunk. The saw falls silent.

"Beautiful."

"This is a real statement."

"Isn't anybody—"

"She can't feel any of it. This is art."

"It's her. Only Anna would do this."

The robot does not teeter, but appears solidly balanced on its metal rump. It turns the saw back on, and starts on the upper right leg. Again the noise of saw on metal shushes the audience. A few minutes more, and another clunk as the limb falls away. The saw is silent again. The crowd analyzes:

"What man makes, he can destroy."

"This is about the limitations of the machine."

"Devolution."

The robot brings the blade up to its neck.

"My god. What's she doing now?"

"Shut up, lady."

"It's not like that. She's immortal now."

"The chip that runs her would be in the ribcage in any case."

The saw hums to life. A few minutes more, and the head falls to the floor, making one and a half rolls before coming to rest on its left cheek. The saw falls silent. Some clapping starts, but immediately stops.

"She's still moving."

"Cool."

The robot, poised, calm and purposeful despite the lack of its head, positions the saw at its chest.

"What the—"

The noise of the saw drowns out the comments. The blade chitters across the surface, unable to find purchase. The robot tips the device and seeks to drive the upper teeth into itself. Sparks arc, miniature fireworks. The saw whines as if in argument. At last, the robot lowers the saw, turns it off. There is some damage on the surface of the chest, exposing the robot's electrical system. A clamp-hand reaches into the breach with a staccato motion. The arm jerks suddenly and the robot collapses backward to the floor. There are "ohs" and a couple of shouts. A tiny object skitters toward the crowd, but stops two feet from the ropes. People bend to peer at it. The object is metallic and flat.

"It's her chip."

"It looks so vulnerable."

There is silence. Then someone starts to clap and everyone joins in. There are shouts of "Brava!" amid less cultured whooping.

"Just look at the wreckage. Unbelievable."

"This has got to be the best thing I've seen in a long time."

"Yeah, it was great. Come on. Let's go see the Pettibons."

A MATTER OF SHAPESPACE

Brian Trent

2013 Apex Magazine Readers' Choice Winner

JACOB STARED AT THE PYRAMID he had not built.

It stabbed up from the center of his otherwise empty room, its three sides so steep they were nearly vertical, converging to a sharp point that aimed toward the skylight. Jacob gaped at it, disbelieving the sight. The rest of his house was a blank desolation, bereft of furniture, color, and of course, pyramids.

"Couch," Jacob said.

His couch formed like gelatin out of the floor. Its default color was cream. He plopped down onto its cushion, steepled his fingers, and contemplated the pyramid he had not asked for.

He had heard of glitches like this occurring, but never in *stationary* homes. Jacob had friends who paid the exorbitant fees for a mobile homespace; wherever they went, they could conjure a modest living pad with whatever furniture, walls, ceilings, and features permitted by their cloudwidth. Oh, there was an undeniable "cool factor" associated with it—snap your fingers and conjure a posh bachelor pad on a Tibetan clifftop or Venetian alleyway or field in the middle of nowhere. Jacob never went in for that. For one thing, it was horrendously expensive. He knew people who had been crippled by the monthly charges and ended up serving time as part of the global cloud, broken down and used by other shapespace projects until they worked off the debt. Law of averages suggested you'd end up being a pipe or a wall or a spate of shingles. Maybe a fence. But there was always the chance you'd end up as someone's toilet for a few years.

"It's all matter," one of his friends, Jocelyn, told him before she was sentenced to shapespace for unpaid debt. "They can have my molecules for whatever they want. I won't know the difference. Consciousness is stored in the cloud."

"Yeah? What if someone makes a mistake?" Jacob asked her. "Then you'd be conscious, unable to move, for the duration of your sentence."

But all she did was laugh. "Then maybe I'll get lucky and end up as a supermodel's sex toy!"

Jacob saw no need for mobile homespace. When he traveled, he used public grids. In the last month alone, he had merged and emerged at a dozen locations around the world. Didn't need to bring a house to show off. Travel and do business, then return to a fixed, dependable castle. That was how Jacob liked it.

He briefly wondered if he could erase the pyramid by conjuring another preset. Jacob uttered the word "Tuscan." The default blankness of his home assumed an earthy hue. Vines burst from the tiles and entwined lovingly around pillars and archways. An in-ground swimming pool dimpled and welled. The walls freckled into faded mosaics. A marble statue grew in the foyer.

But the pyramid remained.

Jacob sighed. "Wine," he said, and a stone goblet formed from the couch, filling with a good red. He sipped it thoughtfully. After a moment, he smacked his lips, enjoying the fruity aftertaste, and said, "House? I think I've been hacked."

"There is no cloudwidth presence detected other than you," his house replied.

Jacob swirled the wine in his goblet. "Anything to report while I was away? Any visitors? Intrusion attempts?"

"No visitors or intrusion attempts detected. Might I interest you in the Caribbean preset?"

"No. Is there a glitch in the mainspace?"

"There are no glitches detected."

Jacob leapt to his feet and jabbed a finger at the immense pyramid. "What do you call that? Why is that in my house?"

"The pyramid is designed to represent the glory of the Amon-Ra, with its slopes stylistically recreating the rays of the sun. All bow and kneel before His glory."

Jacob dropped his goblet. The wine spilled across the floor, soaked into the wood, followed quickly by the goblet itself, like two children fleeing before their parents' impending argument.

"What did you say?" he cried.

"The sun god is the only god," replied his house. "He is the one and only. He is the bringer of life, he is the strength in the hawk's wings, he is the power in the storm, he is the vitality in the bones of the world. Shall I create a House of Healing? Would you like steak for dinner?"

Jacob broke into an icy sweat. "Shutdown," he ordered, his thoughts flying apart in panic. He had heard of poltergeists before. Hackers who somehow managed to invade a mainspace, possess the central processor, and then mess with the owners. Silly pranks, if you were lucky. Rape, torment, or *digestion* if you weren't.

At this thought, Jacob decided to get out. Ordinarily, he would have merged back into his house and simply emerged elsewhere, maybe Toronto or Berlin. But he wouldn't risk dissolving into a hacked mainspace. Wouldn't dare.

"Dissolve," taunted the house. "Dissolve back to the glory of Osiris and defy the serpent of oblivion for all time."

Jacob screamed.

"Jacob! I'm sorry! Jacob!"

The voice had been shouting for some time, but he hadn't heard it over his ragged shrieks. The pyramid in his house flowered open. A woman emerged.

"Hi, Jacob," she began, looking embarrassed. "Forgive me, okay? I wasn't trying to freak you out, I swear!"

He blinked. "Jocelyn?"

"Who else?"

"I thought you were in cloudspace?"

She grinned and flung herself into him, wrapping her arms around his waist. He shrank from the proffered greeting, nerves still firing in anxiety.

Jocelyn cocked her head. "Hey, I said I'm sorry! Come on, don't make a big deal of it! I was just having some fun!" She released him and hopped onto the kitchen counter, perching there like a gargoyle.

"If you're *really* Jocelyn, you would know the last thing we discussed."

She sighed in annoyance. "And I do, you paranoid freak. It was the eve of my debt-sentencing, and I told you that if I remained conscious, it'd be cool if I ended up as a dildo. Does that convince you?

I'm your friend Jocelyn! Stop being an idiot!"

He felt a flash of anger. "You hacked my house?"

"Yep. Can I have something to eat?"

"Figured you would have helped yourself."

"I did," she admitted. "You've got terrific culinary options! I never knew you were such a connoisseur! But I *did* have to download a sushi program while I was waiting for you. What? You don't like raw fish?"

"No. And I don't like being hacked, either."

Jocelyn shrugged—a flippant motion that incensed him. "Well, I didn't like being in cloudspace. You don't think about it usually when you bounce off the cloud. But when you've got to *stay* there for extended periods of time? A fucking nightmare! They have these nanocrystalline tethers that you get uploaded to, and then you just... drift. No ground, no solidity. It's like being a ghost. Everything passes through everything else. They should call it hellspace." She shuddered.

"You were supposed to be there for five years, as I recall."

She shrugged again. "Early release."

"How? Good behavior as a ghost?"

"Something like that."

"Get out," he snapped, "and return homespace control to me."

She made a face. "Yeah? Or what?"

"I'm not kidding, Jocelyn. That shit you pulled almost gave me a heart attack."

"A heart attack! That's good!"

"Still costs money to be resurrected," Jacob said defensively. "And I don't need my premiums going up." He hesitated, measuring her defiant stance. "So what's with the early release? Honestly?"

She grinned. "I made a deal."

"With who?"

"Sun."

He was silent. New fear gathered like icicles in his blood, and he subconsciously edged toward the door, wondering if there were other criminals hiding in his homespace. "You're on Sun's payroll now?"

"And you are on Ragnar's."

"And that makes us enemies."

She laughed throatily. "Not anymore! There's been a merger."

He was stunned. Sun and Ragnar were two of the world's largest megacorps. They were the new hemispheres of an Earth no longer de-marcated by geography or national borders, but by the acquisition lines of the corporate godhead. For him, that was Ragnar. For her, it was Sun.

"I'm an equity baron." His mind raced, considering escape options. "I would have been notified if there was a merger!"

She shook her head. Behind him, his kitchen rose up into a pharaoh's dais with solar motifs dimpling a wall of departmental glyphs. "The merger is secret, Jacob. Sun ran your profile and my name popped up as a known associate. So, they figured it made sense to escort you to…hey!"

In the corpwars, Jacob was aware of grim competitive intelligence reports telling of corporate poaching. A key employee drops his mass and transmits himself to a vacation spot, and suddenly his signal is captured. He's hacked. His brain is absorbed and rewritten. His mass is appropriated for enemy use.

Jacob lived in fear of such a thing.

Without further delay, he dropped his mass and flew through his house circuits, reaching for the outgoing lines. In less than a second he was in the Switzerland grid. He conjured local mass and was suddenly running across a Swiss tarmac into a marketplace. Glass storefronts, neon signs, and a dozen escalators.

Jacob hopped onto an escalator, heading down, his heart pounding.

He had to get to the regional office. If Sun had the ability to hack his home, he needed backup. Ragnar needed to know!

The escalator steps vanished into the floor below him. Jacob sweated, wondering what had happened to the *real* Jocelyn. Or perhaps that *had* been the real Jocelyn, the little self-serving freelancer that she was.

He was nearing the bottom of the escalator. He prepared to step off the vanishing stairs—

—and his legs wouldn't respond.

His shoes seemed to have become glued to the steps. Gasping, he yanked at his legs. He was rooted like a young tree. The escalator flattened out below him, disappearing down the paper-thin gullet of the machine.

"No!" he screamed. "Somebody help me! *Somebody help!*"

As the market's stunned onlookers watched, Jacob melted along with the escalator stairs and disappeared into the floor.

When he reformed, Jocelyn looked plenty pissed.

They were in a Japanese tea room somewhere beneath the market. Red-lacquered walls and shoji dividers and tatami floormats, with Jocelyn sitting lotus-style, glowering at him, while an indifferent waitress poured hot tea into dainty pearl-colored cups.

"She's not real," Jocelyn said sullenly. "So feel free to talk, you paranoid bastard."

"I would have known if Sun and Ragnar were involved in a merger," he cried. "I'm an equity baron, dammit!"

"Put your pride on pause, will you? There's a *reason* it's been kept hush-hush, so drink your damn tea and I'll explain. We're going to an invitation-only strategy meeting. You were *invited*, get it? I was ordered to come get you, so it reflects poorly on me when you freak out like that! You've got all of Switzerland in a panic."

He lifted the scalding tea to his lips and drank. His hands were shaking.

"The godheads of Sun and Ragnar agreed to a merger," she explained. She was flushed from the pursuit, and she snapped up her tea, watching him over the cup's rim. "I was able to get into your homespace because it's not *your* homespace anymore. It's now a property deed jointly owned by both megacorps. The pyramid…that was my idea."

He was feeling a little better. If Sun wanted to absorb him, they would have done it by now. Still, he kept the teacup protectively at his mouth, letting the steam moisten his face.

Jocelyn continued. "All equity barons are being summoned to a strategy call for further explanation."

"Hopefully *you're* not the emissary tasked with fetching them all," he said sourly.

"We can't all be as charming as you." She drank the remainder of her tea. "Come on, we've got to be there in four minutes before the firewall closes." She stood, looked sideways at him. "I like you, Jacob, but if you try to run again I'll turn the tea in your stomach into a block of lead."

The meeting was held in a hive-like structure about one mile underground. At least, it looked like underground, with the hewn rock and veins of ore glinting in a sepia glow. It could have been inside a mountain for all Jacob could tell, or under the sea, or maybe the godheads were doing it in virtual. Nowadays, angels could not only dance on pinheads; they could hold entire conventions atop pinheads that didn't exist.

At any rate, the meeting hall gradually fashioned itself into something like the interior of a massive wasp nest. The vast concavity became pockmarked by thousands of coffers, each containing a person. But they were generic-looking people. No identities were being revealed, and so the meeting hall was filled with faceless, clay-colored attendees like some nightmarish mannequin factory.

"I don't have any arms or legs," Jacob whispered to Jocelyn.

"Neither do I. We're meant to listen, not move around and shuffle our feet."

Slowly, the chamber began to fill with rich, buttery light. The corporate logo of Sun appeared—a dazzling flame sending rays of warmth in every direction. At the same time, Ragnar's eagle-shaped logo materialized alongside it. They were holograms, and as the secret attendees gasped, the two shapes overlapped and became one. An eagle surrounded by fire.

"Welcome to tomorrow," a voice spoke in their heads. It was a crisp, clear voice, and it didn't need to shout. "Let's have an important discussion, you and I. There are twenty billion lives on Earth. Their future must be decided."

The world had been divided into three lobes for as long as Jacob could remember, and you needed to scroll back more than a century to find references that, once upon a time, there had once been other companies too.

In fact, those old references were a historical footnote almost too surreal to be believed. It was easier to think that the Earth had *always* had three megacorps…rather than acknowledge the bygone fables of thousands of corpstates, nations, and tribal enclaves.

Three megacorps struck deep chords of logic and common sense. Earth was the *third* planet in the solar system, after all. There were *three* primary colors. All children had *three* parents—mother, father, and exogenesis pod in which they were incubated.

The Sun godhead spoke, and then the Ragnar godhead joined in what amounted to an intellectual duet. The attendees listened to their grand vision: No more war between the two great empires. The mass of the world would be shared.

"Why keep this secret then?" asked the godhead. Jacob couldn't discern which godhead was speaking, and his eyes fixed on the unified logo. The corporate voices had blended into a single note.

"We have kept it secret," the godhead continued, "because there is still strife and war and cruelty and divisiveness. You know of whom we are speaking."

Jacob nodded. The Sun Ragnar was referring to the third empire of the world. It was referring to Oakbrand.

Sometimes there's a friendly respect that forms between enemies. Sun and Ragnar had engaged in a cold war so long that they knew each other, and there was comfort in that familiarity. By contrast, Oakbrand was an isolated kingdom. Oakbrand laid claim to the mass of the world's northern hemisphere. It maintained a secretive curtain over all it did. You couldn't even transmit to their locations; you had to manifest outside their borders, and then *walk* into Oakbrand territory. If you dared.

"Oakbrand," said the godhead, and there was a murmur through the meeting hive, "is common enemy to us all. They remain the last obstacle to a true, *global* merger."

"*A global merger?*" Jacob whispered, thunderstruck by the idea.

He could sense Jocelyn's smile beside him. "That's right, idiot. One megacorp. One world."

"No one has ever managed that!"

"*We* will achieve it."

"But—"

"You're going to say that Oakbrand will never agree to a merger," she said. "We know."

"Then why even waste time discussing it?"

Jocelyn's smile was pure lechery. "Hostile takeover."

"Like hell."

"We're going to forcibly appropriate their matter. Absorb it into the collective."

Jacob was silent for a stretch of many microseconds, while the corporate godhead droned on in the hive. Then, finding his voice, he said, "You mean we're going to murder three billion people? We're going to…eat them?"

He shuddered to the depths of this legless, armless body that Sun Ragnar was forcing him to occupy. When had humanity been reduced to plankton, susceptible to consumption by a corporate maw? Had it always been the case? When he was just an embryo growing like a bloody tumor on the walls of his exogenesis pod, his fate had already been decided, hadn't it?

Jacob found his voice at last. "Oakbrand is half a continent in size. How do we attack them? They'll never let us transmit across their borders. We can't just emerge like Trojans from a transmit node! What's the strategy?"

Jocelyn spoke, but it seemed like the voice of the corporate godhead was issuing from her sensual lips. "You'll see. It's a matter of matter."

"What do you mean?"

"We'll wash over their lands like a tidal wave," Jocelyn, or the godhead, explained patiently. "Or more precisely, like a tsunami. We'll reduce the collective mass of all Sun Ragnar inhabitants and buildings and trees and streets into a protean apocalypse, racing across the ocean like a shockwave. Right at their shoreline we'll rise up! Oh, it will be beautiful! A towering wave of biomass rising like…like…a pyramid!" There was laughter. "We'll be a wave thousands of meters tall, rushing at hundreds of miles an hour. We'll be across their borders before they know it. We'll cover their lands. Boiling, bubbling, splashing into all crevices and buildings! We'll devour our enemy and add them to our unity. One world!"

The hive chanted, "One world."

"And what of us?" Jacob muttered, surrendering to the grandiosity of the vision. "Where will our consciousnesses be?"

"In cloudspace," came the reply. "We will all dance on pinheads in cloudspace while the attack commences, and then we will descend back to an Earth remade. One world!"

"One world!" echoed the crowd.

The godhead continued through Jocelyn, "We will wait in Heaven while conflict perishes in a mighty wave of righteousness. Global mass will be ours. No more division! No more war! A paradise awaits us all. One world!"

"One world!"

This time, Jacob added his own voice to the rhythmic chant.

They transmitted to cloudspace where there were no bodies. The nanocrystalline substrate was like gossamer wisps, visible only as glittering mica dust beneath the nourishing fusion showers of the sun. Billions of bodiless minds gathered, connected frail tendrils like excited jellyfish, and formed an optical array so they could watch from on high how the war was going.

I can't see the wave, Jacob transmitted to Jocelyn. She was an invisible presence beside him, little more than a compression of neuron-data, like him, and like two-thirds of the human race now.

Jocelyn answered him: *You won't see it until it's about to wash over Oakbrand properties. That's the whole point, idiot.*

Jacob patched into the optic center for the cloud, a single cyclopean eye staring down at the watery expanse of Pacific blue. *You must feel like you're back in prison,* he sent dryly.

Only for a little while longer, she said defensively.

As they would later learn, the wave *did* impact Oakbrand precisely as planned. The dissolved biomass of Sun Ragnar shot up into the sky and boiled over enemy lands like a legendary flood. It seeped into every crack, it assailed every transmit mode, dividing and cordoning off all escape routes. The god Proteus lived and died in a hundred million separate battles.

And then an electric blue umbrella of light mushroomed from Oakbrand properties. The continent froze in mid-battle, the titanic images of monsters and claws and gnashing teeth petrified as if in a feverish snapshot.

And never moved again.

Slowly, the explanation filtered throughout cloudspace.

Electromagnetic pulse.

On a continent-wide scale.

Faced with extinction, Oakbrand must have called upon a doomsday solution. They must have had electromagnetic bombs peppered throughout their nation as a deterrent no one had anticipated. All earthly shapespace was fried in defiant overload. The war froze. Literally. All circuits dead. All bodies, all mass, petrified. Humanity united at last in a picture of eternal struggle.

The populace of Sun Ragnar, floating on high, attempted to contact the world below and found only silence and a picture of frozen rage.

We just witnessed a mass extinction, Jacob thought in horror. The cloudspace drifted above the dead continent. Above a dead world.

A mass extinction, he repeated. *Only we'll still be here, deranged angelic creatures without bodies, floating as formless phantasms. Immortal. Undying. Incorporeal. Floating in the clouds, basking and soaking in the limitless energy from the sun like...*

...like plankton on the seas.

Slowly, Jacob began to laugh for a billion years.

FALLING LEAVES

Liz Argall

Aurealis Award Finalist

CHARLOTTE AND NESSA MET IN Year Eight of Narrabri High School. Charlotte's family were licensed refugees from the burning lands and the flooded coast, not quite landed, but a step apart from refugees that didn't have dog tags.

Charlotte sat on the roof, dangled her legs off the edge and gazed at the wounded horizon, as she did every lunchtime. Nessa, recognizing the posture of a fellow animal in pain, climbed up to see what she could do. The mica in the concrete glittered and scoured her palms as she braced herself between an imitation tree and the wall and shimmied her way up.

She had to be careful not to break the tree, a cheap recycled-plastic genericus—who'd waste water on a decorative tree for children? The plastic bark squished beneath Nessa's sneakers, smelling of paint thinner and the tired elastic of granny underpants.

Nessa tried to act casual once she got to the top, banging her knee hard as she hauled herself over the ledge and ripping a fresh hole in her cargos. She took a deep breath, wiped her sweaty hands, and sat down next to Charlotte.

"'Sup?" said Nessa.

"Go away." Charlotte kicked her feet against the wall and pressed her waxy lips together.

"You gonna jump?"

"No. I'm not an attention seeking whore like you," said Charlotte.

Nessa shrugged her shoulders, as if that could roll away the sting. Rolling with the punches was what she did. "You look sad."

Charlotte bared her teeth. "I said, I'm not like you. Leave me alone."

Nessa wanted to say, "Fuck you," but she didn't. Nessa wanted to find magic words to fix Charlotte in an impatient flurry. She couldn't. Nessa scratched her scars for a while and felt like puking, but she didn't think that would help either. Neither would hitting Charlotte's head against a wall and cracking Charlotte's head into happiness, although Nessa could imagine it so violently and brightly it felt like she'd done it.

Nessa had banged her own head against walls to get the pain out of her head and chest, but it never worked—or rather it never worked for long enough, leading to a worse, moreish pain.

Nessa didn't know what to do, so she just sat there, feeling chicken shit, until the bell summoned them into class.

Nessa found herself back up on the roof the next day, drumming her heels against the wall and reading a book speckled with dry rot. She didn't know how to talk to Charlotte and talking to refugees, even ones with dog tags, was encouraged in a nauseated, be nice to lepers way. She didn't know what to say, but she didn't have any friends either, and the roof was nice and quiet.

Nessa drummed her heels and sent her mind somewhere else, while Charlotte thought about what it would be like to hit the rough tarred yard, how her body would crumple and wondered whether she'd die instantly or bleed out.

Nessa came back the next day, and the day after, to read her book and drum her heels. Nessa liked the roof; she wasn't sure what she felt about Charlotte.

Charlotte hated Nessa's intrusion. Charlotte hated the sound Nessa's heels made against the concrete. She hated the way Nessa turned the page, licking thumb and forefinger, grasping the top page with a peculiar, showy precision. She hated the way Nessa smelled, cheap lemon scented body wipes off-gassing in the sun.

Charlotte thought about leaving, but dammit this was hers, and she wasn't going to let some landed bitch take it from her. But then, after a while, on the days Nessa skipped school and didn't climb up to claim her sun-warmed patch of concrete, Charlotte missed Nessa.

"Stop it," snapped Charlotte after Nessa climbed up onto the roof-top and drummed her heels.

Nessa's sense of peace snapped like elastic. The pain flinging her to her feet, "Fuck you! You don't own the roof. I can sit where I like."

"Just stop drumming your heels," said Charlotte. "God! What's wrong with you?"

"What's wrong with me?" Nessa clenched her hands so tight her nails bit divots into her palms.

"I just asked you to quit making that sound," said Charlotte.

"No you didn't, you just screamed at me."

"I didn't mean it that way," yelled Charlotte.

"You were judging me. Like everyone else, sitting up here so high and mighty."

"I'm not judging anyone," lied Charlotte.

"I thought you were different," said Nessa and she did not say *I thought you were safe.*

"I thought you were different," said Charlotte and she did not say *and so I relaxed and snapped and you saw just how ugly I am.*

"I am different," yelled Nessa.

"Well so am I!"

"Good."

"Fine."

Nessa let herself sigh, breathing out through her nose and softening her fighting stance. Charlotte looked down at Nessa's spot, back up to Nessa and then away to the scrawl of ugly school children below.

Nessa sat down. She started kicking the wall with her heels and then stopped. They sat in silence. Eventually Nessa said, "I guess I overreacted."

"I dunno, maybe." Charlotte shrugged her shoulders. Neither had a clear sense of normal; it made it hard to tell.

They greeted each other in public, acknowledging each other with monosyllabic grunts. Nodding heads, eye contact, perhaps a tiny smile. At some point they became friends. Though they never called it that, the f-word was too potent, impossible and delicate. Sometimes Nessa shared her water ration. When they were slick with refuse from ag class (code for picking over garbage) Charlotte gave Nessa a smear of the anti-bacterial enzyme her parents grew.

On their way to vocational training, a fancy name for free factory labor, a burner slung his arms over their shoulders. The stench of burnt hair and ripe sweat washed over them. He pressed his face close to theirs, eyebrows and lashes singed into uneven chunks, skull a mottled pink, scars on his chin where bumfluff had been burned back. "Are you girlfriends? Can I watch?"

Charlotte shrank away from his draping hands. Refugees that became burners carried their damage strong—keeping themselves hairless using whatever fire came to hand. Pretending to be something until school spat them out and the world mulched over them. She hated and envied the way they remembered and as a dog-tagged refugee she knew they hated her as a sellout.

Nessa grabbed the burner's throat and pushed him against the locker. "Can I watch you bleed?"

The burner tried to punch Nessa in the guts. Nessa felt something happen near her abdomen, but mostly she felt his neck push against her hand and the satisfying thud of his head slamming against the locker. She felt something warm trickle over her fingers and moved her hand up to find its source. She found a fresh cut in his scalp, jagged from the locker's edge, and she poked it.

"You fucking bitch!"

He punched her a few more times in the guts. She went for his eyes and nose with an open palm. He went down first.

Nessa walked away before he got up and before the adrenaline crash took her legs away. The ground felt sloped, full of miniature stumbling blocks.

Charlotte hurried after and whispered in Nessa's ear, "What were you thinking? They'll come after us."

"Maybe solo," wheezed Nessa. "But he won't tell the gang, too embarrassing. Beat by a girl? There isn't enough fire to take away that shame."

"You're mad."

"Yeah."

It was hard to breathe and her guts twisted like snakes, but Nessa felt better than she had in months. An overwound spring uncoiling at last, and if trouble came afterwards, well, at least she'd go down fighting. And it felt good to be able to protect someone, it made her feel like a person.

Nessa saw the burner a few times from a distance, but cat-like he pretended it had never happened. A few weeks later his face disappeared from the school. Part of her was disappointed.

When family got too hard to live with Charlotte and Nessa'd go bush and climb up into the Nandewar ranges—scraps of wilderness too steep or too dry to be cultivated. Let the scrub hold its own and save itself where it can, hold back the weeping salt that crawled up from the earth. The land did not care if they lived or died, but walking the land was a comfort; they became part of a grief bigger than themselves.

Lulled by the bush they often dreamt of running away, but they knew the color of fool's gold. Family held the ration books, the water rights, the ID cards that gave them human rights, and sleeping rough could get damn cold at night.

Once, they came across a wirringan. They damn near died of fright when he appeared in a place they thought of as theirs. He didn't eat them or anything. He just looked like an old man with a beard and gave them strong sweet tea. They sipped from chipped enamel cups as they sat cross-legged on the ground. He told them stories and warned them about places they should not go. They listened for a long time.

Sometimes they hiked up Mount Kaputar, climbing their way past huddled refugee camps, beggars, rain churches, and memorial stones. When they reached the top they yelled songs of love at the land and threw leaves of weather blessings into the wind.

One lazy noon, as they were sitting on the roof sharing a baked bean sandwich, Charlotte realized she wasn't sure when she'd last dreamt of dying. The surprise hit her so hard she laughed.

"What?" said Nessa, her own laugh punctuated by an unladylike spritz of orange baked bean. "Shit, sorry."

"Nothing." Charlotte smiled.

Nessa shook her head and smirked. Her baked beans, slowly melting through the sandwich, chose that moment to fall through the bread and land all over her lap. "Gah!"

"God, I'm sorry."

"S'not your fault," said Nessa as she danced to her feet and emptied the beans all over the rooftop. "Food and I don't like each other much anyway."

Nessa did her best to clean up her shorts using gum leaves that had blown in from a real tree. Charlotte scraped the baked beans off the roof, kicking with the side of her sneakers. Some beans landed on the head of a kid below.

Charlotte and Nessa fled and crouched behind an air conditioning unit on the other side of the roof.

"We are in so much trouble." Charlotte giggled.

"Only if we confess. Oldies see what they want to."

Nessa ground her fingernails against each other and shrugged. Nessa and Charlotte let the concrete's heat lull them into warm stupor.

"What do you want to be?" said Nessa, her voice suddenly ragged.

"Drover," lied Charlotte. "You?"

Nessa pursed her lips and looked up at the empty blue sky. "Rich. I'd board New Venice and never look back."

"Like that'd happen."

Nessa smiled and wriggled her back against the air conditioner's concrete cladding. "Don't ruin my dream. Venice won't float near here for a decade, anyway."

"You don't know what you want."

"Neither do you. Drover? Really? I want to become a big bird and fly across the world."

"Yeah, me to."

Nessa poked Charlotte in the arm and grinned. They hugged each other. Charlotte breathed deeply, enjoying Nessa's lemony scent.

The next spring Nessa got sick and hardly came to school. When she did she didn't have the strength to climb up to the roof, and for the scant days they had together Charlotte had to climb down from her aerie. They huddled on the ugly concrete near the bike cage, accompanied by the overripe scent of banana skins and spilt Cack. Charlotte hated Nessa for being sick. She hated Nessa for abandoning her. She hated Nessa for being her friend and giving her something to lose.

On a sun-bleached Tuesday Charlotte fell from the roof. Slipped, leapt, she wasn't sure. Sometimes it was hard to tell what she was thinking as she played with the edge.

Charlotte felt the concrete edge slip away from her. A numb serenity gave way to convulsive fear roiling up and down her body. Pain shredded her. Asphalt split her skin and bones.

She did not fall unconscious. People kept her awake, pulled her from the dark. She hated them. She hated their sounds. She hated her body. But she also hated the idea of dying and hate was the savage thread she held onto, through broken teeth and flooding ribs, until the paramedics pierced her arm with something that drove sensation away.

If she'd fallen in Newcastle the only consideration would've been how fast would she die, and would her body still have shoes when it reached her family. She was lucky, lucky to be landed, lucky to live in a place with hospitals and schools and without famine.

The ambulance, with Charlotte's bloodied body slipped inside, rushed past Nessa's house. Nessa was eating cereal and watching replays of Sydney burning when the claxons whizzed by. She didn't know her best friend was being revived as the ambulance skidded past their lawn of grey gravel and seaglass.

Nessa didn't find out until the next day at assembly; she limped her way to school, dizzy with the exertion. The news hit Nessa like a gunshot. Her fingernails clawed deep into the scars on her arms. She bit the inside of her mouth and imagined slashing her throat open with a straight razor.

A pretty girl next to her sobbed and was comforted. "I…I sit next to her in…in History…w-w-why?" Nessa wanted to punch the girl in the face. Unwept tears shivered up and down her body, like ice, like fire. Nessa really wanted to punch that girl.

Nessa walked out. Teachers had become accustomed to the erratic attendance record of a sickly child. She walked to the hospital. She didn't like the grounds; the space was too open and too disorienting. People nursing saline bags squandered their rations smoking cigarettes close to the entrance, filling each churn of the rotating doors with a thin ooze of smoke. Nessa braved the reception, the tobacco scent washed away by the sharp smell of bleach and alcohol wipes.

"I'm here to see Charlotte," she said firmly.

"What is her last name, sweetie?" The receptionist wore a tie with cartoon characters on it, and had ugly teeth.

Nessa pursed her lips, awash with shame. She had forgotten, how could she forget Charlotte's last name? Time slowed and her eyes flicked from the crack on the receptionist's left incisor to the crack in the linoleum. "Her name is Charlotte. She fell. Fell real bad." Nessa felt like she was some pathetic little kid. She tried hard not to cry and kicked the floor with her shoe. "Charlotte."

The receptionist patted Nessa on the shoulder. Nessa didn't punch the receptionist. "Don't worry, duck. I'll see if I can find her." The receptionist pulled up details on his monitor. He tapped through a few screens and then sucked his lips inwards. "Are you family?"

"No."

"Do you have a grownup with you?"

"No." Nessa scowled. The last thing she needed was someone treating her like some kid. She turned on her heel and walked away. The receptionist called out something to her, but she didn't hear it.

Nessa went home. The key under the paving stone was missing, so she climbed in through the window. She wondered if this was the season to die. She wondered if she would be allowed that escape, and the thought scared her. Instead she hid inside books until her bones felt like they were going to push through her skin.

The next day everyone at school was wearing jeans as a fundraiser to help Charlotte's family with the medical bills. Nessa was wearing baggy black shorts and hadn't brought any money. She wanted to crawl into a hole and die, but that felt derivative.

She picked a fight with a kid, because she didn't like how angry he was. He walked with a snarl, strutting around like he'd pissed on every tree and sneering at girls who should know their place. She didn't like the way he got in her face, but she only got one good hit in. His fists made her head bleed and her vision went muzzy as she hit the dirt.

Worse than losing the fight, teachers caught them and actually gave a shit for a change. Her people weren't great people, but they were landed. He was refugee scum. She got a band aid. He was expelled.

She hated them for that. Of all the things they didn't see, all the things she took the blame for, and the one time they came to the rescue was when it was untrue and unfair. She didn't even get the chance to apologize.

Two weeks later Charlotte was able to receive visitors, although her status was still tenuous. Charlotte's head was shaved and garish staples held bits of skin together. Her body was a living bruise and her jaw had been wired shut.

Nessa said "Hi." Charlotte waved a finger and blinked. Nessa brushed Charlotte's fingers with her own, scared of the physical contact, scared she would make the tubes come out or something terrible happen. Nothing terrible happened. The wild part of Nessa's brain had the sudden urge to jump up and down on the bed and fling herself across Charlotte's chest.

"Would you like me to read to you?"

The corner of Charlotte's mouth quirked.

Nessa read, self-conscious and awkward, from a book she'd

grabbed from the library, *The Drover's Wife*. Charlotte's grey pallor eased and took on a warmer hue as Nessa read. Her faltering breath became a less ragged counterpoint to the hushed melody of piped oxygen.

"Why am I always waiting for you?" muttered Nessa.

But Charlotte had already fallen asleep and was beyond words. Nessa put the book into her bag as if it were some oily thing. She wiped her hands and watched Charlotte rest.

"Why wouldn't you let me protect you?"

Nessa felt stupid, selfish and ugly. The chill violently crystalized and she didn't care…she was all those things, so she might as well be those things. "It's not fair." Her fingertips brushed Charlotte's. "I hate you."

Charlotte sighed in her sleep, and for a moment Nessa did not see a bruised friend healing. Nessa saw Charlotte smiling smugly, so satisfied by all the pain and harm she'd caused, sleeping like a baby while those around her wept.

"Don't you hear me?" hissed Nessa, her lips almost biting Charlotte's ear. "I hate you."

Charlotte's eyes opened to half slits and she made confused sounds.

Nessa grabbed Charlotte by the shoulder and shook her, shook her like it was screaming. "I hate you." Charlotte's body arched convulsively, her eyes pierced Nessa with their pain and confusion.

Nessa ran, ignoring the dismayed nurses, stumbling down the stairs and vomited out into summer's long bleeding sunset. Nessa ran, fast and fierce with her face to the wind, the hot air drying her tears to salt and sparing her from crying. Her eyelashes clumped into small, hurt spears.

It was dark by the time she got to school, the metallic tang of a dry storm building in the air. Nessa climbed up to the top of the roof, picking around fresh sharp barbwire made it difficult. She sat where Charlotte had always been and looked down. The pavement seemed smugly bland, no stain, no chipping to show it had crushed Charlotte to itself.

Rage, wet and salty, ran down Nessa's face. "I hate you. I hate you. I hate you," she spat. "I will never be your friend. I will never…" Nessa choked on the words and the raw hurting truth. "I will never be anyone's friend. Every thing, every word, every person, every feeling is a lie. And I am better off without you."

And as Nessa said "better off without you," she saw as clear as

daylight Charlotte slipping into death; how her words had made truth.
She huddled next to the air conditioning unit and convulsed with the
depth of her sins, and she begged the empty sky for forgiveness. Her
teeth chattered as she mumbled "please be ok," over and over until her
lips felt numb and blue.

Eventually, storm past and clothes wet, Nessa clambered down
from the roof. The barbwire scratched her arms and legs, biting and
catching on old scars. It was almost accidental, emotion had made her
clumsy, and she pretended the pain didn't make her feel better. The
taste of blood and tears blurred as she sucked her injured palm and
returned to her average house and absent parents.

Nessa spent the next week waiting for news that Charlotte had
died. She waited for the police to come and haul her out of school for
murder.

A week went by and Charlotte was not dead, but Nessa's shame
lingered and coated her lungs. She bought razor blades twice. Her mind
traced their edges, but she managed to throw them away without opening the packet. She had never smoked a cigarette, but the pain of sepa-
ration was similar. Unlike smokes, she couldn't get razor blade patches
to take the edge off. She wanted people to know she was strong, strong
in staying clean, but she stayed quiet. She didn't want people to call her
an attention-seeking whore.

Charlotte's parents came to the school. They looked shrunken and
ordinary. She held her breath as they walked past, but they didn't notice her. They just stood up at the podium and thanked everyone very
much for helping them during this terrible time, after such a terrible
accident. Part of Nessa felt hurt, why didn't they try to talk to her?
Why didn't they yell?

Charlotte's parents accepted the cheque for $257.13 with heads
bowed. Nessa felt instant rage: 257 dollars? That was it? Nessa's rage
was tempered by her own inadequacy. What right did she have to be
angry when she had contributed so little? She raged at the gratitude
Charlotte's parents showed, put on display like some freak show, pros-
trating themselves for tips.

As they left Nessa pushed her way out of the assembly and followed them.

"I'm sorry," said Nessa.

Charlotte's parents looked at her with confusion. They made her think of little grey dolls tumbled in the washing machine too many times. "I'm sorry?" echoed Charlotte's father.

"Is Charlotte ok? I visited and…and…is she ok?"

"Are you Charlotte's friend?" said Charlotte's mother.

Nessa bit her lip. "My name is Nessa."

"Nessa, yes, I think Charlotte mentioned you…" Charlotte's father nodded and shook his head.

"Charlotte's doing much better. Thank you for visiting." Charlotte's mother looked to the ground and flickered up again, eyes as filmy as her thin cardigan. "We…Charlotte's never had a lot of friends. Please, visit her again."

"We mustn't impose on the girl," said Charlotte's father.

Nessa found Burners out by the bicycle cage. Their leader was watching younger ones take turns putting their hand under the lens of a magnifying glass—silently sweating as the dot of light bubbled their skin.

"Burner, respect," she said twitching her chin up for a moment.

The Burner leader looked her up and down for a long minute. He wasn't wearing much, ripped jeans, boots, shirt without buttons. And he was hairless, eyebrows, arms, legs, all dotted with scars from fire and knife. Not many made it all the way. A lean, muscular sixteen with eyes of forty.

" 'spect, landed psycho," he said.

One side of Nessa's mouth twitched. It felt good to be recognized. "Does it help?"

"You work with what you've got."

"What's the in? I could do with some penance."

"We don't need tourists."

A young one pulled her hand out from under the magnifying glass, panting heavy and trying to suck the pain away.

"I'm not," said Nessa.

"You're landed. You weren't there."

Nessa wanted to protest, but the leader cut her off.

"Enjoy it. You don't have to burn. So don't."

The young one was having trouble controlling her pain and started to cry. The Burner pulled her onto his lap and hugged her. The young one's cries became open throated sobs. Her tears splashed his chest. He kissed the top of her head as he cradled her.

Nessa stood there for an awkward moment, then walked away. Behind her she heard tears and soft sounds of comfort.

Nessa snuck into the hospital. She didn't need to, but choosing when she was seen made her feel powerful. Charlotte looked even more like a mess, bruises and swelling shifting into new patterns. The air was pungent with Betadine and wet wounds.

"Why'd you jump?" said Nessa.

"I fell."

"I know what it's like, to want to die," said Nessa. "Why'd you jump?"

Charlotte's gaze flickered to the door.

"It's just me," said Nessa. Charlotte kept her eyes on the door, but Nessa was patient, letting the silence stretch and pull between them.

Eventually Charlotte said, "I can't bear the way people look at me."

"Before? Or now?"

"Yes." Silence grew like a wave; Charlotte's shame a dam against her mouth. The silence sucked and created whirlpool eddies until it was Nessa's turn to speak. Razor words shifting, perhaps kinder, perhaps crueler, they scraped as they came out.

"I know what it's like to want to die. The itch. I don't know what hurts worse. The way things hurt or a numbness that burns."

"It's not like that," said Charlotte. She couldn't tell if she was lying, her body hurt and it was hard to breathe.

"The way people's eyes slide around when they see me," continued Nessa. "See my arms, call me selfish, call me an attention seeking whore."

"You're not."

"You've said it." Nessa's voice was calm and pragmatic. "You don't lie."

"I didn't mean it. I was angry, I was scared." Charlotte's ribs hurt along every break; blood pressed against the staples in her face. "I'm a bad person."

It was Nessa's turn to feel stabbed. "No." Then the pain eased. "Maybe you're just braver. Maybe I am just an attention-seeking whore. It's strange, it's selfish… Even after you jumped, I wasn't brave enough."

"It's braver to live."

Nessa twisted her mouth and shook her head. "Then maybe I'm tired of being brave."

Charlotte squirmed under the sheets. The painkillers were wearing off and everything felt harder, foggier. "We have to be brave. You have to."

Nessa held Charlotte's hand as the pain came and went in waves, building like the tide coming in. After forty-five minutes, nurses came and gave Charlotte an injection that took her away from pain and into sleep.

"I'm tired of feeling angry."

Nessa stood under a cold hose, felt the pounding ice water envelop her. Felt the ice wash her clean and find a quiet core. She moved slowly as she poured the buckets of water back into the tank and added bleach—ready for the next shower. The water was turning sour after too many uses—only the insanely wealthy used water once. Even twisting the cap on the bleach bottle felt holy, as if all emotion had been washed from her.

The night air was cool, and the wind pulled at her damp hair. She walked through the streets in a white shift and bare feet; her pocket full of presents. She let her face relax and her body drift, not even her posture was combat ready. Fire was clear, fire was easy, but she would learn gentleness.

The tree had been cut down, but not yet cleared away. She propped its plastic branches against the wall and climbed to the roof. The tree slid away as her feet sought the gaps between barbs on the wire.

She gazed up at the river of stars and spun around and around, nostalgic for a youth she'd only seen in pictures. Dizzy and luminous she made her way to the rooftop's edge.

"Look!" she held her arms wide. "I'm here."

She breathed deep and dug her hands into her pockets. She pulled out leaves of sweet weather blessing and threw them to the wind and the sky.

Leaves fell down, leaves of words, of "Look." "See." "Feel." "Love."

"I'm sorry."

"I'm sorry."

"I'm sorry."

"I don't want to be angry."

"I'm scared."

"There is more than this."

The wind pulls at her arms. She feels naked to the sky. She could spin and spin forever. But she does not fall.

Charlotte will be a long time recovering. Scars run from nose to jaw and across the ridge of her eyebrow. One cheekbone will always be higher than the other; the hair on her head regrows unevenly over scarring.

The hospital will release her early. Only so many beds, she should be grateful she has her life, her brains, be grateful she can walk.

Charlotte will hobble around the house with an arm in a sling and two ankle casts. The doc will say complete bed rest, her ankles, hips and legs need to heal, but who else will make dinner?

Charlotte's parents will always be working, fresh debt to pay down on top of the old. Charlotte will fall on the kitchen floor and scream with pain and want to die, but she won't. The neighbors won't hear her shouts and she will lie on the ground for two hours.

Nessa will help where she can, and sometimes she will succeed and sometimes she'll fail. Nessa will promise not to get in any more fights. When she breaks that promise her tears will be hot and her teeth bloody. It will be a long time before she makes that promise again.

They will climb up Mount Kaputar. Charlotte's bones will still be healing. It will be a staggering ordeal and more than once they'll think they won't make it. They'll climb their way past huddled refugee camps, fake clevermen, and an Auntie will give Charlotte a chew that helps the pain.

When they reach the top they'll yell everything they want and fear and hate and love. They will laugh and cry and feel the hot sun on their faces. They will hold onto that moment, memorizing the edges of joy, of love, of home. It will be a moment they hold onto in the dark times ahead and when the razor's edge calls. They will be brave.

They will throw down sweet weather blessings and they will sing songs to a land that will one day be whole again.

Blood from Stone

Alethea Kontis

2012 Apex Magazine Readers' Choice Winner

HE HAD NO IDEA THAT I loved him. He barely acknowledged that I existed, a maid twice over, little more than a shadow in empty hallways. Trapped in unhappy marriage and prisoner in his own castle, he did not conceive that anyone loving him was even possible. The baron was a man of war, not of love.

He was also an ass, but as Maman said, so many men are.

He'd borne arms with Jeanne d'Arc in Orléans, had witnessed firsthand the divine power she had wielded. *Sorceress*, they'd called her. Maman had shared a similar fate, for far less a magical offense.

The baron was so much more deserving of that power. If there existed a man with more confidence, more passion about things beyond the realms of heaven and earth, I never knew of him. Prelati was a pompous, hand-waving fool in comparison.

After testing the limits of his seemingly boundless wealth and ultimately finding it, the baron surrounded himself with books and candles and crucifixes in his barren estate, refusing to believe that divine voices could only be heard by the ears of unspoiled females. Yes, it was Prelati who suggested that he was imploring the wrong deity, but it was I who sent him the first child.

"Perhaps those among the fallen might better relate to the sons of Adam."

Prelati's silver-tongued accent echoed through the chimney from which I swept the ashes. The charlatan must have been standing directly in front of the fireplace in the baron's study for his words to have landed so crisply in my unspoiled ears.

I heard the baron's response, rumbled deep from his strong chest, but I did not catch the words. His tone asked a question.

"I will consult my books," replied Prelati, just as he always did. Hidden as I was, I couldn't resist rolling my eyes. Prelati made a far better librarian than an alchemist, or a sorcerer, or a demon-speaker, or whatever color the robes he was wearing today suggested.

Too curious to be privy to half the conversation, I tripped over the ash pail and tore through the cloud of dust out the door and down the hall, hoping to better eavesdrop at the seam between the sitting room doors.

The doors were open.

"I don't care which one, Prelati. Choose whomever—or whatever—you want. I just want some sort of answer, angel or demon or otherwise. There is a way to escape this place, and I will find it. Henriette! You read my mind. Stoke the fire, girl, there's a bit of a chill."

The room was dark; Prelati's idiot form blocked what little light escaped from the dying fire, casting giant shadows of him against the walls hung with thick velvet tapestries to keep out the stones' cold. The air was bitter with the unnatural balsamic tang of Prelati's infernal frankincense.

Prelati scowled at me beneath his great beard and moustaches, so black and thick that he might topple over at any moment with the weight of them. I scowled right back. I didn't care what Prelati thought of me, and he knew it. I worried more that the baron might see an ash smudge upon my cheek, though I was of less note to him than a pebble in his shoe. He ordered me about in the same breath he spoke of summoning demons. I was neither a benefit nor a threat to him and his situation, and he was a skunk for thinking it.

Lord Polecat.

I quickly knelt on the marble hearth, so that only the fire witnessed my grin. I dutifully shoveled the white and grey ashes into the almost full metal bin—the baron often spent long hours in this study, and I was not usually permitted to attend to the fire while his lordship was present. I'd make sure to carry this one away with me when I departed and replace it with the now-empty bin I'd knocked over in the adjacent room. I considered hiding it from Cook for a few days before she set me to making the lye soap again.

"We will need candles, my lord, and soft chalk," said Prelati. "If you will excuse me, I will prepare a few new scents that might persuade more unlikely visitors."

I stifled another grin. They'd have to scrape the bottom of the barrel to summon anything more unlikeable than Prelati. My father might have met those criteria, so it's just as well I'm a bastard child. Perhaps I could persuade the baron that my sire had been a demon; he'd have no choice but to notice me then.

I moved quickly across the room with the quiet grace all servants practiced, allowing not so much as a clank from the exceptionally heavy ash bin. Prelati rattled on about his needs and preparations. I dropped a small curtsey to no one and turned.

"Henriette, please send for Poitou; I need the carpets in this study removed."

My breath caught, my chest ached, and my heart skipped a beat at the sound of his voice and the thrill of being addressed, if not seen.

"Yes, sir," I said politely. I curtseyed again and jauntily swung the metal down the cold, dank hall.

I already had plans to make a far more lasting impression.

Unnoticed in plain sight, I monitored their progress for weeks. Every time I crossed the room, I skipped and hopped over more and more shapes drawn across the marble. What the baron lacked in funds, it appeared he did not make up for in artistic ability. The air, thick with Prelati's incense experimentation, went from spicy to sweet to cloying; I wondered if he'd begun urinating in the thurible as a last resort.

I continued to empty the ashes from the fireplace while the room was unoccupied, an ever-dwindling window of time in the wee hours of the morning while the men pursued their supernatural prey. Spell after spell failed. I collected my ashes and waited. The morning finally came when the study door was locked, barring me from entrance. Beyond, I heard the baron's frustrated, sleep-deprived tones berating Prelati for their constant failure.

It was time.

I excused myself from the palace with a message to Cook that I was to run an errand for the baron. I did not speak untruth—the errand *was* for him, every thought in my head was for him. I covered my hair with a scarf, took a woven basket—so much lighter than ash pails—and walked briskly down the hill into town. The smile never left my face and there was no chill for me that day. The angels had heard my prayers. Patience would deliver me my true love's heart.

I did not have an appointment, but I did not expect to see the furrier himself. "I am sorry, mademoiselle," said the furrier's very new and very young apprentice. "But if it is for the baron, perhaps the master will not mind if I go to him."

Brave child; he looked frightened to death at the prospect of disturbing his master at work. I tried to put him at ease. "What is your name, *chérie?*"

"Jeudon, mademoiselle."

"Jeudon." I smiled. "It is my own fault for arriving unannounced! I do not think we need to bother your master with this. In fact, I think you might be the perfect person for this job." *Angels, hear my prayers.*

It worked. Jeudon's shoulders relaxed. "Anything at all, mademoiselle. For the baron."

"For the baron. Of course! Thank you, Jeudon. But first, I will need to see a sample of your work. I trust your master has started your training on smaller animals, *n'est-ce pas?*"

"*Oui,* mademoiselle. Squirrels and rabbits and the like."

"I don't suppose you've experimented with skunk? Polecat?"

Jeudon's silence at my request answered the question, but I waited him out with a grin.

"Mademoiselle, I would never... For the baron..."

"I insist, dear Jeudon! Take me at my word; the baron will be ever so impressed that you have such a unique specimen on hand." I reached into my apron pocket, removing seven small centimes—my meager life savings—and I sent up another prayer to those mysterious angels. "Please deliver the fur yourself. This is for your trouble."

"Me, mademoiselle?"

"Yes, please, Jeudon. The baron will want to both pay you and thank you in person. I suggest you make haste!"

The boy did not think twice before rushing into the workroom and scampering out the door with no less than three small pelts in his hand. He left no word for his master, written or otherwise. Just as well. It might be days before anyone discovered he was missing.

Assuming, of course, that the baron understood my gift to him, but I trusted my beloved implicitly.

I spent the next few days making ash soap in the stench-ridden bowels of the castle. It didn't go unnoticed that every room in the castle but the study had lain unused for a month's time. Cook had taken me to task for idling in hallways and banished me thence. The rough, oversized gloves scratched at my knuckles, raw from the cruel ministrations of her wooden spoon, but as working without gloves would have been a worse punishment, I bore the pain. I slowly lowered an egg into the still-warm pot of lye, fresh from the fire.

"The baron's called for you."

Cook's announcement from the doorway startled me, and I unceremoniously dropped the egg into the pot, splashing droplets upon my gloves. The egg sank below the surface. I yanked my hand back, pulled the glove off, and fished the egg out with my long-handled spoon. The egg should have bobbed back to the top—this pot would need a bit more time on the fire. But not right now.

I nodded, curtseyed, and slipped beneath Cook's hefty bosom that barred the doorway. I forced my feet to slow, but my heart was flying. I wondered if he'd said my name again, out loud, with those perfect lips, or if he'd just sent a message through Poitou for "the girl who cleans the fireplace." No matter. The baron needed me, far more than he realized.

A full bin of ashes met me outside the study door, so I fetched the empty bin from an adjacent room before knocking on the door.

"Enter."

Oh, if only you would let me. But I dared not meet his eyes. Did he suspect I'd sent the boy? "I'm here for the ashes, my lord." I bent my knees, crossed the room to the fireplace, and stopped dead at a sight I'd never thought I'd see: Prelati on his hands and knees with a scrub brush and bucket.

My hand was too late to hide the smile that betrayed me. Palm firmly clamped over mouth, I skirted around the magician and threw myself down at the hearth. The fire was naught but embers now, but it had burned hot and high and left the ash white. It was also slightly greasy and smelled faintly of brimstone.

Dear, dear Jeudon, I thought, as I shoveled him into my bin. The lard in the mix would undoubtedly make a finer soap. I was too busy wondering how to sneak a batch aside for myself to notice that the room behind me had gone silent. No whispers, no movement, nothing... which could only mean that I was suddenly the center of their attention. I stood tall and dusted my clothes off the best I could before turning to face the two men, both now standing.

The baron was looking at me.

Prelati's gaze slipped to the spot where he'd been scrubbing, and my eyes followed. No doubt they had finally discovered the lengths to which their artistic talent did not go, and chosen to erase the chalk and charcoal and start afresh. True, the lines had been erased, but beneath remained a large, pale pink stain on the perfect white marble.

There was only one thing that stain could be: blood. What would they do with me now that I'd seen it? The baron stared with those intensely hard eyes, sizing me up. I raised my chin and stared right back.

"Do you ever wash floors?" he asked.

"I make the soap," I boasted.

"Have this floor clean by sundown, and we will never speak of this again."

"Yes, my lord." I bent my knees again, collected both ash bins, and went below-stairs to retrieve the soap I'd been stockpiling for this very occasion. I'd considered pocketing some in my apron in preparation for this summons, but I didn't want to play my hand too soon.

Charming, how completely predictable the baron was. But like Maman said, so many men are.

I returned with soap, gloves, and a pot to warm water over the fresh fire I'd built up. I crumbled the lye into powder and set hard to the brush, careful not to get anything on my skin or clothes. It was no easy task, and not quickly done, but before sunset I'd removed every trace of blood from that stone. I stopped on the way back to my rooms only long enough to ask a scrawny young thing to replenish the wood in the baron's study. I didn't bother asking his name.

It was several more days before I was shoveling his ashes out of the fireplace and scrubbing the study floor again. I worked privately and efficiently. As promised, the baron said nothing of the matter.

The third time the baron sent for me, I brazenly spoke without being addressed. "I will clean this floor for you, but I want something."

"We let you keep your life," prattled Prelati. "What more could you possibly desire?"

"In order to properly remove a stain, it's best to catch it right away." My eyes never left the baron's. He knew what I meant.

Or did he? His gaze left mine long enough to gauge Prelati's reaction to my comment.

"Your services are no longer required, girl." Prelati put a hand on the small of my back to lead me to the door and I slapped it away.

I turned to the baron and bowed deeply, in the manner of a *chevalier* and not a scullery maid. My heart beat like a battle drum. "As you wish, Lord Polecat. You may fetch your own errand boys from now on."

I straightened, expecting to see a sly grin upon his countenance with the realization that it was I who'd sent the fitch. What met me instead was a drawn mouth and furrowed brow. I admit I was a little disappointed that such an admirable man like the baron could be so stupid. But like Maman said, so many men are.

Heart in my feet now, I moved to walk away. The bin felt twice as heavy, its scorched refuse now burdened with the leaden weight of my shattered dreams.

"I will do anything."

The baron's voice was low enough to almost be unheard above the crackling of the fresh blaze in the hearth. "I will stop at nothing to regain my fortune, my power, and be free from this place. I will defile heaven and pull demons out of Hell to do my bidding. If you get in my way, I will kill you."

I did not turn back at his words, but I did straighten. The ash bin suddenly felt lighter. "I accept those terms," was all I said before leaving the study.

The next time the baron "sent for a messenger," I accompanied him into the study...and stayed.

Those next few years were the happiest times of my life. Instead of letting our failed attempts at summoning get the best of us, we made a game of it. We gathered young boys from far and wide, for a variety of reasons, and never raised so much as an eyebrow of suspicion. We sometimes drew it out for days, seducing the boys with lavish feasts and mulled wine and games. The baron was pleased to discover that I had a steady hand at runes, despite the hard calluses I earned from scrubbing and soap making. I drew many a circle and lit many a candle. Sometimes we let the boy draw and light them himself. We would stoke the fire high and keep it hot. We always burned the clothes first.

Over time, I even came to tolerate Prelati. It was never anything as bold as "friendship," but we knew each other for what we were, and we each respected the other's loyalty to the baron. Prelati saw that I was a quick study and taught me to read so that I might continue their conversation with new ideas and a fresh perspective. After months of watching me soak ashes in rainwater and strain liquid and boil lye, he invited me to experiment with his incense. I, in turn, taught them both the rudiments of soap making. The baron had a deft hand at floating eggs. I imagined those strong, careful hands on my body many, many more times than I'd like to confess. And the marble was so much easier to clean when we could pour the hot lye right down onto the fresh stain.

I did not let the baron touch me intimately, though I knew at times he wanted to. It was a rush to have such power in one's hands, to literally feel lifeblood slipping from between one's fingers. I drew my best work in that blood. We cleaned the middle of the floor so well and often that I was eventually forced to scrub the rest of the study to match.

Our efforts were not entirely unsuccessful; for otherwise, we wouldn't have wasted so much time. There were days when the candles' flame changed color, or the air filled with tiny starbursts of light. Some chants brought a wind that left the room in complete darkness. One even made it rain indoors—I ran so much that day saving the ash pots and collecting fresh water that I fell asleep in wet clothes on the wet settee and did not wake until the next afternoon. Certain chants made the incense smell strongly of roses, or rot. The flavor of everything we ate on those days was wrong. Not always *bad*, mind you, but roast duck that tastes of chocolate pudding is a shock to any palate.

We celebrated our little triumphs. We danced barefoot in the blood, painted ourselves with red and black and white, finished off the mulled wine and sang every silly song we knew until we'd exhausted our repertoire. Then we pulled on our bootstraps, divined what we could from the entrails, added to Prelati's endless stack of notes, and cleared the stage for the next attempt.

I began to dread the day we actually summoned a demon, when I would lose my place in this exclusive club, and lose the baron altogether. *My* baron. We were close to success; I knew it. I could hear it on the wind. I could taste it in the spiced air. I could feel it in my bones. I feared it so much that I finally let him kiss me.

"Let me in." The words were soft, growled into my neck in frustration. My toes slipped in the blood beneath our feet, but I held my ground.

"Make me your wife," I whispered back.

"I have a wife," he said, and not kindly.

I placed my palm flat on his wide chest, leaving a small red print on the white silk. "Your title is married to her. Not your heart."

The next day, he stole us a cleric.

I took an inordinate amount of time preparing for the ceremony. I believe that Prelati deduced my plans—he was smarter than I'd previously given him credit for, especially with regard to subterfuge and mental manipulation—but he said nothing. He mixed the incense concoction we'd agreed upon and painted my face and arms with the necessary symbols after I'd baptized myself in rainwater.

We exchanged gifts, the baron and I, as per tradition more than as a requirement of the summoning ceremony. I gave him a waxen dolly in his own image, as Maman had taught me to do in life, and then taught me never to do again with her death. From my baron bridegroom I received a solid white egg...that I almost dropped when he placed it in my hands. Upon further examination, I realized it was fashioned out of pure white marble—the perfect symbol of the birth of our love for each other. I slipped it into the pocket of my dress so that no blood would mar its pristine surface.

We built up the fire and lit the candles, and when all was ready, Prelati untied the cleric.

The wise man must have realized his fate, for he did not rush the ceremony. My girlish sensibilities thanked him for every extra moment I was allowed to stand upon the symbols with my beloved's hand in mine.

"Lady Polecat," the baron's breath said into mine.

"Lord Fitcher," I replied.

The second time the baron kissed me, I was his wife. Not his first wife on paper, warden to his prison cell, but the first wife in the way that really mattered: the wife of his heart and soul. This love—our love—was true.

But for all the romance I was a practical young girl. I knew that this union did not exist outside this study, or this castle, or even before the cleric's god. We could lie together as man and wife, but that's exactly what it was: a lie. I could lie beside him for the rest of his days and watch him attempt to summon demon after demon until he killed everyone in the castle, and then Prelati, and then himself. Or I could give him what he wanted—what he needed—and set him free.

In my mind, there was never a choice.

Prelati handed the ebony-handled athame to the baron, but this time those beady black eyes never left mine. My love, my *husband*, drew the blade across his palm with a hiss. I took the dagger myself and did the same without so much as exhaling—I could risk losing neither his belief nor his pride in me for the next few moments. We clasped hands with the strength of two lovers facing the universe.

The candles' flames at the points of the star we'd sketched on the marble turned blue and, as before, the air filled with tiny points of light. The fireplace roared, and the thurible's smoke changed from sandalwood to rosemary. The cleric crossed himself. Thrice.

"It's working," the baron said without breathing, as if he might break the spell with a word. "Henriette, my love, it's working!" I would never tire of hearing my name spoken from those lips.

"I know." I tried to reply without gasping, but my body betrayed me. The baron tore his attention away from the magical room to see the dagger in my hand so covered in blood that it totally obscured the double blade. My virgin bride's blood dripped from my core onto the rune-riddled marble between us.

My true love held me in strong arms; had my silly girlish legs not already given way, they would have then. "What have you done?" He might have screamed this, but I only heard him whisper.

"Freed you," I said, or perhaps I said. Perhaps the only fragment to escape my lips had been "free," but that syllable conveyed the message just as well.

There was no blackness for me to succumb to, nor was there a legendary white light for me to follow. The room stayed exactly as it was, in stark detail, and I tried to commit as much to memory as I could before one entity or another whisked me away to some great beyond. The baron knelt over my limp body, repeating "No" over and over again as if the chant might act as a tether to pull my soul back into my body. Prelati stood to one side of the circle in his solemn violet robes and bowed his head, praying to...something. So neither one of them saw the portal open and the man in black step through.

The man was followed by two angels, both terrible, one with wings of feathers and one with wings of fire. My sacrifice had not summoned a demon, then, it had summoned a *god*. This could only be Lord Death himself.

"We seem to have ourselves a dilemma."

Awestruck, Prelati fell to his knees beside the baron. The cleric passed out cold.

"Bring back my wife." The baron did not implore Lord Death so much as order him to do so.

"See, that's just the thing." Lord Death crossed his legs and sat on the stone, casually before them, before my dead body. The angels remained standing, one to either side of him, as did my ethereal soul. Exactly how much of the room's population could the baron and Prelati see?

"What your loving 'wife' has done here is sacrifice herself for you," Lord Death continued. "To bring her back would undo all that precious magic you've managed to accomplish."

The baron did not reply, but Prelati nodded.

"This girl has made you capable of *love*, of all things. She's also, in one fell swoop, stopped you from ever killing another child again. Am I right?"

The baron gave the idea some thought before nodding his own assent. Of course, my love would no longer bother himself with children. The key to his prison had been there all along in the very thing he eschewed: divinity still had a soft spot for unspoiled females. The marriage ceremony had caught their attention, and the blood had kept it.

"I must honor this sacrifice, as much as it pains me to do so." Lord Death scanned the room, from the well-scrubbed floor to the cinder-strewn hearth. The angel of fire's wings burned ever brighter, and I choked on her ash.

The baron—my baron—took up the bloody athame and looked to a sky that was not there. "Then let me follow her."

Lord Death stayed his hand. "Yeah, let me stop you right there. See, if you do that now, it's not a sacrifice. It's suicide. That particular end will deliver you to a very different place. Am I right?" This was directed at the cleric who, having come to, nodded vigorously. "You will never join her, my dear baron, until you die by a hand other than your own. A death that serves to free the soul of someone else."

The baron looked to Prelati, who raised his own hands in defeat. Prelati's soul was well beyond saving.

"Please," said the baron, and it was a tone I had only ever heard him use to me. "Let her stay with me. There must be some way. Let her haunt me until the end of my days, if you must, but let her stay with me."

"I'm inclined to agree, actually," said Lord Death. "It would be a fitting end for both of you." He gestured to the angel of feathers and that bright light I'd heard so much about finally washed over me. There was a rush of wind and a choir of springtime. I felt blood in my veins and breath in my lungs and strength in my sinew. When my vision cleared, I was viewing the scene from a very new perspective, right in front of Lord Death's face. I screamed, and the dim study echoed with birdsong.

I had wings, indeed, but I was no angel.

"She will stay with you, as requested, until you are relieved of your earthly, fleshy prison." Lord Death stood. "You deserve each other." That mystic portal appeared again, and the angels of feathers and fire sped through the opening before him. Lord Death was halfway through before he turned back for one last remark.

"Oh. And Prelati—cut it out, already."

"Yes, my lord." They were the last words the magician said before they both disappeared.

Overwhelmed, the cleric fainted. Again.

My beloved took my earthly body down, down, down to my rooms in the bowels of his castle, where no one ever saw me but the fire and the ashes and Cook. I fluttered after him on awkward wings. He laid my body on the table: black hair, white dress, red blood and all. He spent a very long time arranging my limbs and clothes. I used the time to find currents of air around the room, getting used to my new body. When he was satisfied, he banked the fire, closed the door to the room, and locked it tight.

He slid the key onto the chain around his neck that once bore a cross—now it held our wedding bands. He pressed his forehead against the door and whispered something, but I didn't catch it. In his hands—larger to me now than they ever had been—was a small white object. My bride gift. He must have rescued it from my pocket when he'd been arranging my dress. My rapidly beating little heart swelled with pride and I burst into song.

The baron raised the perfect white egg to his lips and kissed it, as he had once kissed me. "We have lots of work ahead of us, little bird. There's a floor in my study that needs scrubbing." I perched on his outstretched hand and he stroked my feathers with fingers that would be forced to draw new runes and symbols all on their clumsy own. "And then...let's find a new wife!"

Sexagesimal

Katharine E.K. Duckett

2012 Apex Magazine Readers' Choice Winner

00:41

"You can see summer from here," said Zoya. "On a clear day, anyway. And September's a ten-minute walk."

Teskia looked toward the hills, fingers tapping the sill. "What's your asking price?"

Zoya shrugged her small shoulders. "I'm not asking to sell. You're asking to buy." She morphalated, her hair lightening from deep auburn to the red-gold curls that once shone under the Black Sea sun. Teskia averted her eyes: flashes of her mother's younger self disquieted her.

The season was setting in the west. "Four years."

"I won't take any goldens. They're worthless."

"No, I'll give you sterling. Mid-50s. To own the place."

Zoya closed her eyes. "Okay." She extended a hand. "It's yours."

1:15

Teskia brought Julio to the house in a dawn-driven caravan. He lay motionless on a gold litter she had constructed for a high school play, carried by tanned, solid memories: multiplication tables and easy grammar rules, grounded reminiscences that almost passed for facts. They carried him up the steps and into the empty living room, where she fed him a few minutes through a funnel. He swallowed, but did not open his eyes.

Furniture began to pop up. Oak chairs from their first dining room; a milk-stained futon from pre-school; her grandmother's bed-side table, complete with its icon of a baleful Virgin and Child—nothing matched. Decorating took time, intention: all her energy was focused on Julio. She spent her hours sitting beside him, kneading his limp hand, snatching at bits of the past she might have overlooked. What had his soccer uniform looked like junior year? When did he lose his fifth tooth? How many games of Scrabble had he won against her during the summer of 2013? She thought it was helping—his cheeks seemed ruddier, his breathing easier—but he didn't wake up. They were surviving entirely on her time now, draining her memories twice as quickly. They couldn't afford the strain much longer: Julio had to wake up and remember their life, or they would no longer have one.

3:29

It was Julio who had coined the term "morphalating" to describe how people looked in the Afterlife.

"Flickering's not quite the word for it," Teskia had said as she'd watched Julio's face shift, the wrinkles from his frequent grin creasing and fading, his facial hair receding from full beard into peach fuzz. "It's more like—"

"Undulating—"

"Morphing—"

"Morphalating."

The term had stuck—Julio liked the sci-fi feel of it, and Teskia was a sucker for goofy portmanteaus. As far as they knew, no one had bothered to name the phenomenon before: people were, for the most part, oddly incurious about the weirdnesses of the Afterlife.

Teskia's grandfather chalked it up to nationality. "All Americans believe in immortality," he'd told her. "Even the atheists. The Afterlife doesn't surprise them in the least. They've had everything else handed to them—why not eternity?"

"And what about Russians? Or Greeks?"

He blew out a long plume of cigarette smoke. "We try not to show that we notice. Notice it, appreciate it—someone will take it away from you. I, for one, try to live like I'm dead."

They'd met at his shop, one of the few shared spaces that remained between them. It saddened Teskia to see that her beloved grandfather had traded in the memories of her childhood for those of his own youth, but he had been a respected writer in his earlier years, and dementia had stolen his goldens just as it had taken hers. She had reverted to her younger self, too, of course; but then, she had no children.

That meeting had been their first and only: her grandfather had faded soon after. Teskia knew he was running out of time from the choppy way he morphalated, vibrating back and forth between only two or three states of being. His timeline—what Julio called "the snake"—was losing its tail, shriveling down to its essential segments.

"People's timelines are like long, stringy creatures," Julio had explained as they'd discussed the concept of morphalation. "They contain every moment of that person's life. We *should* be able to see every second of our lives, all at once, but we see each other like this because that's what we're used to. I don't think the brain can handle much more than a flicker."

"We're dead," Teskia had pointed out. "Who knows what our brains can handle?"

It was a question they rehashed frequently in their rambling postlife discussions: why were they conscious now that their brains had, presumably, decomposed? Why did the Afterlife exist? What was its purpose?

"It's a simulation." Julio was a software engineer: this was his favorite hypothesis. "We're all just pieces of virtual reality and the Afterlife is a kind of processor, sorting through all the information we've accumulated to find what's important."

"What do you mean, what's important? What do you think it's looking for?"

"The things that make us human. You know, the most important things. Maybe it discards everything else, all the pain we have to go through, all the mistakes. Maybe it just saves what's good."

"I don't know." Teskia was a student of Russian literature: her theories skewed metaphysical. "I think this could be hell."

Julio furrowed his brow. "Then why would we be together?"

"It's an atonement thing, maybe. Maybe we're supposed to forgive each other our sins."

He shook his head. "But the Afterlife is about second chances. You get to see the people you love again, you get to change things—well, change the way you remember them, at least. I don't think you get second chances in hell."

2:56

Julio got sick in 2001. They had gone there to visit an old friend who had died in November of that year, a high school classmate of theirs who was killed by a bus during his first semester at college.

"I still have that minute right before," Zack told them over dinner at Moneta's, a shabby diner they all remembered from their hometown. "Not the minutes when I was lying there, waiting to die—I sold those off soon as I got here. But right before it hit, when I could see it coming, and it couldn't see me? I kept that one. Might be the last one I ever give up."

Despite herself, Teskia envied him. The decade before her death had been used up by then: it was all fog anyway, empty years with Alzheimer's and without Julio. At least, she thought it was. That was the thing about giving up your time—you retained some sense of it, but it became like a story you heard somewhere, once. Like something you read in a book, but you couldn't remember which one, or when, or why you cared.

Zack morphalated only slightly, hair spiking and lengthening, braces twisting into a mess of unaligned teeth: Teskia guessed that he only had five or six years left. "Your mom still around, Tes?"

"More or less. She's somewhere in the 80s, these days."

He forked a chunk of meatloaf. "You guys see Alex much?"

"Alex?"

"Yeah, Alex. You remember. The third Musketeer? The only other person in English class who actually liked *Dreams of My Russian Summers?*" Zack wiped his mouth. "Wait—*do* you remember?"

"I don't—" Teskia glanced at Julio to see if he recognized the name, but his dark eyes were glassy. "Julio?"

He didn't respond. Teskia put her hand on his. "Julio? What's wrong?"

Tightening his grip on his fork, Julio shook himself, looking through Teskia as if she were one of Moneta's faux-Hellenistic plaster statues. "Who—what?"

"You okay?"

He ran a hand through his hair, exhaling slowly. "Yeah… sorry. Guess I spaced there for a minute."

At Zack's request, Julio began to fill him in on all the geeky news he'd missed ("I can't believe you had to go and die before *Firefly*, man. Seriously bad timing") but his face had a feverish sheen. Sometimes old sicknesses cropped up in ghost form—harmless and temporary, but still irritating. Teskia tried to remember if he'd had the flu in 2001: maybe some figment of it was attacking him now.

Halfway through dessert, though, it became clear the disease was no phantom. Julio had fallen asleep in his chair.

Nobody slept in the Afterlife. It was an enormous waste of

memories: dreams needed huge amounts of fodder, and you could never tell what might be pulled from you while you slept. When Teskia looked up from her key lime pie and saw Julio sitting there, unconscious for the first time since he had died, she knew she wasn't safe. Their memories were wholly communal—without Julio, she had barely enough time to cover their check.

0:35

Teskia had died in her sleep, so her early impressions of the Afterlife were hazy, and she wasn't sure when she'd moved from those last living dreams into her death. She told Zoya that she had felt someone holding her, someone steadying her as she transitioned from life to whatever lay beyond. "It didn't seem like Julio, at first, but…it must have been. It was like those dreams you have sometimes, where you see someone you know but they're two separate people, and you don't recognize them as one being. But it must have been Julio. Who else would it be?"

1:37

When Julio didn't get better after that first week, Teskia knew they needed a house: somewhere for him to convalesce in peace. 2001 was too loud. The crash of the towers, the tolls of freshman year—he couldn't recover in that din.

1981, Teskia recalled, wasn't so bad. They had both been very young then, so the population would be sparse. They took a train (it was five days for the fare) and ended up in July. They traveled north until she found Zoya living in October. Zoya wanted out of 1981; Teskia wanted in.

"It's a nice neighborhood," Zoya said as she ushered Teskia through the wood-paneled ranch house. "But I need to get out of the 80s. Nothing past '79 from now on. That's when life stopped being worth living." She flashed Teskia an abashed smile. "No offense."

Teskia, in urgent need of a house, took none. Trading was uncommon in the Afterlife: most people were self-sufficient and used their own years to house, feed, and clothe themselves. But without Julio, Teskia didn't have nearly enough time to build a house, and Zoya, dead from lung cancer at 54, was desperate for borrowed time. Before Zoya's sister Masha had faded away for good, she sometimes hinted to

Teskia that Zoya made a habit of trading her body for minutes, but sex wasn't popular enough in the Afterlife for her to make much profit off that.

Sex in the Afterlife wasn't physically gratifying, not unless it was with someone whose body you had true, solid memories of. You had to understand a person thoroughly for either of you to get anything out of it. You had to know them, inside and out.

4:34

October was colder than she'd expected. Teskia had never liked the month: the charms of late fall only reminded her that winter was near.

She spent the days sorting through her memories, setting aside what was hers alone, determining how much time they had left. So much had been lost already: she remembered a random phrase from *The Brothers Karamazov*—"I don't want harmony. From love for humanity I don't want it. I would rather be left with the unavenged suffering"—but she didn't know who had written it. She remembered the way her hometown had looked in January, the frost-caked cars driving black snow up against the dirty brown storefronts, but she couldn't recall its name. She remembered that Julio had a best friend, someone whose timeline slithered through their own, but Julio had given up that person's face and name long before Teskia had made it to the Afterlife. "Wasn't important," he'd said, when she asked him about it. "I didn't think you'd mind. I mean, we're what matters, right?"

Other bits of information rattled around in her recollection, too small to be valuable—her locker combination from sixth grade, the names of the streets she used to take on her morning walks, the warning message that used to pop up on her old MacBook before its battery ran out: "Your computer will go to sleep in a few minutes to preserve the contents of memory." Maybe Julio's theory was right; maybe he was just a piece of VR. Maybe he'd shut down to save some crucial file. But what? Teskia thought. What could be worth saving, if it cost them everything else?

There was no one to whom she could voice these questions, no one who had faced a similar plight. The Afterlife was a largely autonomous experience, and most people moved through it alone.

Julio and Teskia, however, were oddities: they had shared almost every moment of their lives together since they were born. Their mothers had been best friends for years, and when Julio's dad died and Teskia's left, they moved in together, each helping to raise the other's child. Julio and Teskia had only spent six years apart in their entire lives and deaths—a year when Teskia studied abroad, nine months in their thirties when she had taken a sabbatical from her position at the university, and the four years that she had survived after Julio passed on.

Both of their mothers had immigrated to the U.S. in middle school, though Zoya, with her pale skin and Baltic-blue eyes, faced less of the prejudice that Julio's mom, Maria, endured. As children Julio and Teskia, both dark haired and olive skinned, were often mistaken for siblings; as teenagers they'd dubbed themselves the "Ambiguously Ethnic Duo."

Teskia used to be able to trace their timelines back across the generations: prompted by an impetus she could no longer identify, she'd gone into research mode in her early thirties, unearthing both of their genealogies in order to catalogue all the coincidences and improbabilities that led to them living in the same house, the movements across four continents that brought them together. All that effort, all those names and dates, were gone now, and only Teskia and Julio remained, the final sum of those erased histories.

When she could no longer bear watching Julio's still form, naked beneath its thin white sheet, Teskia walked to September, watching the red and yellow leaves reverse themselves into the brittle, faded greens of late summer. She could keep walking, she thought. All the way through August, even into July, June—

Her boots scuffed the dirt as she stopped, staring at an apple tree on the edge of August. She thought she saw a shadow, as if someone were hiding behind the trunk, but when she stepped forward, a shiver of September wind passed through her, and she turned back. There was nothing there, she thought. She'd been on her own too long. She needed to return to Julio.

Not long before his illness, they'd lain in the summer grass together, Teskia's head on Julio's chest as his fingers traced small circles on her side. "Do you ever get that feeling," she'd murmured, her eyes falling closed, "when you're in a room with everyone you love, and it still feels like someone's missing? And you feel it so keenly you even count, to make sure you're not overlooking somebody, but everyone's accounted for? And you don't know why, but you're sure someone else was supposed to be there, only you don't know who, or what they look like, or who they are?"

His hand stilled, fingertips brushing her stomach. "No. Not when I'm with you. I don't get that feeling at all."

1:33

They had been married on a rainy day in spring, not long after her grandfather's funeral. Teskia's imminent betrothal seemed to help her grandmother take her mind off her own husband's passing: "It's a fairy tale!" she kept exclaiming. "True love for your whole lives. *Eto horosho, vnoochka. Ochen horosho.*"

Yet as the day approached, Teskia felt a curious lack of excitement. She'd always known, or at least suspected, this day would come, and now she could see everything that came next: the children, the house, the paring down of friends and outside interests until all that remained was their little family unit. To be trapped in one life—even a good one—suddenly seemed a horrible thing. She'd never realized: but now, as the path became narrower, and the means to the end became fewer still, she shivered in the night, wondering how anyone endured this linear passage, one firm step after another, right into the grave. Time, ticking; time, inevitable; time, expiring, for her and for Julio.

Despite her misgivings, Teskia hadn't been tempted to run: she'd walked down the aisle as though stepping onto a stage, keeping perfect poise, her expression a mask of calm exhilaration. As she'd played the part, the feeling had begun to surge up inside her, so that when she reached the altar she was giddy, fighting the urge to stomp her feet and clap her hands like a child. She was getting married to Julio, whom she loved, and who loved her, who knew her, inside and out. Maybe it was a fairy tale, generations in the telling. Maybe it was an ending she should embrace.

1:28

"The AIDS of the Afterlife": that's what they called the thing that was re-killing Julio. It was the only real disease anyone could contract after death, and no one had bothered to find a cure, or even a cause. It was rare and rumor ridden: people said it was everything from a scourge on sinners to the work of time-sucking parasites, who embedded themselves within the victim's body and fed on his memories. Teskia's mother was a believer in the latter.

"I've seen it," Zoya asserted over celebratory cognac the night Teskia bought the house, a theatric touch of her own mother's accent creeping into her speech. "Great *vormy* tings, stealing people's minds. I've seen the husks they leave behind—dried up, *vasted*."

"Where?" Teskia asked. "Where did you see these bodies, Zoya?"

But her mother offered no evidence. She and Teskia had little history left by that point: Zoya had long ago surrendered her memories of Teskia's adolescence and early adulthood. "I love you, darling. And Julio, too, of course—it's just that I got pregnant too young."

Seeming to forget that Teskia was already dead, Zoya morphalated maternal, offering the advice she had so often given her daughter in life: "Wait as long as you can. Don't have a child right away. You have time, Teskia. There's always more time."

Dreaded and damned, the disease Zoya so feared might have been part of why sex was so insignificant in the Afterlife. After all, that was the only way it could be transmitted.

00:17

"You're the only woman I've ever loved," Julio had told her on his deathbed, when her dementia had already set in, when she struggled to remember his name. Then he had coughed, his throat clogged with phlegm. "Remember that. Don't remember anything else." He squeezed her hand. "Only this."

00:06

She didn't want to know who, or where, or why. All she wanted to know was *when*.

1:46

They'd only slept together once after entering the Afterlife. Teskia hadn't thought much of it until Julio had fallen ill. Then she thought about it all the time.

He couldn't have contracted this disease any other way. He must have slept with someone—and not some one-night stand, a brief lapse in judgment. It had to have been someone he knew. Someone he'd known—and loved—in life. All Teskia knew was that it hadn't been her.

Crawling into bed as the season set, curling herself around Julio's body, she sometimes felt she could guess the truth. In that space between wake and rest, possibilities came to her, jerking her upright with hypnagogic force. It felt like the dementia all over again—like those endless mornings before they'd put her in the home, when she'd be walking to the mailbox and a cloud would pass, stopping her in her tracks. Dread would creep up within her, as though something crucial, damning, was about to surface. Then the shadow would pass, dissipating, like all her thoughts, and she would turn back, letters unclaimed.

Teskia leaned in, her lips almost touching his. "When, Julio?" Opening his eyelids with her fingers, she peered into the sightless orbs. "When did you become somebody else?"

His breathing never altered. She thought about slapping him, to jar him into consciousness, but it would be too much like smacking her own face. So, instead, she kissed him, gently. It told her nothing, so she pushed harder, forcing her tongue past his dry lips and searching his teeth for the truth. That's when she felt it—a tug, on the tip of her tongue. She recoiled, gaping at Julio, who was as immobile as before. Hesitantly, she pried open his mouth with her hands, gazing inside. Something red was poking up from Julio's throat. Something new. Something starving.

0:51

It was October. Outside, the streets were sun dazzled, but here in the dark of the bedroom it was colorless, cold. Julio sat on the bed, his head in his hands. "We could keep it. Raise it as our own. We don't have to—"

"No." Teskia swallowed, a sour taste on her tongue, her fingers stretched toward the table as if presaging a fall. "We go through with the adoption. I'll go away, and I'll have it, and—it'll be done. It'll be over."

"And what if we can't—I mean, we're in our thirties, Tes. What if—"

She knelt at his feet, hands on his knees. "We'll have another. Okay? Don't worry, Julio—please. We'll have another, and it'll be ours. Only ours. I promise." Beneath her fingertips, two heartbeats pulsed: hers, and that of another, a tiny, blind, human being.

3:14

She yanked the parasites out of his ears, his mouth, his anus. They were ropy and thick and she could not hold them for long before they scorched her skin. They had been feeding on him all this time, these gigantic, gaping tapeworms, consuming every second he'd ever had. Wrenching the last one from his nose with a clawed hand, she sank her teeth into its tough, engorged body. It gave a hissing caterwaul as its flesh exploded in her mouth, spewing hard seeds down her throat—too fast. She gagged, not just from the force but the fusty, necrotic taste, the bruising texture. Collapsing, she kecked, but nothing fell to the ground—the tiny black suckers that had burst from the creature were taking hold in her esophagus, stabbing barbed pinchers into the mucus-slicked walls of the membranous tube, sliding themselves into her.

They dislodged minutes she hadn't realized were inside her, sets of seconds buried a dozen layers deep. Shaken loose by the burrowing scroungers, the memories fell into place: the first time she and Alex, Julio's best friend, slept together, falling into bed at a college party; the first time they'd had sex after she and Julio had gotten married; the last time they'd slept together in life, because she'd gotten pregnant, because the affair she'd kept up as an escape route, an alternate life, just in case she needed it, had twisted in on itself, constricting her choices.

"Oh," she tried to say, digesting the old, familiar knowledge. It had been her, all along. It had been her Julio had wanted to save: from the memory of what they had become, from the sins she had committed, from the recollection of those last and only moments with her child, of its downy hair beneath her palm.

They'd never had another. They'd never tried. It wasn't the affair; that they could have survived. Alex was nothing but a ghost to them, and they never spoke his name—not until Teskia's dementia set in, not until she began thinking he was there, in the next room, with his grey eyes and silvery hair, waiting for her moments of weakness. No, it wasn't Alex: it was the child, out there, somewhere, the living last sentence in a book it would never read. She didn't think of the child as Alex's—she knew it wasn't, that no matter whose genes it carried it was Julio's, and hers, and she had given it away.

That was what had killed them, in the end. That was what had eaten away everything they were, leaving only the surface, only all those times and places they'd shared together, only the topography of a land that didn't exist. They had suffered decades of denial, of talking around that empty space, with Teskia knowing every moment that she'd failed them: not just Julio and the child, but that long line of her begetters, stretching from here to Stavropol, all those ancestors of whose toil and triumphs her child would never know.

She'd forgotten they were hollow inside, her and Julio. It seemed so obvious, suddenly. It was the kind of fact you couldn't miss—unless, of course, you'd already forced yourself to forget it.

Teskia could feel the leeches nibbling, gnawing at every memory. "Take them," she gurgled, closing her eyes. "They're not mine."

00:24

They didn't take it all. That surprised her—what little of her there was left to be surprised. They left a single moment: gummed, but intact. It was like a photograph, a still frame, of her at age eight, running across the playground, running, as she remembered, from Julio. She could no longer recall if he had caught her.

MULTO

Samuel Marzioli

Apex Magazine Readers' Anthology Selection

MY DAD LIKED TO SAY, *"Ang nakaraan ay hindi kailanman nawawala, na-lilimutan lamang,"* or rather, "The past is never gone, only forgotten." Whether a *salawikain* of the Philippines or something he made up, it seemed to fit. And I'd come across no better example than when I received an unexpected friend request online.

It came with a message: *Adan, we need to talk. There's something you need to know.* And then, *Remember the multo?* The profile included a blurry photo of a forty–something Filipina woman by the name of Dakila Hayes. Hair black, straight, and shoulder length. Lips drawn up in a not –quite–there smile. The image struck me immediately. Though she had a few more wrinkles, and a hardening of her jawline, I could never forget that face.

"That's strange," I said, swiveling my chair around.

My wife Jana lay slumped on the couch, a blanket wrapped around her legs as she watched TV. "What?" she said, catching me out of the corner of her eye.

"A neighbor from…God, maybe thirty years back just contacted me out of the blue."

"What'd they want?"

"She asked me if I remembered the '*multo*,' " I said, using my fingers to indicate quotes. "In Tagalog, that means ghost."

Jana laughed, wrinkling her nose. "Well? Do you?"

My forehead creased as I pored through distant memories. Above all the rest, a single phrase, a name, rose to the surface of my mind. With it, a scattershot of images and emotions I hadn't thought about or felt in years.

"Actually, I think I do. We called it the Black Thing."

When I was six, my family moved from an apartment into the bottom floor of a two–story duplex in Oakland, California. My parents scrimped for ten years before they collected enough for the down payment on that place. As migrants from the Philippines, it became the first piece of U.S. property they owned. And they were proud of it, despite its bowing walls and sunken ceiling. Despite the wood flooring that pitched up and knotted in places, begging to put splinters big as toothpicks in our feet. Proud, despite fearing the boys of *Norteños* who took over the block by sundown, and kept my parents up some nights with the occasional burst of gunfire.

As for me, I was too young to be bothered by such tangible things. My own fear came the day the Jacobes moved into the upper floor of our duplex. Being the only Filipino families in the area, our parents became instant friends, the sort of bond that could only exist when natural-born Pinoy met so far from the homeland. At least once a week, we all came together to eat Filipino cuisine: lumpia, chicken adobo, daing, maybe even balut—because who the hell else wouldn't judge when the egg shell broke, revealing a chicken fetus spilling from its own juices?

When the adults passed out the halo-halo, they convened in the living room and sent us children elsewhere. Since Dakila and Arnel Jacobe were far older than us, we never played. Usually, they just took me and my siblings, Tala and Amado, to the front stoop. There they related stories from the old country and the *mga multo* that haunted our homeland.

They told us about Balete Drive in a place called Quezon City, where the trees are inhabited by spirits, the mansions are haunted, and the apparition of a White Lady stalks the street at night. They told us about the city of San Juan, where the head of the Stabbed Priest searches for his body, the Headless Nun sneaks up on unsuspecting passersby, and the Devil Cigar Man drags victims to hell if they don't offer him a light. They even told us about the special *multo*, the one that followed the Jacobes across the ocean, from city to city and house to house.

"Usually, *mga multo* remain in the places they died," said Dakila. "But sometimes they grow attached to a person and stay with them until the end. This one is attached to our grandma. She says it's different from the others, darker, an evil thing."

"It said it was coming for her when she died," said Arnel. "It said that her soul was his to take, and her flesh and bones his to feast upon, when her body was an empty shell."

"Really?" I said, wide-eyed and breathless. Until then, I'd lived a sheltered life of cartoons and children's books. The idea of tormenting spirits terrified me like nothing else. I didn't want to believe it, but the conviction on their faces made it hard for me to doubt.

"Of course. Grandma never lies," said Arnel with a laugh.

"Never, never," said Dakila.

I've always accepted the fact that life entails growing old, changing in increments that could never be quantified. And so, confronted by this token of the past, the string of subtle changes I'd undergone in thirty years stood out like a glaring metamorphosis. Though I could feel a hint of the boy I'd once been, he had become a stranger to me.

My own children turned six and eight this year. I wondered about the things that kept them up at night. Whether they faced problems much like I did, or if this new generation had different burdens that a young me could never fathom. As I passed by their rooms, I had the sudden urge to peek in and see how they were doing.

I opened Peter's door first. He was lying on his bed, with his shoes on, reading a comic.

"Doing okay?" I said.

"Yeah."

"Good. Then take off your shoes, you know better."

"Yeah," he said. Without a glance in my direction, he kicked off both sneakers to the ground.

Stacy crouched beside her dollhouse, giving a voice to each doll she held, theirs differing from her own only in pitch. She didn't look up when I opened her door either, but my question didn't need answering. I could see she was okay, too.

While heading to my own room, I wondered why I had this sudden concern for their well-being. I thought about it the entire time I stripped and dressed in worn-out clothing more suitable for yard work. The only answer that came could be summarized in one word: fear. As a husband and a father, intangible horrors—like *mga multo*—were meaningless to me now. But my parents' fear of the *Norteños* and the threat of violence acted out against their children? That had come to make sense.

Still, one of the *salawikain* my father taught me lingered in my mind like a warning: "*Ang gawa sa pagkabata dala hanggang pagtanda.*" ("What one learns in childhood he carries into adulthood.") And I wondered how that truth would play itself out.

My house in Oklahoma City was more spacious and preserved than the Oakland duplex, but they had in common a few minor traits. Both were two–story relics built sometime in the 1930s, with wiring that couldn't always keep up with a modern family's electrical needs. Both had the tendency to speak their minds at night, through the groans of hidden pipes, through random thumps, or the creaks of settling wood. And both kept their fair share of idling, dark places.

Here, it was the garage. The sun had almost set, a slivered edge taking one last peek over the horizon, when I stepped through the garage's backyard entrance. The smell of dust and thick, moist air settled around me. It weighed heavy on my lungs and made the room feel somehow smaller. Like a pocket at the back of a long cavern, or the inside of a sealed crypt.

I slid my hand along the dark grooves of the unfinished walls and flipped the light switch. The single bulb dangling from the ceiling swayed from a breeze through the open door. Yet the deepest shadows held their place. They shifted from muddled splotches to tenebrous shapes—a thousand staring faces all focused on me.

In that moment, I could hear the bell toll warning of the headless nun. Could hear the raucous laugh of the Devil Cigar Man, the sigh of the White Lady in my ear, and the distant cries of the Stabbed Priest. All whispers, all figments of my imagination. And yet I couldn't stop the goosebumps rising on my arms, or the tickle at the nape of my neck that made the hairs stand on end.

Once the feelings ran their course, I grabbed my mower and left— quicker than I'd care to admit. It was funny; I'd gone in the garage a thousand times in five years, but never experienced the slightest bit of discomfort. But now, it felt like something more than memories had been stirred up by Dakila's friend request. As if a part of me from long ago had awakened. A part that shuddered at the sight of darkness—that squirmed at its proximity—for the promise, the threat, of what nested in its veil.

The Jacobe grandma only spoke Tagalog. Whenever we visited the Jacobes, she would fix us with a hard stare and shout, *"maiingay na mga bata"* ("noisy children"), before hobbling back to the privacy of her room. Sometimes, through the floorboards, we'd hear her scream, and the muffled voices that comforted her soon after. The details about her harassing *multo* increased and, since she was such an inscrutable character, so did our fascination with the subject.

My siblings and I dubbed it the Black Thing. We spent a lot of time giving substance and meaning to its existence beyond the stories we heard. If someone escaped our purview for a few days, we'd say the Black Thing held them prisoner. Or if someone broke the lock of our fence, shattered a plant's ceramic pot, or otherwise damaged our property, we called it the Black Thing's rage.

Though it had evolved into a shared creation, I may have been the only one in my family who actually believed it. And because I was the youngest by at least three years, my siblings teased me without mercy. Especially when it came to the Black Thing's so-called lair, the basement.

Since it'd been built on a hillside, the duplex lengthened at its rear to match the sloping ground. There, under the southeast corner, the basement lay exposed. Unlike the rest of the house, the room remained untouched through the decades, tinted gray from layered dust, and infested by bugs and vermin. Its windows reflected light in day and absorbed darkness at night, so that it had the habit of resisting peering eyes. Taken altogether, it acted as the perfect focus for our macabre imaginings. The place of idling dark in my childhood years.

Whenever we played by ourselves in our backyard, my brother and sister never failed to steal a glance in its direction. And when they did, the results were always the same.

"Did you see that?" said Tala, eyes wide, jaw hanging open in feigned terror. "Through the window. I think I saw eyes."

"Yes, I saw it too," Amado said. "Something's watching us right now. Something hungry. Something evil."

"Quit it, guys," I said, a subtle tremble beginning in my chest and spreading to my limbs.

"We're serious!" said Tala.

"I think we should tell Mom and Dad," said Amado.

"No, you know how Dad is. He'd only try to investigate and end up getting himself hurt. Or worse, killed," said Tala.

"Come on, guys, stop kidding around," I said, imagining movement from behind the basement windows and feeling the flustered warmth gathering in my face.

"This is no joke," said Amado.

"Do we even look like we're kidding?" said Tala.

Not then, of course. I mistook their lively performance and solemn expressions as honest–to–God truth. And I paid the price for it with many lonely, sleepless nights.

Night fell quicker than I could finish my yard work. I spent the last five minutes mowing in the gloom of dusk. As darkness pooled over the thin stretch of my backyard, my imagination soared with eerie thoughts. The shadows of jostled branches reached out to grab me. A glimpse of movement from behind the fence panels hinted of a figure, dark as absence. It moved around the perimeter of my yard behind a bush. There, I felt its eyes, peering through the foliage as if waiting to catch me unaware.

I gathered my things in a hurry, dragged the mower back to the garage. Though I'd left the light on earlier, its insides now swarmed with black. With a quick shove, I let the mower roll into its proper place—because I didn't dare enter—and rushed into my house.

Jana, seated at the computer desk, turned around when the door creaked open and shut behind me. She must have sensed something amiss because she immediately asked, "What's wrong?"

"Nothing," I said. "Just tired is all."

"I was about to call you in. It's the kids' bedtime."

She headed for the staircase, but halted on the second step. "I almost forgot. I think your old neighbor wrote you another PM."

"Thanks. I'll be up in a second."

I dropped to the computer chair and logged into my account, feeling reluctant to even read Dakila's message. Enough had already bubbled through the cracks of my subconscious for me to know it was better left sealed away. And I worried about what else would slip out before this day had finished.

Dakila's message read: *Kumusta ka? How is your family? I live twenty miles from our old duplex, where my parents still live. They sometimes ask about yours and wonder how they're doing.*

And then it got to the crux:

The reason I contacted you is because my grandma passed away.
Her funeral was last week.

It was sad to find out that someone I knew at such an integral stage of my life had died, but I couldn't understand its relevance to me. I wrote back:

Kumusta kayo? I'm sorry to hear about your grandma. She seemed like a good woman who lived a long life. She will be missed.

I was about to close it down when a new message appeared on the screen.

Dakila: *Do you remember the multo Arnel and I used to tell you about?*

Adan: *Yes.*

Dakila: *And do you remember the story you told us about that multo, shortly before you moved away?*

I did. Of course I did. No matter how hard I'd tried to bury it beneath a mountain of distractions, it didn't take much for it to rise again and shake the dust loose. For a moment, I thought back to a particular day, from those early Oakland years. One I'd hoped and prayed never to think about again.

Some nights, Tala, Amado, and I played superheroes in our bedroom and we always played rough. We'd jump and bounce on our bunk bed and thrash around without a thought for our own safety. One time, I shot a hand out to block an invisible villain's punch and my elbow smashed a sizable hole through the brittle sheetrock wall beside the bottom bunk.

The hole opened up into the house's skeletal frame—an un-insulated passageway that poured in a stale breeze. When my parents heard the noise, they rushed into our bedroom. They didn't yell once they saw the damage, but their irritation was apparent.

"I do not have the tools to fix it right now," said my dad.

"But it's cold," said Amado.

"And it smells," said Tala.

"You should have thought about that before you acted without care," said my mom.

Bedtime came, and we three crawled into the bunk bed: Tala on the top half, and Amado and I on the bottom facing opposite directions. Because I made the hole, Amado made me sleep in front of it. Our parents turned off the light, said their good nights, and closed the door.

I couldn't sleep that night. The constant rush of air from the hole made me shiver uncontrollably. Not because of the cold, but because of what it represented. "The Black Thing sleeps below us," Dakila had once said, and now there was a passageway that spanned the distance from its resting place into our room.

Before long, Tala began to snore, and the deep full breaths Amado made indicated that he, too, had fallen asleep. I was alone with the darkness and, somehow, I could sense it knew.

Every quiet thing amplified into a raucous sound, second only to the staccato thump of my heart. I looked around, but the room was blotted from sight. Not simply unseeable, but as if everything around me had been replaced by empty space.

A thump sounded from where the dresser had been. Somewhere beyond the ceiling, groans erupted in a random pattern that defied the pathway of any normal pipeline. There was silence, and then another rush of air, this time like an exhalation or a sigh spilling out from the hole beside me.

It shifted into the steady sound of scratching against the wooden studs of the inner wall. I thought at first it would go away, like the other sounds before it. Instead, it slowly mounted, as if something below were clawing its way up.

I drew the covers over my head and, at the same time, kicked my brother hard. He didn't move. I whispered, "Amado," but he didn't respond. I kicked him again, this time enough to jar his whole body. He only grunted, shifted to his side, and fell still.

The scratches continued.

I began to shake. Hot tears slid down my face and I silently pleaded for my parents to come back and turn the lights on. To sweep this nightmare away for good.

They didn't.

Another set of scratches.

This time it sounded close, within the hollow just below the gaping hole. The smell of dust, of sweat, of moldering fabric wafted in. A pressure began to build in my throat, a cry that rallied against my self-restraint and threatened to break free. I choked on it, held it down with all my might. If the Black Thing heard me now, it would know I was awake. But if I kept still, kept quiet, maybe I'd be safe. Invisible.

I heard a soft, almost taunting laugh. Then a voice, deep but whispered, said, "*Nakikita kita.*" ("I see you.")

Trying to scream did no good. The cry that fought for freedom only moments before had left me. So I waited beneath my blankets, like a statue, like a boy embedded in ice. And hoped to God it was good enough.

Through the covers, I felt the pressure of hands lean against my chest, so heavy it hurt my ribs and made it hard to breathe. It loomed over me, staring down, with eyes that pierced the thin cloth that separated us by mere inches. The chill of its skin absorbing my warmth.

Again, it spoke in a deep and whispered voice. "When the old woman dies, you and I will meet again. *Sa ibang araw.*"

Its last words trailed off like a fading echo. And with it, the Black Thing disappeared.

After a time—I couldn't say how long—my voice returned. I screamed, over and again, louder and louder, until the bedroom door burst open and lights flooded the room.

"What is it? What is wrong?" my dad said, hurrying to my bedside.

I threw off the covers, jumped from the bed, and mashed myself against his legs. Hugging him tightly, I looked over at the hole again—saw nothing but wood—and then turned to my brother and sister in bed. They were both sitting up, gazing at me, bleary–eyed and disoriented. I had been truly alone, and that realization left me dazed and silent for the rest of the night.

I sat there in front of my computer screen trying to compose myself. Those memories had lain dormant for so long, I didn't know how to take them. As an adult, I knew they couldn't possibly be true, and yet the feelings they invoked, the fears they uncovered, were all too real.

Adan: *Wow. Can't believe you remember that. I'm embarrassed. My imagination was pretty strong as a child.*

Dakila: *So, everything is okay? You're safe?*

Adan: *Of course. Why shouldn't I be?*

Dakila: *You of all people should know how difficult it is for me to share this. But I need you to understand. Grandma was never the same after the multo at-*

tached to her. She grew increasingly distant from the rest of us, disconnected from reality. Tormented by things only she ever heard and saw.

Adan: *Why are you telling me this?*

Dakila: *Because of what it told you. Remember? Sa ibang araw.*

Adan: *Someday.*

Dakila: *Exactly.*

After thanking Dakila for her concern, insisting I was fine and promising that we'd catch up later, I joined Jana and the kids upstairs. We read them a story each, and then tucked them in. Not long after, we went to sleep as well.

While lying in bed before the lights went out, I tried to tell Jana about what Dakila had told me, about the pieces of memory recovered and what it all meant. I couldn't. I told myself there was no need to concern her—it was all superstitious hokum and childhood non-sense—but the greater part of me knew it was a lie. I felt afraid, and to admit it would be to embrace the truth that right now the *multo* could be searching for our house. That somewhere, the Black Thing drew nearer and our lives would never be the same again.

Jana shut off the lights and, within minutes, I heard her winsome snores. As for me, I couldn't sleep, couldn't shut my eyes for fear of what I might find when I opened them again. The darkness seemed to spread throughout our room, blotting out everything except the bed.

Soon, like so many nights before, the house spoke its mind. I heard groans just beyond the ceiling, from hidden pipes. Heavy thumps made their way across the garage beneath us. A thin scuffling in the living room. Then slowly mounting creaks ascended the staircase, one by one, and stopped only when they reached the landing just outside our bedroom door.

I held my breath, felt the sudden urge to cover myself with blan-kets. And I wondered; was it truly just settling wood this time? Or had "someday" finally come?

KEEP TALKING

Marie Vibbert

2014 Apex Magazine Readers' Choice Winner

GERALD'S STOMACH CLENCHED AS HE approached his daughter, Sarah. She sat at her computer, her back to the world, as intent as a cat scenting a mouse. "Sweetie, I have some big news."

She sucked on a lock of her hair, eyes on the screen. He leaned against the desk, as much into her line of sight as he could. "Sarah? I got the job."

"Live feed," Sarah said, angrily, and leaned closer to her screen.

On her screen, a half-dozen text windows showed the usual columns of numbers, her obsession: the daily data streams and reports from SETI, the Search for Extraterrestrial Intelligence. She'd always been so good at math, but when time came to take the SATs, she'd just said, "The problems all have answers," and left her sheet blank.

Gerald turned his daughter's chair toward him. Sarah dutifully turned, but her pupils tracked to the computer monitor, looking out the extreme corner of her eyes. "I got the job, so we're going to move to Japan." Gerald felt the weight of all the things he needed to say, the wall of facts he had to build one stone at a time. "I know you don't want to, but it will be so wonderful, honey. Your computer is coming with us. Nothing will have to change."

Sarah was getting that hard, tight look—the meltdown look. Gerald stepped back. "Remember that I love you. We can talk about this later if you want."

Sarah drew the tip of her hair out of her mouth, letting it sit on her lower lip. "Go away."

When Gerald let go of her, Sarah swung back to the computer like a released spring. She opened a new command-line window and started typing fast strings of figures. Gerald stepped back again. In an age of easy graphics programs, Sarah preferred to draw via line functions. Gerald used to think that was beautiful, a hopeful hint of how brilliant his daughter was, his genes going forth to do things he never could. Now it made him nauseated—the taste of dashed hopes. He left her room. The world of numbers had swallowed her.

Sarah was relieved to get back to her work, but sad her father had left so easily. People always left her. Her father was going to leave her, she knew, if she convinced him not to take her to Japan, and she would be completely alone.

She had a task to do, though, and she was in her room, where the light was dim and she knew where everything was.

The data took the form of pulses at three distinct frequencies. The scientists at SETI had chosen to represent these three signals as 0, 1, and -1. Balanced Ternary. Sarah liked it; it cut down the carry rate in multiplication. There were nine zeroes every seven hundred bytes. The other SETI users on the forum thought this was a tag to help parse the data. Sarah considered this a waste of bytes if it were true. Surely the aliens were smart, like her, not dumb, like forum posters. The data had to be repeating—signal degradation compensated for.

The SETI data would be released to the public soon. She wanted to figure it all out before then. The motion in the numbers had meaning. All math had meaning, but the data was sanitized, cut up in chunks already by the well-meaning SETI engineers. Something was missing, and its absence left a bad smell. She shifted the lines until they linked hands, became dance partners. That was the parsing tag, there, where a negative and a positive lined up exactly opposite. The data fell into neat pentagrams. Dance partners with five hands. Two higher than the other three.

The live feed from SETI announced that someone else had solved the puzzle. A team at Carnegie Mellon announced it could be a video. Sarah pushed back from her keyboard and sulked.

Miranda, Gerald's girlfriend, came over for dinner as usual the next day. She kissed Gerald on the cheek as he opened the apartment door. He looked frazzled as always. He squeezed her hand. She could smell something garlicky cooking.

"Isn't it amazing?" she asked, dropping her purse on the little table by the door. It wobbled and she steadied it with a nudge.

Gerald closed the door. "My cooking?"

"The aliens!"

Gerald squinted at her. "Aliens? That's a good thing?"

"Of course!" Miranda leaned into the kitchenette, really just a corner of the main room of the apartment separated off by a low counter. A pot was about to boil over. She moved it to another burner on the ancient, harvest-gold stove. "Don't you think so?"

Gerald turned off the burner. "What are we talking about?"

"The aliens. The video of the aliens. Dancing. Isn't it wonderful? They communicate through dance! We're beside ourselves at the studio."

He still had that adorable absent-minded-professor expression as he tested the noodles and brought them to the sink to drain. "I had to break the news to Sarah today," he said.

"About first contact with outer space? I find that hard to believe. I bet she was glued to her computer."

Gerald looked helplessly at Miranda. Steam fogged up his glasses.

Miranda spoke slowly. "The SETI news? The video of aliens dancing? You can get it on YouTube now. It's all anyone is talking about. How did you miss it?"

"They offered me the job," Gerald said. He took off his glasses. "Aliens? You mean, like, real space aliens?"

Miranda framed his face in her hands. "Real space aliens," she said. "And they dance!" She couldn't help but kiss him then.

Gerald blushed. "Do you think…they'll need dancers to interpret it, won't they?"

Miranda secretly entertained just this hope, but she waved her hand. "There are plenty of people they'd want before they look at dance instructors in Cleveland."

"You should volunteer. I bet you'd be the best."

"Maybe." Miranda stepped out of the kitchenette. "But Japan! How wonderful for you! Finally a chance to put all that schooling to work!" She pulled a chair out for herself at the dining table and turned to see Gerald slumped against the sink.

"I don't know what to do about Sarah," he said.

"You need this opportunity. You need to do what you were trained to do. Sarah can stay with me."

"You don't mean that."

"It won't be forever. She's eighteen! She can learn to dance. It will focus her, give her a grounding in the physical world, make her less clumsy."

"She isn't going to dance the autism away," Gerald said, angrily. His eyes slid to the corridor that led to his and Sarah's bedrooms. He lowered his voice as he went back to dividing the pasta onto three plates. "She doesn't want to go. She isn't ready to stay on her own. She doesn't even wash her hair if I don't remind her."

Gerry looked so defeated. He hadn't been that way in college, back when he was dating Sarah's mother and Miranda was just a friend. They were just starting on a romance together after years of friendship and they were both closer to forty than thirty. Miranda saw Gerald idling on the on-ramp of life, and traffic was only going to get heavier and faster. "You think I want you to go? I care that much about your future, your potential." She slipped her arm around him. "I trust that you'll come back."

"I should never have applied," he said. He turned out of her embrace and picked up the sauce from the stove. "If I hadn't gotten the job, I wouldn't be tempted."

"What's life if you don't take big risks and do big things? Do you want to live in this crappy apartment forever?"

Gerald set the saucepan down. He looked at her, plainly hurt, but Miranda shook her head. "Don't give me the puppy-dog eyes."

A door opened and slammed. Sarah came into the main area of the apartment. She didn't look at them, but they both watched her walk to the dining table and sit down.

"We'll work it out," Miranda said, and squeezed Gerald's shoulder.

He nodded. "So," he said, with false cheer, "Aliens, huh? Wow."

Miranda left him to pull out a chair next to Sarah. She thought about her father, who had always wanted to be a dancer, but like Gerald had done office work for the sake of his family. "Your father tells me he got the job in Japan. Isn't that great?"

"I'm not going," Sarah said. She stared at her placemat. "I have work to do. They still don't know the message."

Miranda raised her hand, unsure if she should touch Sarah or not.

She ended up setting it on the back of Sarah's chair. "Your father's not strong like us. He needs us to help him. He needs you."

Sarah looked straight at Miranda. "I'm not going, and I'm not stupid."

"I didn't say that. But you can work on your computer project anywhere."

Sarah's eyes squinched up, and then her nose, and then she screamed. Gerald dropped the spaghetti in the sink and rushed to put himself between Sarah and Miranda. Sarah hit him, her fist originally intended for Miranda. And then she lost control, scratching and biting. Miranda had seen it once before, but she thought Sarah had outgrown these fits. It was frightening, how she was not Sarah anymore.

Gerald knelt down, pinned her arms down, hugged her still. "Sh," he whispered. "It's okay. Be calm. We don't hit. Remember? We don't hit."

Miranda stepped back, helpless and locked out. Gerald was calm and focused. He took Sarah back to her room, back where she felt safe with the lights off and the window covered in tinfoil. He came back to get Sarah's dinner. Miranda sat alone at the dining table and wondered how she had ever thought she could take Gerald's place.

A happy monster, all grey fur and smiling teeth, greeted Gerald on his desk at work. It was a plush gift from the movie studio that wanted to hire him. He'd caught their eye because of the free work he'd done for a local independent film. It was a cyberpunk robot romance story and had turned out better than it ought to have, being filmed mostly over two weekends in the Old Arcade downtown. They hadn't gotten the correct permission ahead of time, and a bridal party walked right through the movie's climax. It felt like an essential part, the beauty and the randomness. Pure luck. He'd translated a Japanese poem for the movie, which was used in the credits, and he'd written Japanese dialog for one character and provided Japanese subtitles, even though no one had asked for them.

Now a Japanese movie studio wanted him on board, translating for them. He could remember exactly this sort of job offer in his dreams when he was a college freshman, choosing against all reason to major in modern languages. He should feel like he was on a roller coaster, climbing the first hill, all the joy ahead of him and all the waiting behind.

He was still a little mad at Miranda for talking about "putting his schooling to use," like translating grocery store signs for recent immigrants wasn't useful. Like all the work he'd done raising Sarah on his own wasn't as important as a job.

Business at the Asian American Community Service Agency was slower than usual. Gerald's boss and the delivery girl lingered by the big front window, talking in excited tones about aliens and the future. A pile of pamphlets and manuals sat on his desk, waiting to be translated. Gerald felt the enormity of his personal news dwarfed by the motion of the world, become a rowboat in the wake of a cruise ship.

He opened up a chat window and sent Sarah a message. "Just thinking about you. Hope your day is going well. Home at five. Dad."

Miranda walked barefoot across the dance studio. She still felt tight and unsettled, despite her usual morning yoga. She sat at the computer and opened YouTube. The alien dance was the featured video. Knobby, cactus-like creatures touched a high knob, then a low knob, twisting across a multi-colored floor. It hadn't looked like dance when she'd first seen it, and a lot of her colleagues bristled at the media calling it such. But what else could you call it? Figures moving in space, repeating motions with slight variations, over and over. She wondered if the color was meaningless, a distraction. Maybe the aliens didn't even see color. She picked up a pen and began taking notes.

If Sarah were captivated by THIS dance, if she could see the steps arranged clearly in bright, colorful symbols, she might become captivated by dance itself.

Sarah almost had it. The equations described almost all the motion — each body as a whole, the trajectories of limbs, but there were parts of the dance hidden from view, and you couldn't extrapolate. She didn't want to extrapolate. Extrapolation made her angry. It wasn't fair. It wasn't perfect.

Miranda had entered the room, but Sarah was ignoring her in hopes she'd go away. Miranda was always trying to become her friend, since she wanted to become her mother. It was annoying and unreasonable. Sarah was too old for a mother.

Miranda pulled a chair close to Sarah. "I might be able to help you interpret the dance," Miranda said.

Sarah doubted that, but she had to admit it was nice that Miranda had come right out and said why she'd come instead of saying useless stupid things about the weather and hello first.

Sarah curled a lock of hair around one finger, smoothed it to a point and stuck it in her mouth, feeling the hairs shift against each other, wet with saliva, they became elastic, a new material. She liked elastic things, like numbers.

Miranda set a tablet on the desk. On it were drawings of circles and squares. Sarah stopped sucking her hair and looked at it.

Miranda had made the extrapolations.

Miranda thought Sarah resembled a cat leaping upon a choice piece of fish as she picked up the tablet, eyes moving rapidly. Miranda laughed. "You're welcome," she said. She watched for a while, proud of her own work, before leaving Sarah to it.

Gerald stood in the hallway. "What are you doing?" he asked.

"Just a little girl-time," Miranda said. She kissed Gerald on the cheek, though he looked at her warily. "You and I, we're not a short-term deal. That means I want you as a part of my life, and having you be a part of my life means Sarah being a part of my life. I want Sarah to stay with me while you go to Japan."

Gerald looked past Miranda, into Sarah's room. On the computer screen, cactus-like creatures twirled around each other. He thought it looked like a Eurovision dance number. He had laundry to put away.

He asked Miranda about her day and about the performance her students were putting on at the end of the month. She wasn't deterred. She followed him to the laundry room and back to the apartment, stood by him while he folded clothes on the sofa and followed him into the corridor to put towels in the linen closet.

"It makes sense. She doesn't want to travel. We can move her to my place before you leave, even, give you some transition time to make sure it works."

Gerald couldn't tell her that she doesn't understand; she hasn't been a parent. Because it wasn't parental protectiveness that was pulling him in horror away from her suggestion. It was pride. He didn't want to owe Miranda so much. "What if she never agrees to follow me? What if she's never ready to be on her own? What about you? Do you just follow us? Leave everything you have here?"

"Maybe I will. American dancers could be a novelty in Tokyo. And dance will be big, Gerry. Bigger than big. The world is seeing what dance can do. They'll be hungry for more."

"All of your family is here. You have connections here. I don't want to ask that of you."

Miranda went into the living room and sat down, hands on her lap, a very clear "let's talk" posture.

"I'll order pizza for dinner," Gerald said. "Or do you want to get subs? I didn't take anything out."

"You're scared. I get that." Miranda flattened a hand against her chest. "I'm terrified. But you have to do the things that scare you."

Gerald peeked back down the corridor at Sarah's door. It was closed, and all was quiet inside. If she had ever tried to get a job, if she had taken one of the jobs Gerald tried to arrange for her, maybe he could leave her, but she hadn't. "Let's see what I cook up," he said, and went to the fridge.

Miranda followed him. "How many times have you fed me dinner? Let me give something back."

Sarah's door opened and she marched out in her usual careless, loping gait, all lank hair and swinging arms. She went straight to the refrigerator in the kitchenette and pulled out the orange juice. She was an obsessive orange juice drinker, which was good in a way because she hardly ate enough as it was, and Gerald told himself at least she was getting calories, though he had nightmares where her skin turned yellow.

Sarah turned her back to the fridge and drank.

Miranda smiled a forced smile. "We were just talking about Japan. Your father is going there."

"I'm not stupid," Sarah said. She took another long gulp of orange juice in the awkward silence before adding, "It was a cry for help."

Miranda asked, "What was?"

Sarah shifted, avoiding eye contact. "The aliens. They're dancing for help. For us to come save them. From what isn't clear, but it's definitely an extinction level event."

"Oh," said Gerald.

Miranda grabbed the remote control and turned on the TV, rapidly scanning through channels.

Sarah finished her orange juice. "They're four thousand light years away. It already happened. They're all dead."

Miranda finally found a news channel talking about the aliens, but they were discussing their possible anatomy with a cactus specialist.

"We don't know that," Gerald said.

"Thanks for the extrapolations," Sarah said. "I'll be in my room."

Miranda kept thumbing through channels. "Do you think she's right?" Gerald said nothing. Miranda looked at him. "We should call someone. Maybe NASA. Gerry, they'll want to talk to her. They might offer her a job!"

Gerald felt bloodless. He didn't live in the world Miranda lived in —the world where you tried bold things and they worked out. His daughter was not another Einstein and no one at NASA would want to talk to her. He would not go to Tokyo. The aliens were all dead. He moved the laundry basket off of the couch and sat down next to Miranda.

Miranda had found a channel playing the alien dance. She had her phone out and was searching for phone numbers to call.

Gerald wondered what Miranda saw when she watched the aliens dance. He just saw shapes blurring and thought about all the people who died before you got to know them.

Sarah came back into the room. "Mountain View."

He looked up.

"Mountain View, Daddy. Tell MIT and Caltech I get to work in Mountain View or they can go to hell." And she tossed her vibrating cell phone at her father.

He juggled it, only getting a good grip when it had stopped ringing. "Mountain View?" he asked.

"Where SETI is," Miranda explained.

Gerald felt Miranda's warm, comforting arm around him. He saw the list of recent calls to Sarah's phone without fully processing all the strange numbers. Miranda took the phone from his bloodless fingers.

Miranda paged through received emails. "She's already sent her findings. Gerald...they're really calling her back. This is...what time is it in California?" Miranda muted the TV and fussed through the mess on the coffee table, looking for a notepad and pen.

Gerald looked from Miranda to Sarah's door. His vision wavered in a thin pool of tears. He saw the pattern forming, like a perfect translation. His daughter would be sent like a beacon to parts unknown. Or he would. Or both. There was no path that didn't end in good-bye.

On the television, the cacti were performing their swirling dance, living on as ones, zeroes, and twos.

Remembery Day

Sarah Pinsker

I woke at dawn on the holiday, so my grandmother put me to work polishing Mama's army boots.

"Try not to let her see them," Nana warned me. I already knew.

I took the boots to the bathroom with an old sock and the polish kit. I had seen Nana clean them before, but this marked the first time I was allowed to do it myself. Saddle soap first, then moisturizer, then polish. I pictured Nana at the ironing board in our bedroom, pressing the proper creases into Mama's old uniform.

The door swung open, and I realized too late that I had forgotten to lock it. Mama didn't often wake up this early on days she didn't have to work.

"Whose are those?" my mother asked, yawning.

"Uh—" I didn't know what to say, which lie I was supposed to tell.

Nana rescued me from the situation, coming up behind Mama. "Those were your father's, Kima. I asked Clara to clean them for me."

Mama's gaze lingered on the boots for a moment. Did she think they were the wrong size for Grandpa? Did she recognize them?

"I need the bathroom," she said after a moment. "Do you mind doing that somewhere else, Clara?"

I pinched the boots together and lifted them away from my body so I wouldn't stain my clothes, gathering up the polish kit with my other hand. Mama waited until I slipped past before she wheeled in. Her indoor chair was narrow, but not narrow enough for both of us to fit in the small bathroom.

"I'm sorry," I whispered to Nana once the door closed.

"No harm done," Nana whispered back.

I finished on the kitchen floor, now that there was no reason to hide. It was almost time, anyway. The parade would start at ten by us. In some places, people had to get up in the middle of the night.

Mama came in to breakfast, and I put the boots in a corner to dry. Nana had made coffee and scrambled eggs with green chiles, but all I could smell was the saddle soap on my hands. We all ate in silence:

Mama because she wasn't a morning person, and Nana and I because we were waiting. Listening. At eight the sirens went off, just the expected short burst to warn us the Veil would be lifting.

Mama whipped her head around. "What was that? Oh."

The lifting of the Veil always hit her the same. My teacher said each vet reacted in a different way, but my friends never discussed what it was like for their parents. Mama always went "Oh" first, lifting her hand to her mouth. Her eyes flew open as if they were opening for the first time, and for one moment she would look at me as if I were a stranger. It upset me when I was little. I think I understand now, or anyway I'm used to it.

"Oh," she said again.

She studied her hands in her lap for a moment, and I saw they were shaking. She didn't say anything, just wheeled herself into the bathroom. I heard the water start up, then the creak as she transferred herself to the seat in the shower. Nana came around the table to hug me. When she got up to lay Mama's uniform on her bed, I followed with the boots I had shined. We waited in the kitchen.

Showering and dressing took her a while, as it did on any day, but when she appeared in the kitchen doorway again, she had her uniform on. It fit perfectly. Mama didn't need to know that Nana had let it out a little. I had never seen a picture of her as a young soldier, but it wasn't hard to imagine. I only had to strip away the chair and the burn on her face. This was the one day I looked at her that way; on all other days, those were just part of her.

"Did you shine these for me?" She pointed to her boots.

I nodded.

"They're perfect. Everyone will be so impressed." She pulled me onto her lap. I was getting too old for laps, but today she was allowed. I stayed for a minute then stood again. When she laughed it was a different laugh from the rest of the year, a little lower and softer. I've never been sure which is her real laugh.

At nine, we all got in the van, and Mama drove us downtown.

"Mama, can I ask you a question?"

"Yes?"

"What did you do in the War?"

I saw her purse her lips in the mirror. "There's a long answer to that question, *mija*, and I don't think I can answer it right this moment while I'm driving. Can we talk more in a while?"

I knew how this worked. 'In a while' didn't always come. Still, this was her day. "I guess."

A few minutes later Mama took an unexpected right turn and pulled the van over. "How about if we skip it this year? Go get some ice cream or sit on the pier or something?"

"Mama, no! This is for you!" I didn't understand why she would suggest such a thing. My horror welled up before I thought to see what Nana said first.

She turned to Nana next, but my grandmother just shrugged.

"You're right, Clara. I don't know what I was thinking." Mama sighed and put the van back into gear.

Veterans got all the good parking in the city on the holiday. Mama's uniform got us close. The wheelchair sticker got us even closer. I didn't understand how they all knew where to go, how to find their regiments, but they did. Nana and I stood near the staging area and watched as the veterans hugged each other and cried. Mama pointed to me and waved. I smiled and waved back.

We found seats in the grandstand, surrounded by other families like ours. I recognized a couple of the kids. We had played together beneath the stands when we were little, when we called it Remembery Day because we didn't know better. Now that I was old enough to understand a little more, I wanted to sit with Nana. The metal bench burned my legs even through my pants. A breeze blew through the canyon created by the buildings. It rustled the flags on the opposite side of the street, and I tried to identify the different states and countries.

A marching band started to play, and we all sang "The Ones Who Made it Home" and then "Flowers Bloom Where You Fell." At school I learned that parades used to include national anthems, but since the War our allies everywhere choose to sing these two songs. I can sing them both in four different languages. The band stopped in front of each stand to play the two songs again. It was always a long parade.

Behind them came six horses the color of Mama's boots and every bit as shiny. Froth flew from their mouths as they tossed their heads and danced sideways against their harnesses. Their bits and bridles gleamed with polish, but they pulled a plain cart. It rolled on wooden wheels and carried a wooden casket. The young man driving wore the new uniform designed after the War, light gray with black bands around the arms. Nobody who hadn't fought was allowed to wear the old one anymore.

Then came the veterans. Fewer every year. Nana has promised me Mama was never exposed to the worst stuff; I worry anyway. I imagine there will be a time when there aren't enough of them to form ranks, but for now there were still a good number. Some, like my mother, rode in motorized wheelchairs. Some had faces more scarred than hers. Others waved prosthetic hands. Those too weak were pushed by others or rode on floats down the boulevard. I saw my teacher march past. I had never noticed him in the ranks before, but I guess he wasn't my teacher until this year, so I wouldn't have known to look for him. The way he talked in class I would never have guessed he was a veteran. Of course, that was the case with all of them since the Veil was invented. I don't know why I was surprised.

When Mama passed I mustered a little extra volume, so everyone would know she was mine. She spotted me in the crowd and pointed and waved. We cheered until our throats were raw. It was the least we could do, the only thing we could do.

The same thing was happening at the same time in all the cities and countries left. I pictured children and grandparents cheering under dark skies and noonday sun. It was summer here, but winter in the northern hemisphere, so I pictured the other kids bundled up, their bleachers chilling their legs while the bench I sat on made me sweat behind my knees.

The last soldiers passed us, and we made sure we had enough voice left to show our appreciation to them as well. Behind them, another horse, saddled but riderless, with fireweed braided into his mane. He was there to remind us of the clean-up crews, those who had been exposed after the treaty. None of them were left to march.

We waited in the stands after the parade ended. Nana spoke with some people sitting nearby. Some families left, but others lingered like us. We knew it would be a while. The veterans had gone off to gather at their arranged meeting places as they were supposed to do, in bars or parks or coffee shops at the other end of the route. A couple of people in uniform walked back in our direction and slipped away with family, ignoring the looks we gave them. We all knew they were supposed to be at the vote.

"What do you think they'll decide this year?" asked a boy around my age. I had met him before, but I didn't remember his name, only that both his parents were in the parade. He sat alone.

I shrugged and gave my teacher's answer. "That's up to them. It's not for us to approve or disapprove."

He moved away from me. Nana was still talking. The bench had cleared and I lay back on it despite the heat. We were lucky to have had such beautiful weather. The sky was a shade of blue that got deeper the more I looked at it, like I could see through the atmosphere and into space. I thought about the other girls like me in a hundred other cities, waiting for their mothers and lying on benches and looking up at the sky.

We waited a long time. Nana pulled out her book. Her finger didn't move across the page the way it usually did, so I guessed she wasn't really reading. I closed my eyes and listened to the sweepers come to clear the streets, and the other stragglers chatting with each other. Now and again the bleachers clanged and shook as small children chased each other up and down.

Eventually, I heard the whine of a wheelchair operating at its highest speed. I shaded my face and looked down. Mama. Her eyes were puffy like she had been crying. Some years she smelled like beer, but this year she didn't.

I sat in the backseat and counted all the flags hanging from houses and shops.

"And?" Nana asked after we had ridden in silence for several minutes.

"No."

"Was the vote close?"

Mama sighed, her voice so soft I strained to hear it. "It never is."

Nana put her hand on Mama's arm. "Maybe someday."

"Maybe."

Back at the house, we took in the flag. Mama changed her clothes. She sat in her recliner with her hands folded in her lap, while Nana took the uniform from her to hide until next year. I went to get my father's photo from my drawer. I didn't see Nana on the other bed until I stood up. She was holding her face in her hands.

"That damned Veil," she said. "I'll never understand why they vote for the Veil, year after year."

"Because the memories are too strong." I repeated what my teacher told me. "The war was too brutal."

"But she wants to remember."

"It wouldn't do anyone any good if she ran into one of her friends in the grocery store who didn't remember her. It has to be everybody or nobody, Nana."

"But they push down so many good memories along with the bad ones."

"I think the good memories hurt too." I had seen the tears in my mother's eyes.

"Tell me something about him that I don't know." I climbed onto the arm of the recliner.

My mother smiled and took the photo from me, tracing his jawline and then the buttons on his dress uniform.

"I met him in the gym on base. He was the only guy who would spot me while I lifted without making comments."

"I know, Mama. What else?" I didn't mean for the impatience to show in my voice. "I'm sorry. I don't mean to rush you."

"He liked to play games with the village children outside the compound where we were stationed. The officers hated it, told him he would get kidnapped, but he sneaked out whenever he could."

I smiled. "I didn't know that. What games did they play?"

"The first week we were there, he brought chalk with him. He said there was one little boy, and he went to give him a piece of chalk, and suddenly he had two dozen children climbing all over him with their hands out. He was lucky it was chalk, so he was able to break it into smaller pieces. Some of the little ones tried to eat it. 'At least they got their calcium,' he told me later. After that, he didn't bring them anything, since he didn't have anything else to split so many ways. He made me teach him hopscotch, so he could teach it to them. Can you imagine that? This big soldier playing hopscotch? Then four square, football, anything they could play with a stick or a line in the dirt or the ball they already had. He would sneak back in with his eyes glowing like he had forgotten where we were and why we were there. Then the first attack—" She twisted her hands in her lap.

"Why were you there, Mama?"

A church bell began to chime, and another one, and another.

"Tell me more, Mama, quick!"

There was so much I wanted to know. A tear rolled down her cheek, and she pulled me close. She didn't answer, and I knew it was too late. I thought of my father, the man in the uniform, and tried to picture him teaching hopscotch to me instead of village children. It was hard to imagine somebody I had never known, never could know. I should have started with her instead of my father.

Minutes passed, and the bells stopped. Mama's face closed down like a shutter. She fumbled in the pocket on the side of her chair. The photo of my father slid off her lap and to the floor.

"I don't know why, but I'm in the mood to watch something funny before we make dinner," she said. "Do you want to watch with me?"

"Sure. I'll be right back." I picked up the fallen photograph.

"Who's that?" she asked, glancing up.

"Somebody who fought in the war."

"A school project?"

"Yeah," I said.

"I'm proud of you." She smiled. "Those soldiers deserve to be remembered."

Nana was asleep on her bed. I hid the photo back in my drawer where Mama couldn't reach it or find it accidentally. Why had I asked about him first? I could never know him. He was gone and she was here and I still didn't know any more about the parts of her that went away.

Mama's voice carried down the hall. "Clara, are you watching with me?"

"Coming."

I pulled a chair up beside Mama's and leaned up against her. She leaned back. This was the Mama I knew best. The one who couldn't quite remember why she was in a wheelchair, who thought war was something that had happened to other people. The one who laughed at pet videos with me.

Some year, maybe the old soldiers would vote to lift the Veil. Maybe I'd get to know the other Mama, too: the one who remembered my father, who had died before I was born. The one who could some-day tell me whether it had been worth everything she had lost. Next year, I would try to remember to ask that question first.

BLOOD ON BEACON HILL

Russell Nichols

THE BLACK BOY ON TRIAL smells the blood. That sweet, sweet hemoglobin, boiling now under the blushed skins of the dying race. He can smell mousse, too, and putrid sweat. He can't smell the eyes of this mob of mortals in the courtroom, but he feels them, stabbing like so many wooden stakes into his fifteen-year-old back.

"Mr. Attucks…" The grating voice of Judge Arthur Byron, a balding white man with an O-positive blood type, snaps Teddy from his trance. "What is your full name?"

He swallows hard. "Theodore Christopher Attucks."

"And what is your date of birth?"

"11/5/99."

"Could you clarify the year for the record?"

He clears his throat. "1899."

The judge leans forward, rubbing his knuckles. From the sudden whiff of camphor and menthol, Teddy knows the judge has arthritis. And as he goes on about Massachusetts General Law, Chapter 265, Section 23, his breath reeks of last night's Jim Beam and Fenway garlic fries.

"You are charged with rape and abuse of a child." Mortal murmurs diffuse, and the judge bangs the gavel. "Order. Order, I say!"

The few immortals present sit in the back, still. Among them, Mother appears stoic, wearing a tailored dark blazer with puffed shoulders over a leopard ruffle silk blouse. Wraparound shades hide long-suffering eyes. Beside her, Teddy's older sister, Eliana, also in shades, whispers a mantra for positivity. Father is a no-show. He has a "public image to uphold," considering his historic campaign for state representative for the 8th Suffolk district, an epic battle against longtime incumbent George Murray.

Once the noise dies down, the judge continues: "The statute states that a person who unlawfully has sexual intercourse and abuses a child under sixteen years of age shall be punished by imprisonment in the state prison for life or for any term of years the court finds appropriate." The judge narrows his eyes. "Do you understand what you've been charged with?"

"Yes, Your Honor," says Teddy, but his voice cracks on "Honor."

"All right. How do you plead?"

What follows feels like an eternity. A lifetime swaddled in the span of three seconds. In that forever, Teddy fixes his eyes upon the flag to the judge's right. Star-spangled. Just hanging there, all flaccid. And Father's oft-repeated quote by Thomas Jefferson echoes in his head:

The tree of liberty must be refreshed from time to time with the blood of patriots and tyrants.

Mother, on the other hand, always taught Teddy to take a stand. The stand in this courtroom may not be what she had in mind. But alas, here he is, a martyr in a war he never signed up for. After decades of civil co-existence between mortals and immortals in Boston, this singular case—Commonwealth v. Attucks—has turned the so-called Cradle of Liberty into a hub of bloodlust.

"Not guilty, Your Honor."

All because he fucked a dying girl.

The day he met her was in June, the middle of the hottest heat wave on record. Teddy didn't mind the heat, but prolonged sun exposure wasn't ideal for his kind. For that reason, he usually stayed indoors, working double shifts at the South End's carnivorous flower bistro, Bite Me, Venus. The overtime was helping him save up to get his fangs sanded off, a costly underground operation he knew would make Father proud. Teddy's boss, an unabashed immortal supporter, ran up to him that morning.

"Congrats, bud! I just saw the latest polls on TV," he said, pumped up. "Your father's now got a six-point edge over Old Man Murray! That's wicked awesome!"

"Uh-huh," said Teddy, but he was too distracted by the angel entering the bistro.

Members of the dying race usually came to Bite Me, Venus by accident, enticed by the name, wandering in off Columbus Avenue. Not this girl. She came on purpose that Friday. Teddy could tell because she had on a floral vintage dress, a forget-me-not flower in her blond hair, and the hint of hunger in her wide sky-blue eyes. She was with a giddy group of three other white girls, socialites-in-progress.

"Welcome to Bite Me, Venus," said Teddy at their booth. "My name's Teddy. I'll be your server."

"Excuse me," said the blonde, noticing his smile. "Aren't you, like, a vampire?"

"Oh my God, Wendy!" said the A-positive redhead, then put her hand to her heart, embarrassed. "I'm so sorry, sir, this one doesn't get out much."

Wendy's face turned red.

"It's all right. I'm not offended," said Teddy. "Do you know what you want?"

"Umm," said an O-positive with pearl earrings, "do you have any recommendations for first-timers? The three of us, we've eaten here before—"

"But Wendy's daddy looooaaathes this place," said another O-positive.

"So we wanted to treat her," said the redhead, "for her birthday. And after this, we're taking her to the House of Mirrors. You ever been there?"

Teddy ignored the question, focused on Wendy. "So you're the birthday girl, huh?"

She raised her hand. "Guilty as charged."

"And how old are we today?"

She put her hand on her hip. "Isn't it impolite to ask a woman her age?"

"Says the lady who called me the v-word."

She nodded a touché. "Well, technically, my birthday's on Tuesday. I'll be sixteen. And you?"

Teddy smiled with his mouth closed. "I'll never tell." He put his notepad down. "Now, let me illuminate you on some botany. There are five basic trapping mechanisms found in carnivorous plants. You've got your pitfall traps, fly paper traps, snap traps, bladder traps, and lobster pot traps. Do any of those sound enticing to you, birthday girl?"

"Oh my God, uhh, I don't know," said Wendy, playing with a toothpick under the table as she skimmed the menu. "I would like to try...the deadliest flower you have."

"You want deadly?" Teddy leaned in close, turned the page. "Here..."

He pointed to a picture of a cobra-shaped flower: the Darlingtonia

Californica. The leaves of the plant were bulbous and formed a hollow cavity with an opening situated underneath a swollen, balloon-like structure. It had two pointed leaves hanging off the end like fangs.

Wendy read the description aloud: "Nectar inside the plant's hidden opening attracts insects. Once inside, insects become confused by the transparent areas that appear like exits—"

"After that, it's goodbye fly," said Teddy, close enough to taste her.

Wendy looked up at the girls, exhilarated. "I want this one!"

"You sure, Wen?" said O-positive. "What if you get sick?"

Wendy shrugged. "We're all gonna die someday."

"Not all of us, darling," said Teddy, winking at her.

And as she handed Teddy her menu, Wendy slipped a folded napkin into his palm.

Teddy waited until he reached the kitchen to open the napkin. On it, he saw a blotch of scarlet. AB-negative. Wendy had pricked her finger with the toothpick and dabbed the wound. Her aroma crawled into Teddy's wide-open nostrils, haunting the depths of his olfactory system for the rest of the day.

That night, she came back. Alone, this time. The restaurant was empty, and Teddy was just closing up when he saw her standing there in the doorway.

"Aren't you going to, like, invite me in?"

He caught a whiff of tomato juice on her breath. He said nothing. She stepped inside, locked the door, and moved towards him. He backed up until he hit a wall. He could hear the blood engorging her clitoris. They were inches apart.

"I can't do this," said Teddy, for he knew he'd be in direct violation of Attucks Family Rule #33: Thou shalt not have sexual relations with a member of the dying race.

"You're doing this," said Wendy, sliding his hand under her floral dress, up her thigh for him to feel her slippery insides, that hollow cavity.

Still, he resisted. The Massachusetts general election was five months away, and Father's legacy was at stake. If he could defeat Murray, Father would become the first state representative of his kind. Teddy couldn't jeopardize that.

"My father…" said Teddy as they staggered back through the kitchen. "I can't defy his laws."

She laughed. "His laws?" And started sucking on his neck. "Your father can't control you."

They groped their way to the restaurant greenhouse. Captivated by the exotic display of carnivorous flowers, Wendy gasped. "Where's my darling?"

Teddy lifted her up onto a table next to a small circular garden, its soil filled with ice and dozens of darlingtonias. He picked up an ice cube. Traced the ice down her neck.

"They survive longer in cool temperatures."

She shivered. "Cold…"

Teddy took his time, savoring her until neither of them could take any more. And the hymen blood tasted every bit as good as he thought it would.

❤

TRANSCRIPT OF TRIAL
BEFORE: HON. ARTHUR BYRON, J.S.C. AND JURY
DIRECT EXAMINATION BY: ANNE HAWKINS, PROSECUTION

Q: Mr. Attucks, where do you work?
A: Bite Me, Venus.
Q: And what kind of business is Bite Me, Venus?
A: It's a restaurant.
Q: Specifically, a carnivorous flower bistro named after the Venus flytrap, correct?
A: Correct.
Q: Is it also correct that the Venus flytrap secretes sweet nectar to make insects think they've found a flower? Then traps them in its lobes to feed on the innocent insect's nitrogen-rich blood?
A: Yes, that's, uh…correct.
Q: Like a vampire, no?
MR. HIGHGATE: Objection, Your Honor, that's inflammatory!

THE COURT: Sustained. Mrs. Hawkins, let's leave the v-word out of this.

MRS. HAWKINS: Yes, Your Honor.

Q: Mr. Attucks, are you familiar with German physician Franz Anton Mesmer?

A: He's eighteenth century. Before my time.

(*Response elicits chuckles from the rear of the courtroom*)

Q: But you're familiar with his work, yes?

A: I'm familiar.

Q: Do you subscribe to his theory that bodies ooze an invisible, mysterious fluid-like force that can attract and influence humans?

A: That animal magnetism idea was debunked long ago.

Q: Do you not believe in the power of suggestion?

A: I believe a person can't be hypnotized if they don't want to be.

Q: What if this person is too, er, immature to know what they want?

MR. HIGHGATE: Objection, Your Honor. The question is argumentative.

THE COURT: Overruled. Please answer the question, Mr. Attucks.

A: This isn't folklore, all right? I didn't cast any seduction spells on her. I didn't lure her in with some super-hypnotic loverboy-stare. We were both fifteen, you know? A couple of horny kids just—

MRS. HAWKINS: *She* is a kid, Mr. Attucks! But you? With your 100-plus years worth of experience? No. No, you're something else, I'm afraid.

After the love was made, Teddy felt ashamed as he lay naked in the greenhouse. He had broken the vow and disgraced the family. Father would never forgive him.

"Here," he said, waving Wendy's dress at her, "here."

"What's the rush?"

Teddy hurried to put his clothes on. "I can't be late for supper."

"Supper? But it's past eleven."

He nodded. For the Attucks family, midnight was suppertime, a ritual dating back to the 1910s, established by Father to keep the family united. Teddy dared not add tardiness to his list of transgressions.

Wendy hopped up. "I want to come with you!"

"Huh? No, that's not a good idea."

"Why not?"

"It's just..." Teddy missed a button on his shirt, started over. "Some other time, maybe."

"It's because I'm a mortal?"

"It's complicated, all right?"

"I can't live forever, so I'm not good enough to meet your family. Sounds pretty simple to me."

"Wendy..."

She turned away, covering herself as she dressed. Teddy just knew bringing this girl home would be an epic disaster. But another thought occurred to him: If Wendy saw how sophisticated they lived, Father might be able to gain mortal support.

And Teddy said: "If you're coming, you have to hurry up."

They ran all the way to Beacon Hill. It was 11:57 when they reached the south slope, the seat of Boston wealth and power, where mansard-roofed houses line narrow gaslit streets. Teddy led Wendy to the Attucks residence, a brick Federalist estate, which he still called "the new house" even though his family had lived there sixty years now.

They entered through the French doors. Wendy stood there in the grand foyer under the vaulted ceiling, taking in the magnificent view. Renaissance murals covered the walls. There was a grand piano in the corner. A winding staircase led into a skylit formal dining room. Teddy could smell the blend of black pepper, musk, and citrus from Father's cologne, Penhaligon's Blenheim Bouquet.

"Theodore!" Father called from upstairs, as yet unseen.

"Yes, sir, coming!"

Teddy took Wendy's hand and raced up the stairs, two at a time. Hurried across the creaky hardwood floor, past Father's private study, where the "Wiener Blut" (Viennese Blood) waltz by Johann Strauss II poured out from the phonograph. They arrived, at last, at the long mahogany dining table dotted with burning candles. Chinese porcelain had been set down in four places with designated name tags for each member of the Attucks family. In the middle of the table were plates of prune-stuffed gnocchi. This meal, however, was "for display only," not to be eaten. Instead, the family would be partaking in one of Mother's famous chowder recipes: a rich, tangy dish made from lamb's blood, topped with black pepper, garlic, and a sprinkle of chives.

Wearing a tuxedo with an ascot as usual, Father sat at the head. His back was to the door, so he didn't see them enter, but Teddy knew he could smell her. Seated at the opposite end, in a crimson lace gown with a plunging neckline, Mother froze. Then Eliana saw them, and her eyes grew wide as she started uttering a mantra for peace.

"Hello," said Wendy.

The voice made Father turn around. He was an imposing man in a fifty-two-year-old frame, dark-skinned and robust, with jet black hair, chemically straightened. His jaw was square, his eyes like black holes that Teddy always feared he might get trapped in if he stared too long.

Teddy cleared his throat. "Family, forgive my tardiness. This is Wendy."

Father looked at Teddy.

Then at Wendy.

Then back to Teddy.

After that, he stood up and said: "Excuse me." And walked out.

Nobody moved. The waltz in the background spun through the awkward silence.

Teddy spoke to Wendy to hide his nerves. "So that's my mother down there…"

Wendy went to shake Mother's hand. "So nice to meet you, ma'am."

"Oh please, don't ma'am me. You make me feel old," she said. "Call me Rosemary."

Teddy said: "And that's my sister, Eliana—"

"Namaste," she said.

"—who you might have heard of from—"

"The Bloodline!" said Wendy, rushing over to her. "Oh my God, my friend, Sylvia, calls there, like, all the time. I've never called myself, but she swears you give the best advice ever."

The Bloodline was a suicide helpline Eliana started in Dorchester in the early 1970s. It was her calling, she said, a way to use decades of life experience to give back to the suffering world. Eliana had an extreme sympathy for the dying race. Immortal guilt, Father called it. But people found solace in her wisdom. Her survival stories spanning from slavery in America to the First World War to the Dust Bowl and beyond had a way of making suicidal mortals realize their modern lives weren't so bad after all.

Eliana put her hands together and bowed her head. "I am but a vessel."

Teddy said: "…and, uh, my father is—"

"Mr. Attucks," said Father, returning with an extra hand-carved wooden chair. He set the chair down beside Teddy's seat, then went to shake Wendy's hand. "Wendy, was it? Splendid of you to join us." He motioned for her to have a seat. "Well, then. Let's eat, shall we?"

Father prayed aloud to the Lord, repenting for the sins of the family, asking for the wisdom of Solomon in times of confusion, and giving thanks for the glorious feast before them. "All this, in Christ's name we pray," he concluded, "Amen."

Teddy started to serve Wendy some prune-stuffed gnocchi, but she stopped him.

"Oh, none of that for me, please," she said. "I'll have what you all are having."

Teddy forced a smile. "You really don't have to—"

"Son, let's not be churlish," said Father. "Kindly fix our guest a bowl of Mother's chowder."

Teddy did as he was told as the waltz ended. Father dabbed his mouth with a linen napkin.

"Excuse me," he said, then went out to replay the composition.

Teddy cringed as Wendy lifted a spoonful of blood to her mouth. She squeezed her eyes and pinched her lips as she swallowed the bitter, full-bodied soup. When it was down, she opened her eyes wide, infatuated by the rush.

"This chowder is amazing, Rosemary," she said.

"You are very sweet," said Mother. "I'd share the recipe, but a lady must keep her secrets."

"No, I understand," said Wendy, taking another swallow. "I mean, I guess with Teddy working in a restaurant, I should've known he came from a culinary family."

Father's deep voice seized the room as he reentered. "Is that where you met?" he asked, taking his seat again. "The bistro?"

Wendy wiped her mouth, nodding. "I went there for my birthday today."

Eliana raised a glass of fruitless sangria and quoted Jean Paul, the German Romantic writer: "Our birthdays are feathers in the broad wing of time."

Wendy clinked glasses with Eliana, took a sip, then said: "It was my first time…"

Teddy shifted in his seat. "Uh, coming to the restaurant, she means," he said, then wished he hadn't. "Actually, we've been getting a lot of newcomers. Mostly people coming in to avoid the heat."

Right then, one of the candles went out.

"Christ," said Mother, rolling her eyes as she stood up to get the matchbox.

Father crossed himself. "Dearest, must you desecrate the Lord's name? At the supper table, no less?" Ignoring him, she tried to ignite a match to no avail. Father said: "I'm sorry, son, you were saying?"

"Nothing, I, uh…it was just hot."

"You won't believe how many calls we've been getting about the heat," said Eliana, rubbing her ankh pendant. "Everybody's convinced this is a sign of the apocalypse."

Watching Mother struggle, Teddy grew antsy. "Do you need help, Ma?"

She finally struck the match. "I'm all right…" Then leaned over the table to light the candle, exposing much cleavage.

Father grimaced, tossing a napkin at Mother. "Cover yourself, my dear. Gracious."

The gust of wind caused the candle to go out again.

"Goddammit!" she said, then immediately crossed herself. "Forgive me, children, for I know not what I do."

With that, Mother sat down. The sight of Father's fang-less mouth made Wendy frown.

"Mr. Attucks, how come you don't have fangs?"

Teddy kneed Wendy under the table. Father said nothing. He ran his tongue under his teeth, perfectly straight, immaculately white. Wendy looked around at the others, confused. Nobody else had fang-free teeth like his.

"He had them sanded off," said Teddy, hoping that would suffice, but Wendy wasn't finished.

She looked at Father. "Are you ashamed to be … who you are?" Teddy kneed Wendy again, which made her say: "What?"

Father put down his utensils. For a moment, he was quiet, staring at his bowl, stained red. The waltz carried on. Then Father looked straight at Teddy, but his question was for Wendy:

"Are you a natural blonde?"

"Well, no, but—"

"And surely you didn't color your hair out of shame, did you?"

"But mine is temporary."

"Ah, yes," said Father with a chortle. "Such is life for a mere mortal."

Wendy glowered. Panicking, Teddy grabbed her empty bowl. "I'll start cleaning up—"

Father held out his hand. "Son, we're not finished here. Besides, you have yet to confess."

"Confess? What did I do?" said Teddy, on edge, then turned to Mother for help. But she was too distracted, playing with matches on the table.

Eliana instigated while topping off her glass. "Free yourself, Theodore!"

"I didn't do anything."

All this time, Wendy had been glaring at Father. "You think you're better than us?"

Father stood up, the wooden chair ground against the hardwood floor.

"For centuries," he said, "I've had to watch you people rape Mother Earth, exploit other races, suck the very life out of this … land of the free." He walked around the long table. The floor creaked under each step. "I harbor no resentment, for this is your nature." He held his hands behind his back. He moved clockwise, past Eliana, around Mother. "Do I think I'm better? I wouldn't say that. More qualified? Yes. More civilized? Without a doubt. Enlightened, if you will." Past Wendy and finally stopped behind Teddy. "Because, you see, with age comes wisdom." Father put his hands on Teddy's tense shoulders. "And I'm old enough to know a society ruled by those who die is no place to live."

"Come now, Oscar," said Mother, "let us not put fear in our guest."

Disregarding her, Father raised his voice and his hands as the waltz reached its crescendo.

"The American Dream is deceased, and any hope of its resurrection lies with those of us who were there to witness its complicated birth. The State House needs new blood!" He looked down at Wendy. "Your father's time is up."

Eliana nearly spit out her sangria. "Wait, wait, what?"

The waltz ended. Silence consumed the room.

Teddy frowned at Wendy, whose face was bright red.

Father smiled and returned to his seat at the head. "What's the matter, son? Did you not know your dinner guest was the daughter of State Representative Murray?"

As Father sat down, Wendy wiped her mouth and stood up.

"It doesn't matter how old you are," she said to Father, "or how much you think you know. You can live in this nice house, put on fancy clothes, and act all holier-than-thou. But you'll never be elected to any office because, at the end of the day, you're a fucking vampire."

With that, she raced out of the room and down the stairs. Teddy heard the front door close.

The Attucks family remained still for a moment.

"Well," said Father, "at least she's too young to vote."

TRANSCRIPT OF TRIAL
BEFORE: HON. ARTHUR BYRON, J.S.C. AND JURY
CROSS-EXAMINATION BY: JONATHAN HIGHGATE, DEFENSE COUNSEL

Q: Are you ashamed of your body, Mr. Attucks?
A: What do you mean?
Q: Do you like what you see when you look in…(*clears throat*) Let me rephrase: Are you happy with your physical appearance?
A: I suppose.
Q: You suppose? Mr. Attucks, look at you. You're about,

what, five-seven? In peak shape, with nary a wrinkle in sight. And you've got a full head of hair. Not too shabby for someone born in the same decade as Babe Ruth, eh?

A: Whatever.

Q: Do you know how much Americans would pay to get their teenage bodies back?

A: (*Indiscernible*)

Q: Pardon me?

A: I said it sucks. This body—I'm sick of this peach fuzz and this skin—these zits will never go away and… I'm not supposed to be done…

Q: Done what?

A: Growing.

Q: Throughout the 1990s, you even tried growth hormone replacement therapy, isn't that right?

A: (*Indiscernible*)

Q: Can you repeat that, Mr. Attucks?

A: I just want to feel like a man. (*Voice cracks on "feel."*)

Q: But you're not quite a man, are you, Mr. Attucks? And the truth is, you'll never be one. You were transformed at a young age and now you're fated to forever live as a boy in an endless cycle of puberty. I'd imagine this eternal awkward phase affects your love life. Do you go out on many dates?

A: No.

Q: And why not?

A: I try, but these mortals…they only like the rush.

Q: The rush?

A: Being with me gets their adrenaline going, makes them feel rebellious, free. But the truth is, they're scared of me.

Q: Why would people be afraid of you?

A: People see all those stereotypical portrayals on screen and think that's real. Like we're all just bloodthirsty savages and…that's not the truth.

MR. HIGHGATE: Ladies and gentlemen, if the defendant is guilty of anything, it's trying to live a normal life in a world that discriminates against abnormality. He is neither man, nor monster, but a victim. A lost boy. A child as were we all once upon a time, but he will be a child now and forevermore.

❖

Teddy tried to forget Wendy, but he couldn't.

In the days after the dinner from hell, he couldn't go seven minutes without thinking about what they did in that greenhouse. Intense flashbacks of fleeting images: roaming tongues, random bite marks, his fingers on her lips, back scratches, black skin, white skin, a floral dress on the floor like a puddle.

He'd hide in the bathroom at work to inhale the bloody napkin she gave him. Intoxicated. But then he remembered how she lied. Deceived him, dishonored Father. She used him for political gain. And suddenly, his lustful thoughts made him feel guilty. So guilty that, one afternoon, he used his boss' phone during his lunch break to make a private call.

"Bloodline," said his sister, "this is Eliana speaking."

Teddy disguised his voice to hide his identity. "I'm thinking about killing myself."

"I understand that. First, as a disclaimer, let me say that the Bloodline is not liable for any actions taken by our callers. And second, in regards to wanting to kill yourself, you're not alone."

"I feel alone."

"When was the last time you felt alive?"

Teddy told her about Wendy, explaining in general terms his impossible situation. Eliana went into a drawn-out story about a whirlwind romance she had with a former Confederate general after the Civil War, which ended when she accidentally killed him and sucked him dry during a trip to Yellowstone National Park in 1872.

"Ever since then," said Eliana, "I've been practicing abstinence."

If Teddy didn't want to off himself before, he definitely did now.

"All right, thanks. I'm all better," he said and hung up.

But he didn't feel better, so he told his boss he was sick. His boss let him off early. Teddy put on his hoodie, hopped on the T, and took the Red Line down to Mattapan, where Mother owned a mortuary.

There was a wake going on upstairs, but he didn't see Mother. He went around back and used his key to get to the lower level.

"Ma?" he called out as he stepped down the stairs.

No response. But then he heard a rattle. He pressed on, peeking into the cold chamber.

There, he spied Mother pulling a sheet off a gurney, where a fresh corpse lay naked. The twenty-one-year-old man had a broken neck from hanging himself, and his penis was completely erect-a condition known as postmortem priapism, often caused from the noose putting pressure on the cerebellum. Teddy wondered if this man had been one of Eliana's callers. But the thought flew from his mind when he saw what Mother did next.

She hiked up her black dress, climbed up on the gurney, and lowered herself, carefully, onto him, sliding his stiff penis into her. Then started churning. She closed her eyes. Lifted the dead man's arm and slapped herself in the face with his limp hand, again and again, snarling all the while.

Teddy could watch no more. He backed away into the hall, bumping against another gurney.

"Hello?" Mother called out, but he gave no response as he ran up the stairs to the exit.

Teddy rode the Red Line to the Common, the oldest city park in the States. He used to play catch here with Father, who made him practice running slower and dropping the ball to "look normal." It was only four now, another muggy afternoon. The elm trees provided some cover, but not enough to protect his sensitive skin. And as he took off his hoodie to let the sun burn him, he heard the chants:

"If you can't stand the heat, get out of our streets!"

He looked across the way, where the State House rose up like something majestic, its golden dome seizing a spot of sunlight. Out in front of the steps, protesters in star-spangled bikinis and speedos held signs that said IMMORTALITY with the letter T crossed out. This scantily clad group was part of the anti-fang movement, public demonstrators who called themselves People Of The Sun.

Watching them, Teddy thought about Father, about everything his old man had fought for, everything he's had to overcome to stand here on the tipping point of history. Thinking about these things helped Teddy put his life in perspective. Dying girls come and go, he thought, but his family is forever. With that, he put on his hoodie and rushed home to rest his stinging body.

Later that night, Teddy woke to muffled yelling. The voice was desperate, raging against the walls beneath his floor, trying to break free from the master bedroom. It was Mother.

"I don't want to live like this!"

"And how, pray tell, are you living, my dear?" said Father, calm and monotonic.

"Like this! Like I can't be myself. All this acting and posing and pretending we're something we're not. For what? Why? So you can get elected to the House? What then, huh?"

"Then we move on up. We've discussed this."

"Do forgive me, Representative Attucks—I mean, Governor At-tucks—oh, here comes President Attucks! Behold, the leader of the free world is black and Catholic and a closet blood-sucker!"

"I do not *suck*," said Father. "I *partake*." Then he recited 1 Corin-thians 10:16: "The cup of blessing which we bless, is it not the com-munion of the blood of Christ?"

Teddy sat up in bed. His room was a makeshift gym with an Ever-last punching bag, dumbbells, and weights for bench pressing. In the corner sat a blue pot filled with dirt in a glass display case, labeled: "Thomas Jefferson's Venus flytrap"—a birthday gift from Father when Teddy turned fifty in 1949.

It was nearly dusk. Getting his bearings, Teddy touched his face. He'd been asleep for almost four hours. The sun damage had mostly healed. Teddy emerged in the hallway, adjusting to the light from the wall-mounted lanterns. On the opposite end, he saw Eliana in her un-furnished bedroom, meditating on a mandala rug. She sat in the lotus position, chanting Om, the ancient Sanskrit mantra. Sensing Teddy's presence, she opened her eyes and called him over.

"Brother," she whispered, "tell me it isn't true."

"It's not true."

"So you and a mortal aren't making the beast with two backs?"

"What?!"

"Because earlier this afternoon, I got a call from a boy, talking about how he was into this 'forbidden' girl. And I gave him advice, and he didn't sound like you, but he sounded like you, you know? Was that you?"

"Why would I call the Bloodline? We live together. That makes no sense at all."

"I know. You're right..." She rubbed her belly. "...but you know when you have a feeling about something that just won't go away?"

Teddy thought about Wendy. Eliana caught the shift in his eyes. Teddy knew she caught him.

"Brother, let me help you."

Teddy scoffed. "You can't even help yourself. You're old and lonely and bitter and all you do is hide on the other end of the phone, trying to get people to like you by acting like you know everything."

Insulted, Eliana laughed. "Least I'm not sleeping with the dying to feel alive."

"Nobody wants a spinster like you, that's why."

"And you're gonna get impaled as soon as I tell Daddy!"

Teddy stormed out. He needed to speak with Father right away to confess everything. As he crept down the stairs, avoiding creaks in the hardwood, he heard Mother scoff in the bedroom.

"Oscar, you've been alive for over 400 years, but I swear to God, you act sometimes like you were born yesterday. They don't want us here, don't you get that?"

Teddy inched closer as Mother rambled on.

"These fucking mortals, they're scared of our power: We're stronger, faster, smarter. We can fly, goddammit! Yet and still, you're so desperate for their approval. Does that not sound backwards? And for what? To be in the club? With the Brahmin? The same crowd who'd rip your fangs out?"

"I haven't any fangs, my dear."

Teddy tiptoed through the passageway, past the main library and the museum of artifacts.

Mother said: "You want so badly for that race to accept you. You're so thirsty for validation, you're willing to suppress who you truly are."

Teddy approached the wooden door at the end of the hall. He peeked inside.

The master bedroom was an ornate space, illuminated only by

claws of flames in the grand fireplace. Ruby velvet drapes swooped down from the high ceiling. There were marble sculptures around the room, busts of some of history's greatest minds, from Aristotle to da Vinci to Darwin. In the center of the room stood an elaborately carved wooden canopy bed, where Mother was sprawled out wearing a silk negligee. Father had his back to her, in white briefs and sock garters, facing a full-length mirror as he combed his slick hair.

"My dearest wife, can you not see? The Lord calls us to lay aside our old selves, which are corrupted by lusts and deceit."

Hearing this, Teddy thought twice about knocking. He watched as Father put on his cilice, an undergarment made of goat's hair and prickly wires. It looked painful to wear, which it was supposed to be as it was a sign of repentance and atonement. Over that, Father put on a perfectly starched white shirt as he said: "Beloved, it is God's will that we be not savages, but civilized beings. Whoever humbles himself shall be exalted."

And she said: "But a city set on a hill cannot be hidden."

Father gave no response as he fastened his cummerbund.

Mother put the back of her hand on her forehead. "Oh, for the love of plasma, I can't go on like this, Oscar. I am tired of lying just to fit in. Acting like these urges are unnatural. Being forced to believe something's wrong with...the way I am."

Father said nothing as he tied his bow tie.

Mother rolled over, in dramatic fashion, letting her head hang upside-down off the bed. Her locks cascaded to the wooden floor. "I feel sooooo repressed in this place, Oscar. All those prophesies about fiery lakes and burning sulfur? No. This, right here, this is hell. And God said—" Then Mother spotted Teddy in the doorway. "Fuck! Theodore, you scared me."

Teddy entered. "I'm sorry, Ma, but I, uh...I need to speak with Father please."

A flash of guilt swept over her face, and Teddy knew she knew it was him at the mortuary.

"Um, Mommy and Daddy are talking right now. What is this regarding?" she said, covering her exposed parts with embroidered leaf throw pillows.

"It's kinda..." He cleared his throat. "It's kinda personal."

Father said: "You'll have to make this quick, son. I've got a very important fundraiser to get to and I'm expecting some big campaign donors to be there."

Teddy took a breath. He didn't want to discuss Wendy in front of Mother.

"Could we speak in private?"

"I have to get dressed."

"You can talk in front of me," said Mother, daring her son to betray her. "I won't bite."

Teddy swallowed hard. He felt the eyes of the marble busts upon him, like history staring him down. An eerie moment of silence filled the room. Breaking through, suddenly, the phone rang.

Father, still at work on the bow tie, said: "Dearest, would you get that?"

Mother glared at Teddy. Neither of them moved at all.

It rang a second time.

"Rosemary, please…" said Father. "That might be important."

Mother, eyes fixed on Teddy, shouted upstairs: "Eliana! Get the phone!"

Eliana fired back: "I'm off duty!"

It rang a third time.

"For heaven's sake…" said Father, rushing over to answer. "Attucks residence…" Father listened to the caller, standing there, half-dressed. He said nothing for a long time. Then finally, he said: "No. Thank you for telling me. God bless you." And the line went dead.

Mother said: "Who was that?"

Father hung up the phone and stared at Teddy.

At that point, Mother sensed something was very, very wrong. "Oscar…"

"Our son is being charged with statutory rape."

Teddy spent three days in jail, awaiting trial. After that time in a private cell, he was escorted to a private bus and driven to Pemberton Square, where the Suffolk County Courthouse stands like an Art Deco giant with white brick exterior. Teddy could still remember when this tower was built, back in the late 1930s as World War II was breaking out.

Without precedent, this case was wide open. And Teddy felt sick to his stomach in the courtroom, fielding question after question, trying to prove his innocence in front of those who have prejudged him.

PROSECUTION:

Q: Mr. Attucks, have you never considered dating *inside* your race?

A: I'm not attracted to immortals.

Q: So you're exclusively hemosexual?

A: What's your point?

Q: I'm just wondering why you feel compelled to prey on— I mean, pursue—humans when you can be with your own kind. It seems like every other night, there's a new bloodpub popping up in this city. And that new immortal club just opened in the Theatre District, uh, what's it called?

A: House of Mirrors.

Q: I've never been myself, but I hear it's all the rave.

A: Not really my scene.

Q: An old geezer such as yourself wouldn't know what to do in a place like that, would you?

MR. HIGHGATE: Objection!

DEFENSE COUNSEL:

Q: Mr. Attucks, have you ever been to House of Mirrors?

A: No.

Q: Only because it's not your scene?

A: Even if it was, I couldn't get in.

Q: Oh? Why not?

A: They serve alcohol, so it's 21 and over.

Q: So even though you were born in 1899, biologically you're not old enough to get into a 21 and over club, isn't that right?

MRS. HAWKINS: Objection!

And the trial went on for hours with no end in sight.

But at four p.m., just when the judge is about to call for recess, the prosecution introduces a method to prove whether Teddy should be tried as a human at all.

"Ladies and gentlemen," she says, "the defense wants to paint Mr. Attucks as the victim, subject to the same laws of justice as human beings. But Mr. Attucks is not human. Mr. Attucks is a monster, which I intend to prove with this." She holds up a green plant with two red connected lobes, fringed by stiff hair-like cilia. "Presenting the Venus flytrap, Dionaea muscipula. Native to the Carolinas, the Venus flytrap is known for eating insects and arachnids, but what you may not know is this carnivorous plant also has a penchant for human flesh." She smiles at Teddy. "Ladies and gentlemen, what I'm proposing is a test: If Mr. Attucks agrees to put skin from his finger in this trap, and the plant eats the flesh after one week, then we will honor the age of his fifteen-year-old body."

Mortals object, and she raises her hand and adds:

"If, however, his skin remains more or less intact, then he shall be deemed a monster and punished accordingly."

The courtroom erupts with those in favor.

"Order!" says the judge, banging the gavel. "Order, I say!"

Then calls both attorneys to the bench. Teddy can only watch as these members of the dying race decide his fate. He turns to look for Mother and Eliana in the back, but can't see them through the crowd. Finally, the judge sanctions the test. Mr. Highgate helps Teddy cut off a piece of his pointer finger. Carefully, he sets the dark skin on the lobes. The trap snaps shut.

The judge says: "We'll reconvene in seven days," and bangs the gavel.

But the mortals present are in such a frenzy that guards have to escort Teddy through the pack. On the way out, he spots Wendy, crying by the door, a forget-me-not in her hair. State Representative Murray, whose aged skin looks to be melting, holds her close, smirking at Teddy.

Teddy shoulders on through the mob, but as he passes behind Wendy, catching a whiff of her AB-negative, she discreetly slips something into his hand. A note.

Teddy waits until he reaches the lobby to read the note:

Daddy made me do it. :_(

He rips up the note, drops the scraps in a recycle bin, then goes outside.

The July air is suffocating, but not as bad as those crowding the entrance, barely dressed and sunblock-slathered: People of the Sun beaming him with silver metallic UV reflectors.

"Just die already!" somebody hollers.

The private bus is waiting to take Teddy back to Beacon Street. But he stands still, caught in the hate-filled gaze of the dying. And that's when he smells it, those familiar notes: black pepper, musk, and citrus. The scent of Father's Blenheim Bouquet. Teddy scans the crowd, thinking Father has come to save him from this mortal chaos.

"Father!" Teddy cries out, but he's nowhere to be found.

Then another thought occurs to him. That Father didn't come to save Teddy, but to save himself, to protect his legacy. He can hear Father's voice in his head now:

The tree of liberty must be refreshed from time to time with the blood of patriots and tyrants.

Martyrdom would make Father very proud, Teddy thinks. His only son slayed by barbaric mortals. Such a sacrifice would surely swing enough empathy votes for Father to win come November. Oscar Attucks would go down in history! But what then? Would anything truly change? Or would Father be doomed to repeat the sins of the forefathers? Teddy thinks about Wendy and wonders if we're not all just victims of those who raise us, cultivated. Conditioned to be controlled in a deadly environment.

He steps out of the shadows. He lifts his head to the wide-open sky.

"Get the vampire!" somebody screams.

The people crowd around to hold him down. Out for blood, dying of thirst.

He inhales the clear summer air and whispers: "Goodbye, my family."

And the black boy on trial flies away.

THE GREEN BOOK

Amal El-Mohtar

Nebula Award Nominee

MS. Orre. 1013A Miscellany of materials copied from within Master Leuwin Orrerel's (d. Lady Year 673, Bright Be the Edges) library by Dominic Merrowin (d. Lady Year 673, Bright Be the Edges). Contains Acts I and II of Aster's *The Golden Boy's Last Ship*, Act III scene I of *The Rose Petal*, and the entirety of *The Blasted Oak*. Incomplete copy of item titled only THE GREEN BOOK, authorship multiple and uncertain. Notable for extensive personal note by Merrowin, intended as correspondence with unknown recipient, detailing evidence of personal connection between Orrerel and the Sisterhood of Knives. Many leaves regrettably lost, especially within text of THE GREEN BOOK: evidence of discussion of Lady Year religious and occult philosophies, traditions in the musical education of second daughters, and complex reception of Aster's poetry, all decayed beyond recovery. Markers placed at sites of likely omission.

My dear friend,

I am copying this out while I can. Leuwin is away, has left me in charge of the library. He has been doing that more and more, lately—errands for the Sisterhood, he says, but I know it's mostly his own mad research. Now I know why.

His mind is disturbed. Twelve years of teaching me, and he never once denied me the reading of any book, but this—this thing has hold of him, I am certain plays with him. I thought it was his journal, at first; he used to write in it so often, closet himself with it for hours, and it seemed to bring him joy. Now I feel there is something fell and chanty about it, and beg your opinion of the whole, that we may work together to Leuwin's salvation.

The book I am copying out is small-only four inches by five. It is a vivid green, quite exactly the color of sunlight through the oak leaves in the arbor, and just as mottled; its cover is pulp wrapped in paper, and its pages are thick with needle-thorn and something that smells of thyme.

There are six different hands in evidence. The first, the invocation, is archaic: large block letters with hardly any ornamentation. I place it during Journey Year 200-250, Long Did It Wind, and it is written almost in green paste: I observe a grainy texture to the letters, though I dare not touch them. Sometimes the green of them is obscured by rust-brown stains that I suppose to be blood, given the circumstances that produced the second hand.

The second hand is modern, as are the rest, though they vary significantly from each other.

The second hand shows evidence of fluency, practice, and ease in writing, though the context was no doubt grim. It is written in heavy charcoal, and is much faded, but still legible.

The third hand is a child's uncertain wobbling, where the letters are large and uneven; it is written in fine ink with a heavy implement. I find myself wondering if it was a knife.

The fourth is smooth, an agony of right-slanted whorls and loops, a gallows-cursive that nooses my throat with the thought of who must have written it.

The fifth hand is very similar to the second. It is dramatically improved, but there is no question that it was produced by the same indi-

BEST OF APEX MAGAZINE

vidual, who claims to be named Cynthia. It is written in ink rather than charcoal—but the ink is strange. There is no trace of nib or quill in the letters. It is as if they welled up from within the page.

The sixth hand is Leuwin's.

I am trying to copy them as exactly as possible, and am bracketing my own additions.

Go in Gold,

Dominic Merrowin

[First Hand: invocation]

HAIL!

TO THE MISTRESS OF CROSSROADS, [blood stain to far right]

THE FETCH IN THE FOREST

THE WITCH OF THE GLEN

THE HUE AND CRY OF MORTAL MEN

WINSOME AND LISSOM AND FEY!

HAIL TO THE [blood stain obscuring] MOTHER OF CHANGELINGS

OF DOUBLED PATHS AND TREBLED MEANS

OF TROUBLED DREAMS AND SALT AND ASH

HAIL!

[Second Hand: charcoal smudging, two pages; dampened and stained]

Cold in here—death and shadows—funny there should be a book! the universe provides for last will and testament! [illegible]

[illegible] I cannot write, mustn't [illegible] they're coming I hear them they'll hear scratching [illegible] knives to tickle my throat oh please

They say they're kind. I think that's what we tell ourselves to be less afraid because how could anyone know? Do **[blood stain]** the dead speak?

Do the tongues blackening around their necks sing?

Why do I write? Save me, please, save me, stone and ivy and bone I want to live I want to breathe they have no right **[illegible]**

[Third Hand: block capitals. Implement uncertain-possibly a knife, ink-tipped.]

WHAT A BEAUTIFUL BOOK THIS IS. I WONDER WHERE SHE FOUND IT. I COULD WRITE POEMS IN IT. THIS PAPER IS SO THICK, SO CREAMY, IT PUTS ME IN MIND OF THE BONES IN THE IVY. HER BONES WERE LOVELY! I CANNOT WAIT TO SEE HOW THEY WILL SPROUT IN IT—I KEPT HER ZYGOMATIC BONE, BUT HER LACRIMAL BITS WILL MAKE SUCH PRETTY PATTERNS IN THE LEAVES!

I COULD ALMOST FEEL THAT ANY TRACE OF INK AGAINST THIS PAPER WOULD BE A POEM, WOULD COMFORT MY LACK OF SKILL.

I MUST SHOW MY SISTERS. I WISH I HAD MORE OF THIS PA-PER TO GIVE THEM. WE COULD WRITE EACH OTHER SUCH SE-CRETS AS ONLY BONES GROUND INTO PULPY PAPER COULD KNOW. OR I WOULD WRITE OF HOW BEAUTIFUL ARE SISTER-GREEN'S EYES, HOW SHY ARE SISTER-SALT'S LIPS, HOW GOLDEN SISTER-BELL'S LAUGH

[Fourth Hand: cursive, right-slanted; high quality ink, smooth and fine]

Strange, how it will not burn, how its pages won't tear. Strange that there is such pleasure in streaking ink along the cream of it; this

paper makes me want to touch my lips. Pretty thing, you have been tricksy, tempting my little Sisters into spilling secrets.

There is strong magic here. Perhaps Master Leuwin in his tower would appreciate such a curiosity. Strange that I write in it, then-strange magic. Leuwin, you have my leave to laugh when you read this. Perhaps you will write to me anon of its history before that unfortunate girl and my wayward Sister scribbled in it.

That is, if I send it to you. Its charm is powerful-I may wish to study it further, see if we mightn't steep it in elderflower wine and discover what tincture results.

[Fifth Hand: ink is strange; no evidence of implement; style resembles Second Hand very closely]

Hello?
Where am I?
Please, someone speak to me
Oh
Oh no

[Sixth Hand: Master Leuwin Orrerel]

I will speak to you. Hello.

I think I see what happened, and I see that you see. I am sorry for you. But I think it would be best if you tried to sleep. I will shut the green over the black and you must think of sinking into sweetness, think of dreaming to fly. Think of echoes, and songs. Think of fragrant tea and the stars. No one can harm you now, little one. I will hide you between two great leather tomes—

[Fifth Hand-alternating with Leuwin's hereafter]

Do you know Lady Aster?
Yes, of course.
Could you put me next to her, please? I love her plays.
I always preferred her poetry.
Her plays ARE poetry!

Of course, you're right. Next to her, then. What is your name?

Cynthia.

I am Master Leuwin.

I know. It's very kind of you to talk to me.

You're—**[ink blot]** forgive the ink blot, please. Does that hurt?

No more than poor penmanship ever does.

Leuwin? are you there?

Yes. What can I do for you?

Speak to me, a little. do you live alone?

Yes—well, except for Dominic, my student and apprentice. It is my intention to leave him this library one day—it is a library, you see, in a tower on a small hill, seven miles from the city of Leech—do you know it?

No. I've heard of it, though. Vicious monarchy, I heard.

I do not concern myself overmuch with politics. I keep records, that is all.

How lucky for you, to not have to concern yourself with politics. Records of what?

Everything I can. Knowledge. Learning. Curiosities. History and philosophy. Scientific advances, musical compositions and theory—some things I seek out, most are given to me by people who would have a thing preserved.

How ironic.

...Yes. Yes, I suppose it is, in your case.

[[DECAY, SEVERAL LEAVES LOST]]

Were you very beautiful, as a woman?

What woman would answer no, in my position?

An honest one.

I doubt I could have appeared more beautiful to you as a woman than as a book.

...Too honest.

[[DECAY, SEVERAL LEAVES LOST]]

What else is in your library?

Easier to ask what isn't! I am in pursuit of a book inlaid with mirrors—the text is so potent that it was written in reverse, and can only be read in reflection to prevent unwelcome effects.

Fascinating. Who wrote it?

I have a theory it was commissioned by a disgruntled professor, with a pun on "reflection" designed to shame his students into closer analyses of texts.

Hah! I hope that's the case. What else?

Oh, there is a history of the Elephant War written by a captain on the losing side, a codex from the Chrysanthemum Year (Bold Did it Bloom) about the seven uses of bone that the Sisterhood would like me to find, and—

Cynthia I'm so sorry. Please, forgive me.

No matter. It isn't as if I've forgotten how I came to you in the first place, though you seem to quite frequently.

Why

Think VERY carefully about whether you want to ask this question, Leuwin.

Why did they kill you? …How did they?

Forbidden questions from their pet librarian? The world does turn. do you really want to know?

Yes.

So do I. perhaps you could ask them for me.

[[DECAY, SEVERAL LEAVES LOST]]

If I could find a way to get you out…

You and your ellipses. Was that supposed to be a question?

I might make it a quest.

I am dead, Leuwin. I have no body but this.

You have a voice. A mind.

I am a voice, a mind. I have nothing else.

Cynthia… What happens when we reach the end of this? When we run out of pages?

Endings do not differ overmuch from each other, I expect. Happy or sad, they are still endings.

Your ending had a rather surprising sequel.

True. Though I see it more as intermission—an interminable intermission, during which the actors have wandered home to get drunk.

[[DECAY, SEVERAL LEAVES LOST]]

Cynthia, I think I love you.

Cynthia?

Why don't you answer me?

Please, speak to me.

I'm tired, Leuwin.

I love you.

You love ink on a page. You don't lack for that here.

I love *you*.

Only because I speak to you. Only because no one but you reads these words. Only because I am the only book to be written to you, for you. Only because I allow you, in this small way, to be a book yourself.

I love you.

Stop.

Don't you love me?

Cynthia.

You can't lie, can you?

You can't lie, so you refuse to speak the truth.

I hate you.

Because you love me.

I hate you. Leave me alone.

I will write out Lady Aster's plays for you to read. I will write you her poetry. I will fill this with all that is beautiful in the world, for you, that you might live it.

Leuwin. no.

I will stop a few pages from the end, and you can read it over and over again, all the loveliest things...

Leuwin. no.

But I

STOP. I WANT TO LIVE. I WANT TO HOLD YOU AND FUCK YOU AND MAKE YOU TEA AND READ YOU PLAYS. I WANT YOU TO TOUCH MY CHEEK AND MY HAIR AND LOOK ME IN THE EYES WHEN YOU SAY YOU LOVE ME. I WANT TO *LIVE!*

And you, you want a woman in a book. You want to tremble over my binding and ruffle my pages and spill ink into me. No, I can't lie. Only the living can lie. I am dead. I am dead trees and dead horses boiled to glue. I hate you. Leave me alone.

[FINIS. Several blank pages remain]

You see he is mad.

I know he is looking for ways to extricate her from the book. I fear for him, in so deep with the Sisters—I fear for what he will ask them—

Sweet Stars, there's more. I see it appearing as I write this—unnatural, chanty thing! I shall not reply. I must not reply, lest I fall into her trap as he did! But I will write this for you-I am committed to completeness.

Following immediately after the last, then:

Dominic, why are you doing this?

You won't answer me? Fair enough.

I can feel when I am being read, Dominic. It's a beautiful feeling, in some ways—have you ever felt beautiful? sometimes I think only people who are not beautiful can feel so, can feel the shape of the exception settling on them like a mantle, like a morning mist.

Being read is like feeling beautiful, knowing your hair to be just-so and your clothing to be well-put-together and your color to be high and bright, and to feel, in the moment of beauty, that you are being observed.

The world shifts. You pretend not to see that you are being admired, desired. You think about whether or not to play the game of glances, and you smile to yourself, and you know the person has seen your smile, and it was beautiful, too. Slowly, you become aware of how they see you, and without looking, quite, you know that they are playing the game too, that they imagine you seeing them as beautiful, and it is a splendid game, truly.

Leuwin reads me quite often, without saying anything further to me. I ache when he does, to answer, to speak, but ours is a silence I cannot be the one to break. So he reads, and I am read, and this is all our love now.

I feel this troubles you. I do not feel particularly beautiful when you read me, Dominic. But I know it is happening.

Will you truly not answer? Only write me down into your own little book? Oh, Dominic. And you think you will run away? Find him help? You're sweet enough to rot teeth.

You know, I always wanted someone to write me poetry.

If I weren't dead, the irony would kill me.

I wonder who the Mistress of the Crossroads was. Hello, I suppose, if you ever read this—if Dominic ever shares.

I am going to try and sleep. Sorry my handwriting isn't prettier. I never really was myself.

I suppose Leuwin must have guessed, at some point. Just as he would have guessed you'd disobey him eventually. I am sorry he will find out about both, now. It isn't as if I can cross things out. No doubt he will be terribly angry. No doubt the Sisters will find out you know something more of them than they would permit, as I did.

It's been a while since I've felt sorry for someone who wasn't Leuwin, but I do feel sorry for you.

Good night.

That is all. Nothing else appears. Please, you must help him. I don't know what to do. I cannot destroy the book—I cannot hide it from him, he seeks it every hour he is here—

I shall write more to you anon. He returns. I hear his feet upon the stair.

L'ESPIRIT DE L'ESCALIER

Peter M. Ball

RAT OPENS THE DOUBLE DOORS and the stairwell smells of baking, the air thick with dull warmth and the smell of yeasty dough. He wrinkles his long nose and wonders if it will be like this for the entire way down, or if the doughy stink will gradually transform itself into the aroma of fresh-baked. He hopes not. Rat worked in a bakery one summer, and he hasn't enjoyed the smell of bread since. It reminds him of the finger burns and the thick coats of lard painted into hot bread trays to keep the dough from sticking as it cooked.

He flexes his fingers. The big backpack is so heavy it's cutting off the circulation to his arms, so he has to remember to keep his fingers moving.

Someone has bolted a sign to the mahogany balustrade, warning people not to throw coins or pebbles down the centre of the stairwell. The guidebook says this is for the safety of fellow climbers. Every year someone is struck on the head when they're 130 flights below, and there's no chance of getting help in time when you're that far down.

There's another sign that warns people not to jump. Rat's guidebook says this isn't, in fact, the warning to the habitually stupid that it appears to be on the surface. Originally it was posted as a warning to the suicides that come to contemplate the twisting drop of the stairwell's core. It is easy to assume the stairwell has an end because that's what stairwells do, but the fact that no-one has ever reached the bottom leaves the question open. No-one ever thinks of stairwells as being bottomless, not even the people who stand on top of big buildings like the Empire State where the ground is a distant and hazy memory over 1,800 steps below. There's a hierarchy to such things determining what truly can go on forever. Wells? Yes. Pits? Yes. Trenches in the seabed where giant squid may live? Sure. But stairwells? No. Never. Hence there's a sign, a warning, to make the suicides rethink before leaping.

Rat isn't thinking about jumping over the railing. He turns around and looks at the first step. It's a foot high and four feet wide, a lump of grey marble that's cracked and covered with a random assortment of tags and graffiti. Rat looks at some of the things people have written and snorts. It's easy to write graffiti on the first step; it's the lower ones that require commitment. He wonders how far he'll need to descend before he reaches virgin territory.

The guidebook says that the lowest step anyone has reached is 120,828 steps down. People have probably gone lower, but they haven't come back. It's assumed that the suicides make it to the bottom.

If there is one.

If they were lucky.

The stairwell requires a lot of assumptions. The guidebook tells you to get used to that.

Rat figures the guy that hit the low-point 120,828 steps down probably had better things on his mind than leaving graffiti. He shrugs off the backpack and starts searching for his sharpie. It's a big backpack full of cunning pockets and hidey-holes for passports. The sharpie is in one of the cunning pockets Rat never uses, right next to the outer pocket that contains the plastic baggie filled with Marlo's ashes.

The smell of the uncapped sharpie is soothing. Its mentholated tang cuts through the yeasty heat. Rat chews on the cap for a few minutes, thinking, then leans over and writes *But I love you* on a blank patch of the first step. His handwriting is awkward, full of childish loops and a tendency to curve without the benefit of a ruled line.

Rat wishes he had something better to write; *But I love you* seems trite, and it probably didn't need to be said. He'd lost arguments with it before, with Marlo and others. He could have skipped the first step and used the first 500 to think of something better. He could have used the time to think of something poetic and elegant.

"No," he says, and his voice echoes down the stairwell. "No poetry."

Poetry would defeat the object. Just because something is trite, possibly even expected, doesn't make it any less true. He hasn't spent the last month preparing just so he could sacrifice truth for elegance. Marlo deserves better than that. So does he.

Rat puts the lid back on the sharpie and returns it to the backpack. He snaps everything shut and makes sure it's secure, twice. He's only packed three sharpies. It wouldn't do to lose them; he may need all of them before his descent is done.

He pulls the backpack onto his shoulders again, sagging with the weight. His hands are slippery. The air's not that hot; the guidebook says it'll get hotter, but Rat sweats easily. He spent a whole week planning ways he can stay hydrated. One hand rests against the railing, holding him steady. Rat places his left foot on the next step and lowers himself down.

"Two," he says, thumb hitting the click-counter at his belt. He keeps clicking away as the descent begins in earnest. "Three, four, five, six…"

The guidebook is small enough to fit in Rat's pocket, but he keeps it tucked into the backpack. Just in case.

They found the guidebook together, Rat and Marlo. It was hiding in the bottom of a used book bin, out the front of a Salvation Army store. Marlo found it; Rat has never been a big reader. The guidebook is the only book he's ever read all the way through. It's the only book he's ever attempted to read more than once.

"Check it out," Marlo said. "A book about the Endless Stairwell."

"What?" Rat said.

"The Stairwell. You know about the Stairwell, right?"

Rat shook his head. He'd never heard of the Stairwell before Marlo found the guidebook. That wasn't unusual. Rat rarely knew about the things Marlo knew about. Marlo was smart. Rat was smart, too, but he didn't think on his feet. Marlo said his talent lay in cunning, and Rat was okay with that.

"We should go one day," Marlo said. "Promise me we'll go."

Rat didn't promise. He thought an endless stairwell sounded stupid.

Rat meets six young couples coming up the stairs, all before he reaches step 500. The couples are young and giddy, with young men dressed with understated elegance. They are men dressed in casual clothes that are meant to look impressive. One of the couples has a camera.

Another couple, the second-last couple Rat passes, looks dour. They stand on separate sides of the steps, maximizing the space between them. Rat is forced to cut between, muttering an "excuse me" between clicks of his click-counter.

Rat's surprised by the number of couples he passes, but he shouldn't be. The guidebook says that step 657 is a popular place to propose, a landmark right up there with Niagara Falls and New Year's Eve fireworks.

When he reaches step 500, Rat uncaps a sharpie and thinks about the dour couple, unhappy in their long climb back to the surface. He leans over the step and writes *That would have been us, I think, if only things had gone differently*. He stands up and looks at his scrawl. Better, but still not great. Rat wonders if this really needs to be said.

"Five hundred and one," he says, "five hundred and two."

He descends. There are no more couples. He has a smooth run between step 500 and step 657.

The romance step; the step where proposals happen. The guidebook gushes about its ambiance.

Rat schedules a rest stop on step 658. He drinks his water and looks up the stairwell, trying to work out what makes the step just above him so special. The step smells of old prophylactics. When Rat peers over the banister, he can see used condoms stuck to the side of the stairs. The stink mingles with the dough smell, turning Rat's stomach. There's nothing special here; grey marble with a worn patch on the centre; endless graffiti that links two sets of initials with a crude heart around the outside and the number "4" between the names.

Rat digs Marlo out of the backpack, cradles the plastic against his cheek.

"Will you marry me," he says. "You should say yes, you know. It's traditional to say yes when you love the person who asks you."

The baggie says nothing. It's cool against his cheek, but he feels cold talking to it.

It's hard to have a conversation with Marlo these days. Somehow, it just doesn't seem right.

Rat digs the ring out of a pocket in his jeans. There's only one diamond, small and flawed. It should have been better. Rat was going to propose to Marlo outside a cinema after a really good film, but the moment slipped away before he got the chance. He puts the ring on the romance step, the proposing step, right in the corner where step meets wall. Its yellow band is pale, hard to see against the darkness and the marble's whorls.

"Last chance, babe. You should have said something if you wanted the ring." Rat takes a long sip of water and shoulders the pack. "Six hundred and fifty-nine…"

At step 1,000 he writes out the lyrics to a Leonard Cohen song and underlines the refrain. He stops 500 steps later and writes out the number of times he thinks Marlo faked orgasm during their time together. He stares at the number, unsure of its accuracy, then adds a question mark. At 2,000 steps he admits in writing that Marlo was right, that he did sometimes fantasize about dating her sister.

There is a plaque on step 2,109. It tells Rat that he's climbed the length of the Sears tower. Rat doesn't look at the plaque; he knows what it says because he's read the guidebook.

He stops again at step 2,500. He writes: *I wish you were here. I'd like to kiss you right now.*

Rat stops when he reaches step 3,000. According the guidebook, most people turn before they reach step 3,000. A lot of people lie about reaching it. Rat takes out a sharpie and writes: *I wasn't sure if I would cry for you, but it appears that I can.*

It's a lie; Rat hasn't cried yet. Rat isn't a crier, not really.

He stops and camps on step 5,418. He drinks water and pecks at trail mix for dinner, saving the substantial fare in his pack for further down. Nights are cold on the Stair; the guidebook has warned him of this. He unpacks a green sleeping bag and nestles against his pack, using it as a pillow. He listens to the wind echo as it slides down the stairwell.

A Rastafarian is there when Rat wakes up, lounging against the balustrade while Rat struggles to open his eyes. Rat looks up, noting the long line of the Rastafarian's body, the black dreadlocks that brush against the marble step.

"Your hair must weigh a lot," Rat says. The Rastafarian grins, and his teeth are a flash of white amid his face. Marlo dated a Rastafarian once. She used to tell Rat stories about kissing him, letting her hands get lost in the tangled chords of his hair.

"It's light," she had said. "So much lighter than you'd expect hair like that to be."

Rat wonders whether it was this Rastafarian. It seems unlikely, but so does an endless stairwell. Rat is prepared to embrace the unlikely at present.

"Good morning," the Rastafarian says. He has an English accent, upper crust. Rat keeps waiting for him to say "Mon," but he doesn't. The silence seems awkward.

"Hi," Rat says. He sits up, still wrapped in the sleeping bag. "Sorry, am I in your way?"

"Not at all," the Rastafarian says. "Maybe you were, once, but I've adapted, yes?"

The Rastafarian drops into a crouch, his face filling Rat's vision.

"Up or down?" the Rastafarian says.

"Down," Rat says.

"How far?" the Rastafarian says.

"As far as I can," Rat says. "Then a few steps further, just for good luck."

"Brave," the Rastafarian says.

"Maybe," Rat says. "Maybe I'm just stupid."

The Rastafarian grins again. His dreadlocks are pooled around, spreading over step 6,417. He looks at the backpack that Rat's been using as a pillow.

"Big pack," the Rastafarian says. "You're prepared, so you aren't stupid. Foolish, maybe, but not stupid."

The Rastafarian looks at Rat, his brown eyes so dark they look like giant pupils. Rat squirms.

"So," Rat says. "Up or down?"

"Both," the Rastafarian says. "Neither. Depends on my mood."

"You're a strange man," Rat says. The Rastafarian nods, dreadlocks sliding across the marble. He stands up and offers Rat a hand.

"Come on," the Rastafarian says. "Big day ahead."

Rat nods. He lets the Rastafarian lift him onto his feet. He folds the sleeping bag and stows it in the backpack while the Rastafarian watches. It's hot again, the air thick with yeast, but the Rastafarian smells like hair-oil and cinnamon.

The Rastafarian ascends. Rat descends. Both of them have their hands on the mahogany banister. Rat can hear the Rastafarian's hair swishing against the marble as the Rastafarian walks away.

Step 6,500: *I never wanted to hear about your exes.*

Marlo loved her Rasta boyfriend because he scored her free weed. She'd told Rat as much when she was explaining her ex-boyfriends. The revelation made Rat feel inadequate. He'd never scored Marlo weed, free or otherwise. The only greenery he'd given her was a potted plant, and that died on her windowsill after three weeks of neglect.

Step 7,000: *I loved you. I didn't love you. I can't really remember anymore.*

Rat stops for lunch. It isn't much; a cheese sandwich on rye bread, slightly squashed after two days in the pack. It tastes great. A day-and-a-half over, and Rat is already sick of trail mix. The cheese is waxy, a little flavourless, but it hits the spot. He wasn't supposed to eat it to-day, but the stairwell is hotter now, and the cheese wasn't travelling well.

He sips water from a flask. It's tepid. He digs through the pack and pulls out the guidebook, looking for the pink post-it tag that marks Rat's notes for the second day.

The guidebook says that this is the toughest part, the second day of descent. It's the part where most people start to think about turning around, heading back up to the surface in order to escape the heat. A day-and-a-half of climbing means you've lost sight of the top of the stairs.

Rat stands up and leans over the balustrade. He looks down. He looks up. The guidebook is right-both directions look the same. He knows the top is up there, somewhere, but he can't see it.

Rat checks the clicker. He has covered 8,369 steps. He could turn around now if he wanted. No-one would really know. It's not like he told anyone his plans. It's not like he should be ashamed. He's already eaten the sandwich he was saving for the third day. Most people turn around on the second day of climbing. Rat has always been good at giving up.

He can't think of anything to write on step 8,500. He sits on the marble, chin in his hands, staring at Marlo's ashes. Eventually he uncaps the sharpie and writes *Happy birthday*. It doesn't really work. Rat crosses it out. Then he writes *Happy Birthday Happy Birthday Happy Birthday*.

Marlo always said that repeating something thrice meant you didn't really mean it.

The world's second-longest stair is in Switzerland, dug into the side of a mountain. Rat knows this because the guidebook told him, and because someone has put a plaque on the appropriate step. The world's second-longest stair has 11,674 steps.

Rat stops to read the plaque this time, trying to feel like he's accomplished something.

He doesn't. He just feels sore. His legs are burning

He stops for the night on step 11,700. He writes *I'm sorry. I did love you* on the marble because he's too tired to think of anything better. He sets up his sleeping bag and uses it to cover the declaration. He tosses and turns all night, bothered by the heat. The yeasty smell gets worse at night. It makes Rat's nose twitch.

Marlo was going out with one of Rat's friends. He probably shouldn't have slept with her that first time, even after she said she was broken up. He wasn't always called Rat, but he'd earned himself the name and it suited him too well to go away.

On step 12,073 he sees his first suicide. The body whistles past, not even screaming anymore. Rat's surprised by the way the arms and legs twist, struggling against the fall.

On step 50,500 he writes *There were many expressions you used that drove me crazy. I still think of killing someone every time I hear the words "done and dusted" in conversation. Nothing is ever done. Nothing is ever dusted.*

He is on his second sharpie. He killed the first after forgetting to replace the cap while writing on step 15,000.

He runs out of sandwiches on the fourth day of climbing, but there's plenty of trail mix and tins of beans. The plan was to descend until he ran out of things to say. Rat never bothered thinking about how he'd ascend once the task was done.

On step 120,000 he writes *Fuck cancer.* He crosses this out and writes *It wasn't my fault.* Deep down, he believes neither of these things, despite the fact that he should. The doctors were wrong; it wasn't the cancer that killed her.

The heat turns slick and humid 300 steps later. His rubber soles squeak against the moisture coating the ancient marble.

At step 120,828 he pauses and pulls the guidebook out of his backpack. He flicks through the worn pages, looking at the detailed notes he's scrawled into the margins. Pauses on the photograph of the step he's reached. The point of no return, the deepest step anyone's reached and still returned to the surface. He's followed the guidebook's advice when it comes to supplies. His pack is lighter now, easier to handle, but he could still return.

Rat tosses the book over the balustrade. He looks up the stairwell, then down. Sweat streams across his forehead, soaks through his T-shirt. Rat's been wearing the same outfit for days. He's pretty sure he smells.

"Hello?" he says, and his voice echoes across the stairwell. His throat is dry, so he drinks some water. More than he should, regardless of his decision. Rat figures he can extend his supply a little this far down, assuming he's willing to lick condensation off the stairs.

He pulls Marlo out of his pack and holds her in both hands. Better to do it now, regardless of the decision. This is where they were headed when they'd first planned to come here. Too many things could go wrong once he moved into uncharted territory.

"We made it, babe," Rat says. His thumbnail punctures the plastic and sets the ashes free. The cloud disperses across the empty space, descends on the breeze. Slow-moving, delicate, waiting for the next suicide to freefall through its mass. Even in death Marlo is beautiful. Rat misses her more than anything.

He sits down on step 120,829 and grieves, shedding tears for the first time.

Step 121,500: *We were never meant to be happy. I'm no longer sure that matters.*

On step 200,000 Rat commits an act of poetry. He chooses to keep descending. Poetry bothers him less this far down the stairwell.

Rat knows three things to be true. The first is this: he will run out of food and water before he runs out of things to say. Two: what goes down need not emerge at the surface. Three: there will be no ending. The ending lies above, at the first step, in the life he'd live if he walked away. Endings are destinations and the Stairwell has but one, found only by backtracking and returning to the beginning.

The heat gets worse as he hits the lower depths. The balustrade is hot enough to redden his palms. Rat sheds clothing, equipment, leaves his sleeping bag on a step. The sharpies leak in his pockets, bleeding ink across his thighs.

STILL LIFE (A SEXAGESIMAL FAIRY TALE)

Ian Tregillis

EVERY EVENING WAS A *FIN DE SIÈCLE* in the great sprawling castle-city of Nycthemeron. But, of course, to say it was evening meant no more than to say it was morning, or midnight, or yesterday, or six days hence, or nineteen years ago. For it was every inch a timeless place, from the fig trees high in the Palazzo's Spire-top cloud gardens all the way down to the sinuous river Gnomon encircling the city.

Nycthemeron had tumbled from the calendar. It had slipped into the chasm between tick and tock, to land in its own instantaneous eternity. And so its residents occupied their endless moment with pageants and festivals and reveled in century-long masques, filled forever with decadent delights. They picnicked in the botanical gardens, made love in scented boudoirs, danced through their eternal twilight. And they disregarded the fog that shrouded their city with soft grey light.

As for time? Time was content to leave them there. It felt no pity, no compassion, for the people stuck in that endless *now*. This wasn't because time was cold, or cruel, or heartless. But it had no concern for that glistening place, no interest in the people who existed there.

Except one. Her name was Tink.

And it was said (among the people who said such things) that if you sought something truly special for your sweetheart, or if you yearned for that rarest of experiences—something novel, something new—you could find it at Tink's shop in the Briardowns. For Tink was something quite peculiar: she was a clockmaker.

Indeed, so great were her talents that normally staid and proper clock hands fluttered with delight at her approach. Time reveled in her horological handiwork. If it had to be measured, quantified, divvied up and parceled out, it would do so only on a timepiece of Tink's design.

How could this be? She was a clockwork girl, they said. And indeed, if you were to stand near Tink, to wait for a quiet moment and then bend your ear in her direction, you might just hear the phantom *tickticktickticktickticktick* serenading every moment of her life. Who but a clockwork girl would make such a noise, they said. And others would nod, and agree, and consider the matter settled.

But they were wrong. Tink was a flesh and blood woman, as real as anybody who danced on the battlements or made love in the gardens. She was no mere clockwork.

Tink was the object of time's affection. It attended her so closely, revered and adored her so completely, that it couldn't bear to part from her, even for an instant. But time's devotion carried a price. Tink *aged*.

She was, in short, a living clock. Her body was the truest timepiece Nycthemeron could ever know; her thumping heart, the metronome of the world.

But the perfectly powdered and carefully coifed lovelies who visited her shop knew nothing of this. They made their way to the Briardowns, in the shadow of an ancient aqueduct, seeking the lane where hung a wooden sign adorned with a faceless clock. Midway down, between an algebraist's clinic and a cartographer's studio, Tink's storefront huddled beneath an awning of pink alabaster.

Now, on this particular afternoon (let us pretend for the moment that such distinctions were meaningful in Nycthemeron) the chime over Tink's door announced a steady trickle of customers. The Festival of the Leaping Second was close, and if ever there was an occasion to ply one's darling with wonderments, it was this. Soon revelers would congregate on the highest balconies of the Spire. There they would grasp the hands of an effigy clock and click the idol forward one second. Afterward, they would trade gifts and kisses, burn the effigy, then seek out new lovers and new debaucheries.

If you were to ask the good people of Nycthemeron just how frequently they celebrated the Festival of the Leaping Second, they would smile and shrug and tell you: *When the mood descends upon us.* But Tink knew differently. The Festival came every twenty years, as measured by her tick-tock heartbeat. She felt this, knew it, as a fish feels water and knows how to swim.

To a marchioness with a fringe of peacock feathers on her mask, Tink gave an empty, pentagonal hourglass. "Turn this after your favorite dance, and you'll live that moment five times over," she said.

To a courtier in a scarlet cravat, Tink gave a paper packet of wildflower seeds. "Spread these in your hair," she said. "They'll blossom the moment you kiss your honey love, and you will be the posy she takes home."

Tink requested only token payments for these trinkets, expecting neither obligation nor gratitude in return. Some, like the marchioness, paid handsomely; others, such as the tatterdemalion scholar, gave what they could (in his case, a leather bookmark). And sometimes she traded her wares for good will, as she did with the stonemason and gardener.

Though she was young and strong and did not ache, Tink spent what her body considered a long day rummaging through her shop for creative ways to brighten static lives. Her mind was tired, her stomach empty.

Unlike the rest of Nycthemeron's populace, Tink had to sleep. She announced her shop closed for the remainder of the day. Cries of dismay arose from the people queued outside (though of course they had long ago forgotten the meaning of "day").

"The Festival!" they cried; a chorus of painted, feathered, and sequined masks. Everyone wore a mask, as demanded by the calculus of glamour.

"Come back tomorrow," she said (though of course they had forgotten the meaning of this, too). But a tall fellow in a cormorant mask came jogging up the lane.

"Wait! Timesmith, wait!"

Nobody had ever called her that, but the phrase amused her. Few people dared to let the word "time" touch their lips. The rest of Tink's petitioners grumbled at the bold fellow's approach. They dispersed, shaking their heads and bemoaning their bad luck.

"Sorry, pretties. Sorry, lovelies," said Tink. "You'll get your goodies tomorrow."

The newcomer laid a hand upon the door, panting slightly. His breeches, she noticed, displayed shapely calves. "Are you Tink?"

"I am."

"Fabled maker of clocks and wonderments, I hear."

"Let me guess," said Tink. "You're seeking something for the Festival. Something with which to impress your lady love. You want me to win her heart for you, is that so?"

His shrug ruffled the long silk ribbons looped around the sleeves of his shirt. Some were vermilion, and others cerulean, like his eyes. "It's true, I confess."

"The others wanted the same," she said. "I told them I could do no more today. Why should I become a liar?"

"Do it for my flaxen-haired beauty."

Tink thought she recognized this fellow. And so she asked, knowing the answer, "Will you love her forever?"

"Forever? That is all we have. Yes, I will love her forever, and she me. Until the Festival ends."

Aha. "You are Valentine."

He bowed, with a flourish. The ribbons fluttered on his arms again. "You know me?"

"Everybody knows you."

Valentine: the legendary swain of Nycthemeron. Valentine, who could spend centuries on a single seduction. Valentine, famed for his millennial waltz. Charmer, lothario, friend of everyman, consort of the queen.

Though it was against her better judgment, Tink beckoned him inside. Valentine's eyes twinkled as he examined her space. The shelves were stacked with odds and ends culled from every corner of Nycthemeron: strange objects floating in yellow pickle jars; workbenches strewn with gears and mainsprings, loupes and screws and a disassembled astrolabe; the smell of oil and peppermint.

He said, "Your sign says 'Timepieces'."

"Is that somehow strange?"

"But you gave that fellow with the scarlet cravat just a packet of wildflowers."

"You know this how?"

"I stopped him and asked. I knew he'd come from your shop because he looked happy." He crossed his arms. "Flowers are nice, but they're no timepiece."

"Everything is a clock," said Tink. "Even the buckles on your shoes and the boards beneath your feet. But this place," she said, with a gesture that implied all of Nycthemeron, "has forgotten that."

"The stories are true. You are a peculiar one." And then he cocked his head, as if listening to something. "They say you are a clockwork, you know. "

His gaze was a stickpin and Tink a butterfly. She shrugged, and blushed, and turned away.

clockmaker create one of her fabled wonderments.

Thus, when she returned to his forge, he presented her with thirty inches of gleaming steel. It was, he proclaimed, the finest and sharpest blade he'd ever forged. Sharp enough to shear the red from a rainbow.

She thanked him. But it was not sharp enough.

And so, in the months before the next Festival (measured, as always, by the thumping of Tink's broken heart), she spent every moment in her workshop. Things took longer these days. Her eyes strained at the tiniest cogs; her grip quavered as it never used to do.

People again reported odd noises in her shop. At first, the grinding of a whetstone. Later, a rasping, as of sand on steel. Then, the susurration of cotton on steel. And finally, if they pressed their ears to her shop, they might have heard the whisper of breath on steel.

And those who stayed until Tink emerged might have noticed something different about her. For where before there had always been the phantom *tickticktick* that followed her like a devoted puppy, now, when she carried the pendulum blade, there was sometimes only a phantom *ti-ti-ti*, and other times a *ck-ck-ck*, depending on how she held it.

Tink loaded her cart with a crate the size of a grandfather clock, then drove to the Spire. By now, of course, she was one of the queen's most favored subjects, and so the ballroom had a place of honor reserved for Tink. There, she assembled her contribution to the Festival.

The revelers advanced the effigy. Tink wound her clock; the pendulum swung ponderously across its lacquered case. It was silent. Not even a whisper accompanied the passage of the pendulum. It sliced through the moments, leaving slivers of *ticks* and tatters of *tocks* in its wake.

At Tink's request, the queen posted guards around the clock, for the pendulum blade was a fearsome thing. Its edges were the sharpest things that could ever be, sharp as the *now* that separates past and future.

But only time, and time alone, understood what she had done. Tink had given Nycthemeron something it had lost.

She had given it the present: a knowledge of now.

❤

Tink returned to the Briardowns. Her body would be eighty years old at the next Festival, while Valentine would still be a stunning twentysomething. How many lovers had he charmed since his visit to Tink's shop? How many stolen kisses, how many fluttering hearts? Her life had none of these things. Her pillow never smelled of anybody but Tink.

What chance had she of winning him now? It was a foolish hope. But she had spent her life on it, and couldn't bear to think it had all been for nothing.

She tried to concentrate. But time's desperation had become jealousy, so it had imbued the pendulum blade with a special potency. Anything for Tink's attention.

The man in the scarlet cravat returned. He asked Tink for a trinket that would "set him moving" again. She couldn't help him. Nor could she help the pregnant woman whose belly suggested imminent labor and whose eyes were the most sorrowful Tink had ever seen. She'd been that way, Tink realized, since time had lost its interest. Since the moment Nycthemeron had fallen from the calendar.

Tink was passing beneath the aqueduct, on her way to the Palazzo, when a man in a cobalt-colored fez crashed onto the street before her cart. The wind of his passage ruffled her hair, and he smashed the cobbles hard enough to set the chimes in Tink's clock to ringing. Plumes of dust billowed from between the paving stones. She screamed.

Not because he had perished. He hadn't, of course. Tink screamed because his sorrow had driven him to seek death, the ultimate boundary between past and future. And because he'd never find it.

He shambled to his feet, for his body was timeless. But when the poor fellow realized that nothing had changed, that he hadn't bridged the gulf between *was* and *will*, he slumped to the ground and wept. He waved off Tink's offers of a ride, of conversation, of commiseration.

A quiet gasp of dismay reached her ears. She looked up. People lined the tallest edges of the aqueduct.

The pendulum blade carved a personal *now* for every soul in Nycthemeron. And drove them mad. Tink had shown them they were entombed in time, and now they were suffocating.

Which was odd. Time had never seen her fall shy.

"As for your lady love," said Tink, changing the subject, "I know what to do. Come with me."

She led him to shelves stacked with clocks of sand, and candle wax, and other things. (Time frequently sprawled here, like a cat in sunlight.) She stopped at a grandfather clock carved in the guise of a fig tree. Tink set it to one minute before midnight.

"Hold out your hand," Tink said. She gave the clock a nod of encouragement, and it began to tock-tick-tock its way toward midnight. Valentine watched with fascination. But, of course, he had never seen a working clock.

A miniscule hatch opened above the twelve and a seed *plinked* into Valentine's hand. Tink repeated the process.

"What are these?" he asked.

"Intercalary seeds. At the Festival, put one under your tongue. Have your lady do the same. The seeds will release one minute that belongs solely to the pair of you."

Valentine tucked the seeds into the tasseled sash at his waist. He took her hand. His touch, she noticed with a shudder, was warm and gentle. With his other hand he removed his mask, saying, "I am in your debt."

He winked and kissed her hand. Now, Tink was prepared for this, for Valentine was nothing if not notorious for his charms. But when she saw the laugh lines around his eyes, and felt his breath tickle the back of her hand, and felt his soft lips brush against her skin, her metronome heart—

...diners in a sidewalk café marveled at a turtledove hanging motionless overhead, just for an instant...

—skipped—

... the candles in a Cistercian chapel, all 419 of them, stopped flickering, just for an instant...

—a—

...all the noises of life and love and revelry and sorrow, the voice of Nycthemeron, fell silent, just for an instant...

—beat.

Tink did not sleep that night. Lying on a downy mattress just wide enough for one—she had never needed anything more, having never known loneliness—she replayed those few minutes with Valentine in her head, again and again. She smelled the back of her hand, imagined it was his breath tickling her skin.

Tink could win his heart. All she needed was time.

She awoke with a plan.

In order to win Valentine's heart, she had to know him, and he had to know her. In order to know him, she had to be near him. To be near him, she had to get into the Palazzo. She could get into the Palazzo if she brought a birthday gift for Queen Perjumbellatrix.

Of course, birthdays held no meaning in a place exiled from the calendar. But the eternal queen was fond of gifts, and so she held masques and received tributes once per year (measured, as always, by the ticking of Tink's heart). And Valentine, her consort, attended each. Even so, Tink would be fortunate to get more than a few moments with him.

Thus, after the Festival, Tink went to work on a special series of clocks. Each was designed to delight the revelers in Her Majesty's grand ballroom.

And each was designed to steal one minute from Her Majesty. Each clock would swaddle Tink and Valentine in sixty purloined seconds. Nor was that all.

For Valentine—pretty, perfect Valentine—minutes held no meaning. One was much the same as another. Thus, it would be nothing odd for him to experience a conversation strung across the decades, one minute per year.

But Tink—mortal, metronome Tink—had to *live* her way from one stolen minute to the next. So she designed the clocks to string those moments together like pearls on a necklace, forming one continuous assignation with Valentine.

The first clock was a simple thing: a wind-up circus. But Her Majesty disappointed courtiers throughout the Palazzo when she declared it her favorite tribute.

Tink curtsied, feeling like a dandelion in a rose garden. The braids in her silvery hair had unraveled, and her gown—the finest from the second-hand shop in the Briardowns—was not fine at all in this company.

She retreated to a corner of the ballroom. Tink had never learned to dance.

Valentine danced with every lady in the hall, always returning to Perjumbellatrix in the interim. He hadn't changed one tock from the way he'd appeared at Tink's shop. The ribbons on his sleeves traced spirals in the air when he twirled his partners so, the feathers of his cormorant mask fluttered when he tipped his ladies thus. Tink fidgeted with her embroidery, waiting until the clockwork elephants on the queen's gift trumpeted midnight.

Everything stopped. The ballroom became a sculpture garden, an expressionist swirl of skin and feathers and jewels and silks. Beads of wine from a tipped goblet sparkled like rubies suspended in midair; plucked harp strings hung poised to fling notes like arrows.

"Well done, Timesmith." Tink turned. Valentine bowed at her. "It is a wonder," he said, marveling at the motionless dancers. "But I think your wonderment has missed its mark, no?" He pointed: Tink's clock had made a statue of the statuesque monarch.

Tink swallowed, twice. She found her voice: "The clock is for her. But this," she said, "is for you." *And me.*

Valentine smiled. "I've never seen its equal." He took her hand. Her skin tingled beneath his fingertips. "Thank you." Her metronome heart skipped another beat when he touched his lips to the back of her hand. But the world had stopped, so nobody noticed.

He asked, "How long will they stay like this?"

"That's complicated," said Tink. "But they're safe."

The room blurred about them. Merrymakers blinked into new positions around the ballroom. The eternally tipping wine goblet became an ice sculpture of the queen. And her gift, the clockwork circus, became an orrery.

A year had passed.

"I see! I see, I see!" Valentine clapped. He understood, for every moment was the same to him.

"Do you like it?" she asked.

"It's marvelous," he said. "Now let *me* show *you* something you've never known. Dance with me."

She wanted to waltz with him, but feared to try. She had impressed him. But could that be undone by a single awkward step? Valentine was a graceful creature, accustomed to graceful partners.

"I don't, that is, I've never—"

"Trust me," he said.

Valentine pulled her to the center of the ballroom. His hand warmed the small of her back. He smelled like clean salt, like the distant sea. Dancing, she discovered, came naturally. It was, after all, a form of rhythm. And what was rhythm but a means of marking time?

The room blurred around them. The orrery became an hourglass. They wove and whirled amongst the motionless dancers. Tink laughed. It was working.

"Look," said Valentine. "Look at their eyes."

Masks hid their faces, but not their eyes. She looked upon a man who wore the burgundy cummerbund of a baronet. His eyes glistened with hidden tears. They pirouetted past a countess with a diadem on her brow, butterfly wings affixed to her cheeks, and soul-deep weariness in her eyes.

Valentine asked, "What do you see?"

"Sorrow," said Tink.

"They've lost something. We all have."

"Three things," said Tink. For suddenly she knew what Valentine wanted and needed. He didn't know it himself.

Yet still they danced. It was wonderful; it was magical. But his eyes returned again and again to Perjumbellatrix. He danced with Tink—and what a dancer he was—but his heart and mind were elsewhere.

The final timepiece expended its stolen minute. The bubble of intimacy popped under the assault of music, laughter, and voices raised in tribute to the queen.

"Truly marvelous," said Valentine. "Thank you for this dance, Timesmith." With a wink, a bow, and a kiss, he returned to his place beside the queen.

Tink's feet ached. Her lungs pumped like bellows. Her skin wasn't quite as smooth as it had been when their dance began. She had aged twenty years in twenty minutes. But it was a small price for the key to somebody's heart.

She returned to her shop, deep in thought. And so she did not notice how the hands of every clock bowed low to her, like a bashful admirer requesting a dance. Time had seen how she had laughed with joy in Valentine's arms. It yearned, desperately, to dance with her.

Tink spent months (measured, as always, by the thumping of her heart) holed up in her shop. She labored continuously, pausing only for food and rest. And, on several occasions, to climb a staircase of carved peridot and dip a chalice in the waters atop the aqueduct.

Far above the city, craftsmen and courtiers built an effigy clock atop the Spire. Valentine, Tink knew, was there. She wondered if he ever gazed from that aerie upon the Briardowns, wondered if his thoughts ever turned from queen to clockmaker.

When the Festival of the Leaping Second returned to Nycthemeron, and a crowd again milled outside Tink's shop, they found it locked and the storefront dark. Her neighbors, the algebraist and the cartographer, told of her forays along the aqueduct and of strange sounds from her workshop: splashing, gurgling, the creak of wooden gears.

By now, of course, the queen had grown quite fond of Tink's wonderments. And when she heard that the clockmaker had arrived, promising something particularly special for the Festival, she ordered a new riser built for Tink's work.

There, Tink built a miniature Nycthemeron: nine feet tall at the Spire, six feet wide, encircled by a flowing replica of the river Gnomon, complete with aqueducts, waterwheels, sluices, gates, and even a tiny clockmaker's shop in a tiny Briardowns. There, a model clockmaker gazed lovelorn at the Spire, where a model Valentine gazed down.

When the revelry culminated in the advance of the effigy, Tink filled the copper reservoir on her water clock. And everybody, including the queen and lovely Valentine at her side, marveled at Tink's work.

The water flowed backward. It sprang from the waterwheels to leap upon the aqueducts and gush uphill, where special pumps pulled it down to begin again.

It was a wonder, they said. An amazement. A delight.

Only time, and time alone, understood what she had done. Tink had given the people of Nycthemeron something they had lost.

She had given them their past.

Tink went home feeling pleased. Just a few more clocks, just a few more stolen moments, and Valentine would express adoration. But she couldn't work as many hours at a stretch as she had in her youth. She had to unlock his heart before time rendered her an unlovable crone.

But there were interruptions. People peppered her with strange requests: vague notions they couldn't express and that Tink couldn't deliver. The fellow in the scarlet cravat returned, seeking a means of visiting "that place."

"What place?" Tink asked.

"That—" he waved his hands in frustration, indicating some vague and distant land "—place." He shrugged. "I see it in my head. I've been there, but I don't know how to return. It's here, and yet it's not here, too."

Tink could not help him. Nor could she help the baroness who requested a clockwork key that would open a door to "that other Nycthemeron." At first they came in a slow trickle, these odd requests. But the trickle became a torrent. Tink closed her shop so that she could finish the next sequence of birthday clocks for Queen Perjumbellatrix.

Valentine invited Tink for another spin around a ballroom filled with motionless revelers. He was, of course, as handsome as ever. But when he doffed his mask, Tink saw the crease of a frown perched between his cerulean eyes. Her metronome heart did a little jig of concern.

"You look troubled," she said as he took her hand.

Valentine said, "Troubled? I suppose I am."

"Perhaps I can help," said Tink. "After all, my skills are not inconsiderable." She added what she hoped was a coquettish lilt to these words.

Valentine wrapped his arm around Tink's waist. They waltzed past a duchess and her lissome lover. "I find my thoughts drifting to a new place. A different Nycthemeron."

Tink faltered. The dancers blurred into a new configuration. Another precious year had passed.

Valentine danced mechanically. His movements were flawless, but devoid of the grace that had made Tink swoon when first they had danced together. And for her part, her whirring mind couldn't concentrate on one thing or the other; she stepped awkwardly, without poise or balance.

It wasn't supposed to be like this. Her gift was meant to impress Valentine, not confuse and distract him. But she had her pilfered minutes and intended to use them.

She rested her head on his shoulder, enjoying his scent and the fluid play of muscles in his arm. "What sort of place?" she asked.

"I don't know," he said. "It's a place I've been, someplace close, even, but I don't know how to get there."

The revelers snapped into new arrangements; another year lost. Valentine led her in a swooping two-step around the ballroom. There was, it seemed, more room to move.

"Is it here in Nycthemeron? A forgotten courtyard? A secluded cloister?"

"I can't say. I feel like it may be…everywhere. Strange, isn't it?" He shook his head and smiled. "No matter. Once again you have done a magnificent thing."

But Tink barely heard his praise. She had given the people of Nycthemeron their past. But what did that mean to timeless people in a timeless city? Nothing. They were afflicted with strange thoughts they couldn't comprehend: memories of times past. To them, the past was a foreign place they couldn't visit.

They waltzed. Tink's feet ached, twinges of betrayal from her aging body. Blur. They danced a sarabande. Her back ached. Blur. Her lungs burned. Blur.

Tink *saw* the thinning of the ballroom crowd.

"Valentine, have you noticed there are fewer people in this ballroom every year?"

"Yes."

"Where are they going?"

"They're trying to leave Nycthemeron," he said.

"Oh, no," she said, and crashed to the floor.

"Timesmith!" Valentine leapt to her side, cradled her head in his hands. "Please forgive me. Are you hurt?"

The ballroom floor was hard and her body less resilient than it had been minutes and years ago. But she disregarded her bruises, because Valentine was sopping wet. His slippery hands had lost their grip on her. He smelled of river grass and mud.

"What happened?" she asked.

"The queen sent me to stop her half-brother from trying to swim his way out of Nycthemeron. That's where they're going. To the river."

But, of course, nobody could leave Nycthemeron. Not even Tink. The luminous fog was chaos, its touch deadly.

In a tiny voice, she asked, "Did you save him?"

"No. He entered the fog before I was halfway across."

And at that moment Tink realized her gift, bestowed upon the people of Nycthemeron with love and intended to win love in return, was killing people.

Tink's clock chimed midnight. Their stolen time had lapsed. And when Tink saw herself in the golden mirrors of the ballroom, she saw that her hair, once a lustrous silver, had tarnished to grey. She had aged another twenty years, but had gained nothing from it.

Tink returned to the Briardowns and her lonely, narrow cot, unaware of the clocks that capered for her attention. Time ached to comfort her, to console her. It sang her to sleep with a lullaby of ticks and tocks.

She'd been so foolish. She might as well have given a penny-farthing bicycle to the koi in the fishponds. The people of Nycthemeron couldn't comprehend her gift. Right now they had the past bearing down on them like a boulder rolling toward a cliff. But that time had nowhere to go, no safe landing. It was disconnected. Meaningless.

She could salvage this. She could cure the malady she had created. She could still win Valentine. She could fix everything. All it required was a simple pendulum clock.

Tink paid a visit to the smithy in Nycthemeron's Steeltree district. There, she commissioned the finest double-edged blade the smith could forge. No hilt—only the blade, with a tang for fastening it. A strange request. But it was considered no small honor to help the

Tink rushed to the Palazzo. The ballroom was emptier than she had ever seen it. Couples still danced, but just a fraction of those who had toasted the queen in pageants past.

The ribbons on Valentine's arms still fluttered; his shapely calves still flexed and stretched when he waltzed with the queen. But was it Tink's imagination, or had his eyes lost their sparkle? Was it her imagination, or did he seem distracted and imprecise in his movements?

An earl in an owl mask requested a dance, but she declined him and all the others who sought a few steps with the famous clockmaker. She might have been flattered, but now, with age weighing upon her, she lacked the energy for much revelry. She saved herself.

Her clock chimed. Once more, Tink and Valentine were alone together in a private minute. He took her hand.

"You look worried," he said.

"How are you? Are you well?" She studied his face.

"I am the same as ever," he said, a catch in his voice.

He was silent for what felt like eternity. Blur. Blur. Blur. It broke her heart, every wasted instant. This was her last chance. It wasn't meant to be like this.

"Something is bothering you," she said. "Will you tell me about it? You'll never have a more devoted listener."

That, at least, elicited a slight sigh, and a weary chuckle. "What is it like?"

"What is what like?"

"Aging."

Tink said, "My body aches. I can't see or hear as well as I could. My mind isn't as sharp, my fingers not as nimble." She paused while he gently spun her through a pirouette. "But I am more wise now."

"More wise?"

"Wise enough to know that I'm a foolish old woman."

Grief clenched her chest, ground the gears in her metronome heart. The years had become a burden too heavy for her shoulders. She faltered. Valentine caught her.

He asked, "Are you ill?"

She shook her head. "Just old. Will you sit with me?"

"Of course."

They watched motionless dancers blink through the celebrations.

Tink rested her head on his shoulder. She wanted to remember his scent forever. That was all she'd ever have of him; her efforts to win his heart had failed. Worse than that: she had transmuted his joy into melancholy.

"May I ask something of you, Valentine?"

"Anything, Timesmith."

"Your ribbons. I would like to take one, if I may."

"Allow me," he said. He removed a vermilion ribbon and tied it into her grey hair. "Remember me, won't you?"

That made her smile. She would remember him until the end of her days. Didn't he realize this? Had she been too oblique in her bids for his affection? Blur.

Tink turned to thank him for the token, and to tell him that he was ever on her mind. But she didn't. His shirt was tattered, his ribbons were frayed. Feathers had come loose from his cormorant mask. He was dusty.

"What happened to you?" she asked.

"I…I fell," he whispered.

"Oh, Valentine—" She reached up to touch his face. His changeless, beautiful face. Her stolen time came to an end. It left her very old, very tired, and very alone.

Valentine's heart would never be hers; she could accept that. But it would never be pledged to anybody ever again, and that she couldn't bear. It was broken. Because of her.

If Tink could do one final thing before she succumbed to old age, she wanted to mend him. Mend everybody. But though she knew what that would require, she did not know how to do it. The future was an abstract thing, built of possibilities and nothing else. It was impervious to cogs, springs, pendulums, blades, sand, beeswax, and water.

She paced. She napped. She ignored the urgent knocking of would-be customers. More napping. More pacing.

And then she noticed the model castle-city she had built years earlier. Her water-clock Nycthemeron sat in a corner, draped in cobwebs and dust.

Tink looked upon the Spire, and the surrounding gardens, and knew exactly what to do.

First, she paid a visit to the stonemason. He welcomed her. But when she told him what she needed, he balked. It was too much work for one person.

But Tink had not come alone. For she was famous, and drew a small crowd when she ventured outside. Some followers, such as the fellow in the scarlet cravat, had been waiting outside her dark and shuttered store, hoping to wheedle one last wonderment from the aging clockmaker. Others had followed the siren call of her *tickticktick*, hoping it would lead them to a novel experience.

Next, Tink called upon the gardeners who maintained the parklands along the river. Their objections were similar to the stonemason's. But she solved their concerns as she had those of the stonemason: she presented the gardeners with strong and beautiful volunteers.

She supervised as best she could. But often the volunteers found her dozing in her cart because she had succumbed to weariness. They took turns bringing her home and tucking her into bed.

The changes to the outskirts of Nycthemeron drew more volunteers, and more still, as people abandoned their decadent delights. But nobody knew why Tink needed so much granite carved *just so*, nor why she needed the gardens landscaped *just so*.

Only time understood her plan. Only time, which had felt first confusion, then jealousy, then heartbreak while she squandered her short life yearning for Valentine.

Tink awoke with Valentine's hand brushing her cheek. At first she thought she had died and had gone to someplace better. But when she touched his face and saw her aged hand, she knew she was still an old woman. Her pillow was moist with tears.

His eyes gleamed. Perhaps not as brightly as they once had, but enough to cause a stutter in her metronome heart. "I've come to take you to the Festival."

That caused a jolt of alarm. "But my work—"

"Is finished. Completed to your every specification. Although nobody can tell me what your instructions mean."

His face was smudged with dirt.

"What happened to you?" she asked.

"I've been gardening," he said, and winked.

Valentine carried her to her cart. She dozed with her head on his shoulder as he drove to the Palazzo. Once, when the jouncing of the cart roused her, she glimpsed what might have been an honor guard with shining epaulettes and flapping pennants. It may have been a dream.

Tink dozed again during the funicular ride up the Spire. The view did not transfix her: she had seen it every year for the past sixty (measured, as always, by the beating of her failing heart). She preferred the drowsy sensation of resting in Valentine's arms, no matter how chaste the embrace. Her glimpses of Nycthemeron, between dreams and sighs, showed an unfamiliar city.

Ah, she recalled. *Yes. The Festival.* It had seemed dreadfully important once, this final gift. But she was too exhausted and too full of regrets to care.

"Why do you cry, Timesmith?"

"I'm a foolish old woman. I've spent my entire life just to have one hour with you."

She closed her eyes. When next she opened them, Valentine was setting her gently upon a cushioned chair in the gilded grand ballroom. It was, she noticed, a place of honor beside Queen Perjumbellatrix. The queen said something, but it was loud in the ballroom. Tink nodded, expressed her thanks, then returned to her dreams.

A jostling woke her, several minutes or decades later. Her chair floated toward the balcony. Valentine lifted it, as did the courtier in the scarlet cravat, and several others whom she felt she ought to recognize but didn't.

Silence fell. All eyes turned to Tink.

She stood, with Valentine's assistance. (His hands were so strong. So warm. So young.)

"This is for you," she said to Nycthemeron.

The fog brightened, then thinned, then dissipated. A brilliant sun emerged in a sky the color of Valentine's eyes. The Spire cast a shadow across the sprawling castle-city. Its tip pierced the distant gardens where so many had labored according to Tink's specifications.

Nycthemeron had become a sundial.

Cheers echoed through the city, loud even to Tink's feeble ears high atop the Spire.

Everyone understood what Tink had done. She had ended Nycthemeron's exile. She had given the people a future.

Tink collapsed. Her metronome heart sounded its final *tickticktick*. Her time had run out.

But not quite.

Time understood that this magnificent work, this living sundial called Nycthemeron, was an expression of her love for Valentine. She had set him free.

Tink found herself in a patch of grass, staring up at a blue sky. The grass was soft, the sky was bright, and her body didn't ache.

"Ah, you're awake." Valentine leaned over her, eclipsing the sky with his beautiful face. He wasn't, she noticed, wearing the cormorant mask. Nor his ribbons. And his shirt was new. "I have something to show you," he said.

When Tink took his hand, she saw that her skin was no longer wrinkled, no longer spotted and weak.

These were the Spire-top gardens. But everything looked new and different in the sunlight. Even the trees were strange: row upon row upon row of them. Strange, and yet she felt she somehow knew them.

Valentine saw the expression on her face. He said, "They're intercalary trees. It seemed a waste to toss the seeds after they'd been spent. So I planted them."

Seeds? Ah... Tink remembered when she'd first met Valentine, decades ago, when he'd wanted to charm a flaxen-haired beauty. Back when Tink had been young.

The *first* time she had been young.

And time, knowing it had failed to win Tink's heart, had given her a parting gift, then set her free.

BUILD-A-DOLLY

Ken Liu

AS SOON AS SHE OPENS the door of the bedroom, I jump up and down on the bed in excitement. All day I've been lying here, watching the square of sunlight drift slowly across the room. But this is when I come alive.

I adore Amy. I love Amy. Amy is the purpose of my life.

But as I look into her face, I see that this is a bad day. I stop jumping and try to shrink against the pillow, to melt into the bedspread.

Amy drops her backpack and closes the door. I shudder. She doesn't want people to hear.

She stops in front of the bed, looking down at me.

"Hi, Amy," I say. I open my arms for a hug. Sometimes this works.

"Hi, Stella," Amy says. Her voice is cold, angry, sad.

My name is Dolly.

Stella is the name of another girl in Amy's class. Amy showed me a picture of her once. In that picture she was very pretty. But I heard longing and fear in the way Amy talked about her, and I've learned that those loved by many have a kind of power.

I'm programmed to play any role that Amy wants me to play with gusto and joy. When she was younger, sometimes she wanted me to play a baby, and sometimes she wanted me to play her mom. Most often I just played me, Dolly. But she is older now.

I assume a pose that I think Stella would assume. I stand on my tiptoes, as though I'm wearing high heels, one foot crossed over another, my hands lightly resting on my hips.

But my twelve-inch-tall body is designed more for hugs than realism. My body, made out of a plastic skeleton covered by stuffing and soft cloth-skin, is flat and wide. My legs are short and thick. My eyes are wide open and smiley. I'm not much of a Stella.

"You're here," I say, trying for a disdainful tone.

Amy steps closer. She leans down so that her face is level with mine. I can see redness around her eyes.

"You're a bitch, Stella," Amy hisses.

The next thing I know, I'm flying. Amy grips me by my nylon hair, twirls me around in the air, and then lets go. I slam into the wall, fall, crumble against the ground in a heap. I struggle to stand up, motors whining, gears grinding.

Amy is on me in a few steps. "*You* are ugly. *You* are dirty. *Your* clothes look like they came from the homeless shelter. No one wants to be friends with *you.*"

"I'm sorry," I squeak out. Her words hurt, even though I know she no longer sees *me.*

"I'm soooo-rry," she says, mimicking my squeak. She picks me up and throws me across the room.

Something breaks inside me as I hit the wall this time. I struggle to stand up. But no matter how hard I try, my legs don't obey. I lift my head to look at Amy's approaching figure, and I lift my arms to shield my eyes.

Amy kneels down. "Stella," she whispers, "why are you so mean? We could be such great friends."

She cradles me in her arms, and hugs me tightly.

And I'm happy, so happy, even though I can't move my legs any more. I wrap my arms around her neck and don't ever want to let go.

Robbie laughs as he straps me to a firework rocket. The rocket is stuck into the beach and pointing out at the sea.

He hasn't bothered to turn me off. He likes hearing me beg. So I've stopped.

"You're going to the moon, Dolly," Robbie says. "You're going to be an astronaut. Bet my sister never played this game with you."

I close my eyes.

"You can have her," Amy said as she handed me to Robbie. "She's broken and out of warranty. I'm getting too old anyway."

"No, no, no, no," I squeaked. But Amy never even turned around. Robbie lights the fuse.

A brief, dizzying flight, and then cold, wet, darkness.

For months I drift in the ocean.

The salty waves and the curious fish and seagulls have ripped away my clothes, my nylon hair, my cloth skin, my stuffing. I am reduced to my metal parts and my plastic skeleton, now bleached white by the sun. Inside, my gears and motors have rusted so that any movement is difficult.

Miraculously, the batteries still send electrical currents to my chips.

Endlessly, I replay the scenes between Amy and myself. Helplessly, I adore her, I love her, the imperative an indelible part of me from the moment when she had picked me out at the shop and named me and the sales clerk had burned her name and image into my circuits.

It's evening. I reach out—there's something to hold onto, land. I force my motors into overdrive and climb onto these new shores.

Around me, I see a tangle of milk jugs, nylon stockings, drinking bottles, bobbing barrels, shopping bags like floating jellyfish, plastic sheets, vinyl strips. I'm on a floating island of discarded plastic, of trash thrown away by people and gathered here by the currents.

"Amy," I croak. I miss her so much that I sound like a recording. "Amy, Amy, Amy." I want my batteries to run out so the missing will stop.

Around me I see the broken plastic bodies of other dolls, stripped down to their skeletal selves: a missing eye socket here, a crushed, misshapen head there, a stump for a lost limb. All over the island, abandoned dolls wriggled jerkily with the last of their dying electricity.

The sun goes down; the stars twinkle in the sky. And I hear nothing but the howling of the wind and the faint rasping voices of the dolls: "Talia…" "Jenny…" "Maddie…"

Amy, oh my Amy.

ARMLESS MAIDENS OF THE AMERICAN WEST

Genevieve Valentine

THERE'S AN ARMLESS MAIDEN IN the woods beyond the house.

She doesn't wail or weep the way you'd think a ghost or a grieving girl would. Her footsteps are heavy—sometimes she loses her balance—but that's the only way to hear her coming.

It happens in plenty of time that you can grab the bucket of golf balls you're collecting (the golf course buys them back for beer money) and get out of the woods before she reaches you.

If you do see her, it's because you lingered when the others ran, and you hid behind the largest oak, the one you and your dad once built a fort under, and waited for her.

The first thing you see is that her hair is loose. That strikes you as the cruelest thing, that whoever did this to her couldn't show even enough mercy to fasten her hair back first, and cast her into the forest with hair so long and loose that it's grown into corded mats down her back. The knots at the bottom are so twisted and so thick they look, when she's moving, like hands.

(No, you think, that's the cruelest thing.)

But her face is clean, as these things go. You imagine her kneeling beside the creek that runs all the way out past the golf course, dipping her face in the water.

There are dark stains down the sides of her dress, all the way to the ground, where she bled and bled and did not die after they cut her arms off at the shoulders.

The armless maiden has hazel eyes, or maybe brown.

She says, "Hello."

There's no telling what the armless maiden did.

It doesn't matter now. To her father, it was offense enough to warrant what happened. To anyone else, what happened was a crime beyond measure; what happened to her was a horror.

(Where they were when her father picked up the axe, there's no telling.)

She's been living in the woods as long as you can remember, though no one talks about it much where you are. Live and let live. If she stays off the golf course, no one minds her.

Nobody in town talks about her to strangers, but still, word gets out.

Sometimes one of the news crews from a bigger city would get wind of her and send a crew to do a story about the woman who haunts the woods. Usually it was Halloween, but sometimes it was International Women's Day, or something horrible had happened to a woman where they were from, and they wanted to find as many crime victims as they could to round out the story so it could last.

Once someone came all the way from Indianapolis to write her up; she asked if anyone had caught her, like she was a rabbit or a disease. The station could pay for testimonials, she said. She gave a dollar number that meant Indianapolis was serious about it.

She left empty-handed. The neighborhood didn't like the implications.

The armless maiden has never spoken, that anyone has ever said, and someone would have said. There's no need to tell strangers from Indianapolis about her, but she belongs to the town, sort of, and it's nothing strange to talk about your own.

Suzanne from the hairdresser's talked sometimes about how she couldn't imagine how that poor girl was looking after herself, and how she'd go out to the woods asking if the maiden needed anything, except that it would be butting in. Usually she said this when she was cutting your hair; she said, "I hear she's a blonde," and then there was no sound in the whole place but her scissors, and you watched your hair falling and held your breath.

At least once every year, someone from the PTA stood up in a meeting and asked if she was still of the age where she needed to be in school, even though she'd been in the woods so long that even if she'd started out that young, she wasn't now.

Tommy from the motel told everyone about the time the bird watchers came down to look for some warbler that was hard to find except in the forested region where they were, and ran into her, and got so frightened they left town without paying their bill. But they left most of their things in the room, too, so he sold the binoculars and the cameras and it came out all right.

He told the story like it was funny, how scared they had gotten, like any of them had ever really seen her and there was something to compare.

You start to think that you're the only one who has ever seen her.

It's a terrible thing to think, and you hope for a long time that it isn't true, but in all the stories people tell about her, no one says a word about seeing her themselves. Maybe she's just the kind of person whose privacy people respect, you think.

(But you know already, long before you admit it, that you're the only one who's ever seen her, and that she must be so lonely it makes your stomach hurt.

When she said hello, you've never heard anyone so surprised.)

That year, a researcher comes.

She isn't like the newscasters, with their navy or pastel skirt-suits, and their hair that got blonder the farther south they came from, and their camera crews who said nothing and tipped poorly.

She comes alone, with a roll-along suitcase that Pete from the diner said was mostly just full of notes and books and a laptop. She read papers the whole time she ate, Pete said, and after she paid the bill she asked him if the rumor was true.

"I'm studying armless maidens of the American West," she said. "I hear there might be one in the area. If anyone has any information about her, I'd like to meet her."

Pete said it like she was the weird one, but some of the people he told the story to thought she sounded different.

Meet, she had said, which sounded very civilized, and which none of them, the more they thought about it, had ever really done.

You kind of hate Pete for not asking more about it. You worked Wednesday through Saturday; if she had come in a day later, you would have asked her plenty.

Because it was as though no one heard the part you hear, the part that sends you down to the motel after work Friday to leave a wadded-up note with Carla, who does the night shift, and who would be more likely to actually pass the word along. (Tommy works days, and he'd let it get lost out of spite, because some guys are just nothing but spite, aren't they?)

She had said, armless maidens.

There are more.

There's comfort in an armless maiden.

In the stories about one armless maiden or another, her suffering is finite; because she is a girl of virtue—or was, before her father got to her, but allowances are made—we know she won't always wander the forest, bleeding and solitary.

While she does make the forest her home, angels part the water for her to walk through, so she'll never drown, and drape their heavenly cloaks on her, so she'll never freeze. It's a comfort.

The birds drop berries into her open mouth, and the rain falls past her grateful lips, so that when the prince finds her she won't be starved (princes in stories don't like maidens whose bodies are eating themselves).

The comfort of the armless maiden is how well you know she's being cared for; how easy it is to understand which parts of her are not whole.

When the researcher actually calls you back, you're surprised.

"It was kind of you to contact me," she says. "And yes, I'm still very interested in speaking with her, if it's possible."

You ask, "Why?" like she was the one who left you a note instead.

She says, "I'll show you the structure of the study, if you want. It's very respectful of privacy. It's still at the research stage at the moment—we're a little low on funding—but I hope that we're doing important work."

The guys at the golf course probably do important work, and you hope she's after something besides golf-course money. (You feel like you wouldn't even know what really important work was.)

"Sure," you say.

The armless maiden is alone.

Even in dreams, no one comes near her; even if there are forests teeming with armless maidens, each one is in a world only she knows for certain.

If the woods were teeming with them, the armless maidens wouldn't believe it, somehow; they would pass by and pass by, each thinking of the others, What a lonely girl, how like a ghost.

(In the good dreams, the world of an armless maiden is a world of silence; it's a world filled with rings of silver; it's a world where the axe couldn't hold.)

The researcher comes in on a Thursday night with her rollalong, looking just like Pete described her, and orders a cup of coffee, and asks you to have a seat.

There are some people who stopped off on their way to the antique fair, so you can't right away, but you stop by to refill her coffee about a dozen times, and finally she pushes a document toward you.

You flip open the first page, standing right there at the table because you can't wait any longer to know what's going on.

You scan the page quickly—the corner booth ordered omelets and the toast gets stone cold if it sits out for more than ten seconds.

It reads, "The armless maidens of the American West are not, despite the title of this study, a geographically-defined phenomenon. The concentration on this region merely allows for a reasonable sample size to be defined and, if possible, interviewed."

Then, farther down, "For purposes of this study and in the interests of maintaining privacy for participants, all names have been changed."

Then there are lists of names; there are charts and graphs full of more data points than you ever thought were possible to gather about anything.

(One axis is labeled "Age at Dismemberment." You can't breathe.)

Next to her, there are stacks of paper fastened with clips, with names like ANNA or CARLIE or MARIA written in large block letters across the front, maybe so they're easy to find.

They're not real names; you wonder if she picked them, or they picked their own.

"What happened to them?" you ask, finally, after you've decided there's not enough money in the world to make you pick one up and read it.

(Your fingers are still resting on CARLIE. Underneath her name it reads: AGE 13.)

She considers her answer, like she doesn't want to frighten you.

She says, "Different things."

That's sort of worse—you had tried to take comfort in the old story that only a father did this kind of thing. Your dad was okay; you thought you were fine.

You swallow. "Are they—are they all right?"

"Some of them," she says. "It depends a lot on what happens to them afterward—who they know, how much they feel they have support to rejoin the world. Sometimes their arms even grow back, eventually, depending."

You guess a little bit about what that depends on, but it's not hard; the armless maiden has been around a long time, and nothing has healed, and everybody you know says things about her but never to.

"I'd like to speak with her, if you know where to find her," she says. "It's a good starting point. The more we talk to them, the easier it is to take note of their progress."

Progress.

There could have been progress already, if someone had ever walked out past the golf course and looked her in the eye, just once.

You don't want to talk about this anymore.

"I'll get your check," you say, and fill her coffee cup too full, and clock out for your smoke break twice in a row by accident because your hands are shaking.

You suck the cigarette down to the filter, making up your mind about it.

You go back out to the woods, late in the day, when no one is likely to be on the course.

(You don't like the golfers. They never come into the diner, even though it's right down the highway and they have to drive past it, and it seems more trouble to avoid it than to stop.)

You wait near the tree. You've brought some things that make you feel stupider than you've ever felt, including the time you had to give an oral report on the French Revolution in history and blanked, and Tommy never let you hear the end of it.

(You've brought scissors, a comb, vitamins, a dress with sleeves.

You want to be prepared; when you tell her about the researcher, she might say yes.)

Near dark, just before it's really night, she comes by all the same, with careful footfalls.

When she sees you, she stops.

"Hello," says the armless maiden.

You say, "Hello."

POCOSIN
Ursula Vernon

Author's Note: Pocosins are a type of raised peat wetland found almost exclusively in the Carolinas. The name derives from an Eastern Algonquian word meaning "swamp on a hill."

They are a rare and unique ecosystem, today widely threatened by development.

THIS IS THE PLACE OF the carnivores, the pool ringed with sundews and the fat funnels of the pitcher plants.

This is the place where the ground never dries out and the loblolly pines grow stunted, where the soil is poor and the plants turn to other means of feeding themselves.

This is the place where the hairstreak butterflies flow sleekly through the air and you can hear insect feet drumming inside the bowl of the pitcher plants.

This is the place where the old god came to die.

He came in the shape of the least of all creatures, a possum. Sometimes he was a man with a long rat's tail, and sometimes he was a possum with too-human hands. On two legs and four, staggering, with his hands full of mud, he came limping through the marsh and crawled up to the witchwoman's porch.

"Go back," she said, not looking up. She had a rocking chair on the porch and the runners creaked as she rocked. There was a second chair, but she did not offer it to him. "Go back where you came from."

The old god laid his head on the lowest step. When he breathed, it hissed through his long possum teeth and sounded like he was dying.

"I'm done with that sort of thing," she said, still not looking up. She was tying flies, a pleasantly tricky bit of work, binding thread and chicken feathers to the wickedness of the hook. "You go find some other woman with witchblood in her."

The old god shuddered and then he was mostly a man. He crawled up two steps and sagged onto the porch.

The woman sighed and set her work aside. "Don't try to tell me you're dying," she said grimly. "I won't believe it. Not from a possum."

Her name was Maggie Grey. She was not so very old, perhaps, but she had the kind of spirit that is born old and grows cynical. She looked down on the scruffy rat-tailed god with irritation and a growing sense of duty.

His throat rasped as he swallowed. He reached out a hand with long yellow nails and pawed at the boards on the porch.

"Shit," Maggie said finally, and went inside to get some water.

She poured it down his throat and most of it went down. He came a little bit more alive and looked at her with huge, dark eyes. His face was dirty pale, his hair iron gray.

She knew perfectly well what he was. Witchblood isn't the same as godblood, but they know each other when they meet in the street. The question was why a god had decided to die on her porch, and that was a lousy sort of question.

"You ain't been shot," she said. "There's not a hunter alive that could shoot the likes of you. What's got you dragging your sorry ass up on my porch, old god?"

The old god heaved himself farther up on the porch. He smelled rank. His fur was matted with urine when he was a possum and his pants were stained and crusted when he was a man.

His left leg was swollen at the knee, a fat bent sausage, and the foot beneath it was black. There were puncture wounds in his skin. Maggie grunted.

"Cottonmouth, was it?"

The old god nodded.

Maggie sat back down in the rocking chair and looked out over the sundew pool.

There was a dense mat of shrubs all around the house, fetterbush and sheep laurel bound up together with greenbrier. She kept the path open with an axe, when she bothered to keep it open at all. There was no one to see her and the dying man who wasn't quite a man.

Mosquitos whined in the throats of the pitcher plants and circled the possum god's head. Maggie could feel her shoulders starting to tense up. It was always her shoulders. On a bad day, they'd get so knotted that pain would shoot down her forearms in bright white lines.

"Would've preferred a deer," she said. "Or a bear, maybe. Got some dignity that way." Then she laughed. "Should've figured I'd get a possum. It'd be a nasty, stinking sort of god that wanted anything to do with me."

She picked up a pair of scissors from where she'd been tying flies. "Hold still. No, I ain't gonna cut you. I ain't so far gone to try and suck the poison out of a god."

It had likely been another god that poisoned him, she thought— Old Lady Cottonmouth, with her gums as white as wedding veils. She saw them sometimes, big, heavy-bodied snakes, gliding easy through the water. Hadn't ever seen the Old Lady, but she was out there, and it would be just like a possum to freeze up when those white gums came at him, sprouting up fangs.

Even a witch might hesitate at that.

She waited until he was a man, more or less, and cut his pant leg open with the scissors. The flesh underneath was angry red, scored with purple. He gasped in relief as the tight cloth fell away from the swollen flesh.

"Don't thank me," she said grimly. "Probably took a few hours off your life with that. But they wouldn't be anything worth hanging on for."

She brought him more water. The first frogs began to screek and squeal in the water.

"You sure you want this?" she asked. "I can put a knife across your throat, make it easy."

He shook his head.

"You know who's coming for you?"

He nodded. Then he was a possum again and he gaped his mouth open and hissed in pain.

She hesitated, still holding the scissors. "Ain't sure I want to deal with 'em myself," she muttered. "I'm done with all that. I came out here to get *away*, you hear me?"

The possum closed his eyes, and whispered the only word he'd ever speak.

"...*sorry*..."

Maggie thrust the scissors into her pocket and scowled.

"All right," she said. "Let's get you under the porch. You come to me and I'll stand them off for you, right enough, but you better not be in plain sight."

She had to carry him down the steps. His bad leg would take no weight and he fell against her, smelling rank. There were long stains on her clothes before they were done.

Under the porch, it was cool. The whole house was raised up, to save it from the spring floods, when the sundew pool reached out hungry arms. There was space enough, in the shadow under the stairs, for a dying god smaller than a man.

She didn't need to tell him to stay quiet.

She went into the house and poured herself a drink. The alcohol was sharp and raw on her throat. She went down the steps again, to a low green stand of mountain mint, and yanked up a half dozen stems.

They didn't gentle the alcohol, but at least it gave her something else to taste. The frogs got louder and the shadows under the sheep laurel got thick. Maggie sat back in her rocking chair with her shoulders knotting up under her shirt and went back to tying flies.

Someone cleared his throat.

She glanced up, and there was a man in preacher's clothes, with the white collar and clean black pants. The crease in them was pressed sharp enough to draw blood.

"Huh," she said. "Figured the other one'd beat you here."

He gave her a pained, fatherly smile.

She nodded to the other chair. "Have a seat. I've got bad whiskey, but if you cut it with mint and sugar, it ain't bad."

"No, thank you," said the preacher. He sat down on the edge of the chair. His skin was peat colored and there was no mud on his shoes. "You know why I've come, Margaret."

"Maggie," she said. "My mother's the only one who calls me Margaret, and she's dead, as you very well know."

The preacher tilted his head in acknowledgment.

He was waiting for her to say something, but it's the nature of witches to outwait God if they can, and the nature of God to forgive poor sinners their pride. Eventually he said, "There's a poor lost soul under your porch, Maggie Grey."

"He didn't seem so lost," she said. "He walked here under his own power."

"All souls are lost without me," said the preacher.

Maggie rolled her eyes.

A whip-poor-will called, placing the notes end to end, whip-er-*will!* whip-er-*will!*

It was probably Maggie's imagination that she could hear the panting of the god under the porch, in time to the nightjar's calls.

The preacher sat, in perfect patience, with his wrists on his knees. The mosquitos that formed skittering sheets over the pond did not approach him.

"What's there for a possum in heaven, anyway?" asked Maggie. "You gonna fill up the corners with compost bins and rotten fruit?"

The preacher laughed. He had a gorgeous, church-organ laugh and Maggie's heart clenched like a fist in her chest at the sound. She told her heart to behave. Witchblood ought to know better than to hold out hope of heaven.

"I could," said the preacher. "Would you give him to me if I did?"

Maggie shook her head.

His voice dropped, a father explaining the world to a child. "What good does it do him, to be trapped in this world? What good does it do anyone?"

"He seems to like it."

"He is a prisoner of this place. Give him to me and I will set him free to glory."

"He's a possum," said Maggie tartly. "He ain't got much use for glory."

The preacher exhaled. It was most notable because, until then, he hadn't been breathing. "You cannot doubt my word, my child."

"I ain't doubting nothing," said Maggie. "It'd be just exactly as you said, I bet. But he came to me because that's not what he wanted, and I ain't taking that away from him."

The preacher sighed. It was a more-in-sorrow-than-in-anger sigh, and Maggie narrowed her eyes. Her heart went back to acting the way a witch's heart ought to act, which was generally to ache at every damn thing and carry on anyway. Her shoulders felt like she'd been hauling stones.

"I could change your mind," he offered.

"Ain't your way."

He sighed again.

"Should've sent one of the saints," said Maggie, taking pity on the Lord, or whatever little piece of Him was sitting on her porch. "Somebody who was alive once, anyway, and remembers what it was like."

He bowed his head. "I will forgive you," he said.

"I know you will," said Maggie kindly. "Now get gone before the other one shows up."

Her voice sounded as if she shooed the Lord off her porch every day, and when she looked up again, he was gone.

It got dark. The stars came out, one by one, and were reflected in the sundew pool. Fireflies jittered, but only a few. Fireflies like grass and open woods, and the dense mat of the swamp did not please them. Maggie lit a lamp to tie flies by.

The Devil came up through a stand of yellowroot, stepping up out of the ground like a man climbing a staircase. Maggie was pleased to see that he had split hooves. She would have been terribly disappointed if he'd been wearing shoes.

He kicked aside the sticks of yellowroot, tearing shreds off them, showing ochre-colored pith underneath. Maggie raised an eyebrow at this small destruction, but yellowroot is hard to kill.

"Maggie Grey," said the fellow they called the Old Gentleman.

She nodded to him, and he took it as invitation, dancing up the steps on clacking hooves. Maggie smiled a little as he came up the steps, for the Devil always was a good dancer.

He sat down in the same chair that the preacher had used, and scowled abruptly. "See I got here late."

"Looks that way," said Maggie Grey.

He dug his shoulder blades into the back of the chair, first one, then the other, rolling a little, like a cat marking territory in something foul. Maggie stifled a sigh. It had been a good rocking chair, but it probably wasn't wise to keep a chair around that the Devil had claimed.

"You've got something I want, Maggie Grey," he said.

"If it's my soul, you'll be waiting awhile," said Maggie, holding up a bit of feather. She looped three black threads around it, splitting the feather so it looked like wings. The hook gleamed between her fingers.

"Oh no," said the Devil, "I know better than to mess with a witch's soul, Maggie Grey. One of my devils showed up to tempt your great-grandmother, and she bit him in half and threw his horns down the well."

Maggie sniffed. "Well's gone dry," she said, trying not to look pleased. She knew better than to respond to demonic flattery. "It's the ground hereabouts. Sand and moss and swamps on top of hills. Had to dig another one, and lord knows how long it'll last."

"Didn't come here to discuss well-digging, Maggie Grey."

"I suppose not." She bit off a thread.

"There's an old god dying under your porch, Maggie Grey. The fellow upstairs wants him, and I aim to take him instead."

She sighed. A firefly wandered into a pitcher plant and stayed, pulsing green through the thin flesh. "What do you lot want with a scrawny old possum god, anyway?"

The Devil propped his chin on his hand. He was handsome, of course. It would have offended his notion of his own craftsmanship to be anything less. "Me? Not much. The fellow upstairs wants him because he's a stray bit from back before he and I were feuding. An old loose end, if you follow me."

Maggie snorted. "Loose end? The possum gods and the deer and Old Lady Cottonmouth were here before anybody thought to worship you. Either of you."

The Devil smiled. "Can't imagine there's many worshippers left for an old possum god, either. 'Cept the possums, and they don't go to church much."

Maggie bent her head over the wisp of thread and metal. "He doesn't feel like leaving."

Her guest sat up a little straighter. "I am not sure," he said, silky-voiced, "that he is strong enough to stop me."

Maggie picked up the pliers and bent the hook, just a little, working the feathers onto it. "He dies all the time," she said calmly. "You never picked him up the other times."

"Can only die so many times, Maggie Grey. Starts to take it out of you. Starts to make you tired, right down to the center of your bones. You know what that's like, don't you?"

She did not respond, because the worst thing you can do is let the Devil know when he's struck home.

"He's weak now and dying slow. Easy pickings."

"Seems like I might object," she said quietly.

The Devil stood up. He was very tall and he threw a shadow clear over the pool when he stood. The sundews folded their sticky leaves in where the shadow touched them. Under the porch steps, the dying god moaned.

He placed a hand on the back of her chair and leaned over her.

"We can make this easy, Maggie Grey," he said. "Or we can make it very hard."

She nodded slowly, gazing over the sundew pool.

"Come on—" the Devil began, and Maggie moved like Old Lady Cottonmouth and slammed the fish-hook over her shoulder and into the hand on the back of her chair.

The Devil let out a yelp like a kicked dog and staggered backwards.

"You come to *my* house," snapped Maggie, thrusting the pliers at him, "and you have the nerve to threaten me? A witch in her own home? I'll shoe your hooves in holy iron and throw *you* down the well, you hear me?"

"Holy iron won't be kind to witchblood," he gasped, doubled over.

"It'll be a lot less kind to *you,*" she growled.

The Devil looked at his hand, with the fish-hook buried in the meat of his palm, and gave a short, breathless laugh. "Oh, Maggie Grey," he said, straightening up. "You aren't the woman your great-grandmother was, but you're not far off."

"Get gone," said Maggie. "Get gone and don't come back unless I call."

"You will eventually," he said.

"Maybe so. But not today."

He gave her a little salute, with the hook still stuck in his hand, and limped off the porch. The yellowroot rustled as he sank into the dirt again.

His blood left black spots on the earth. She picked up the lantern and went to peer at the possum god.

He was still alive, though almost all possum now. His whiskers lay limp and stained with yellow. There was white all around his eyes and a black crust of blood over his hind leg.

"Not much longer," she said. "Only one more to go, and then it's over. And we'll both be glad."

He nodded, closing his eyes.

On the way back onto the porch, she kicked at a black bloodstain, which had sprouted a little green rosette of leaves. A white flower coiled out of the leaves and turned its face to the moon.

"Bindweed," she muttered. "Lovely. One more damn chore tomorrow."

She stomped back onto the porch and poured another finger of whiskey.

It was almost midnight when the wind slowed, and the singing frogs fell silent, one by one.

Maggie looked over, and Death was sitting in the rocking chair.

"Grandmother," she said. "I figured you'd come."

"Always," said Death.

"If you'd come a little sooner, would've saved me some trouble."

Death laughed. She was a short, round woman with hair as gray as Maggie's own. "Seems to me you were equal to it."

Maggie grunted. "Whiskey?"

"Thank you."

They sat together on the porch, drinking. Death's rocker squeaked in time to the breathing of the dying god.

"I hate this," said Maggie, to no one in particular. "I'm tired, you hear me? I'm tired of all these fights. I'm tired of taking care of things, over and over, and having to do it again the next day." She glared over the top of her whiskey. "And don't tell me that it *does* make a difference, because I know that, too. Ain't I a witch?"

Death smiled. "Wouldn't dream of it," she said.

Maggie snorted.

After a minute, she said, "I'm so damn tired of *stupid.*"

Death laughed out loud, a clear sound that rang over the water. "Aren't we all?" she said. "Gods and devils, aren't we all?"

The frogs had stopped. So had the crickets. One whip-poor-will sang uncertainly, off on the other side of the pond. It was quiet and peaceful and it would have been a lovely night, if the smell of the dying possum hadn't come creeping up from under the porch.

Death gazed into her mug, where the wilting mint was losing the fight against the whiskey. "Can't fix stupid," she said. "But other things, maybe. You feeling like dying?"

Maggie sighed. It wasn't a temptation, even with her shoulders sending bright sparks of pain toward her fingers and making the pliers hard to hold steady. "Feeling like resting," she said. "For a couple of months, at least. That's all I want. Just a little bit of time to sit here and tie flies and drink whiskey and let somebody else fight the hard fights."

Death nodded. "So take it," she said. "Nobody's gonna give it to you."

Maggie scowled. "I was," she said bitterly. "'Til a possum god showed up to die."

Death laughed. "It's why he came, you know," she said. Her eyes twinkled, just like Maggie's grandmother's had when she wore the body that Death was wearing now. "He wanted to be left alone to die, so he found a witch that'd understand."

Maggie raked her fingers through her hair. "Son of a bitch," she said to no one in particular.

Death finished her drink and set it aside. "Shall we do what's needful?"

Maggie slugged down the rest of the mug and gasped as the whiskey burned down her throat. "Needful," she said thickly. "That's being a witch for you."

"No," said Death, "that's being alive. Being a witch just means the things that need doing are bigger."

They went down the stairs. The boards creaked under Maggie's feet, but not under Death's, even though Death had heavy boots on.

Maggie crouched down and said, "She's here for you, hon."

She would have sworn that the possum had no strength left in him, but he crawled out from under the porch, hand over hand. His hind legs dragged and his tail looked like a dead worm.

There was nothing noble about him. He stank and black fluid leaked from his ears and the corners of his eyes. Even now, Maggie could hardly believe that God and the Devil would both show up to bargain for such a creature's soul.

Death knelt down, heedless of the smell and the damp, and held out her arms.

The possum god crawled the last little way and fell into her embrace.

"There you are," said Death, laying her cheek on the spikey-furred forehead. "There you are. I've got you."

The god closed his eyes. His breath went out on a long, long sigh, and he did not draw another one.

Maggie walked away, to the edge of the sundew pool, and waited.

A frog started up, then another one. The water rippled as their throat sacs swelled. Something splashed out in the dark.

"It's done," called Death, and Maggie turned back.

The god looks smaller now. Death had gathered him up and he almost fit in her lap, like a small child or a large dog.

"Don't suppose he's faking it?" asked Maggie hopefully. "They're famous for it, after all."

Death shook her head. "Even possum gods got to die sometime. Help me get him into the pond."

Maggie took him under the arms and Death took the feet. His tail dragged on the ground as they hauled him. Death went into the water first, sure-footed, and Maggie followed, feeling water come in over the tops of her shoes.

"If I'd been thinking, I would've worn waders," she said.

Death laughed Maggie's grandmother's laugh.

The bottom of the sundew pool was made of mud and sphagnum moss, and it wasn't always sure if it wanted to be solid or not. Every step she took required a pause while the mud settled and sometimes her heels sank in deep. She started to worry that she was going to lose her shoes in the pool, and god, wouldn't that be a bitch on top of everything else?

At least the god floated. Her shoulders weren't up to much more than that.

In the middle of the pool, Death stopped. She let go of the possum's feet and came around to Maggie's side. "This ought to do it," she said.

"If we leave the body in here, it'll stink up the pool something fierce," said Maggie. "There's things that come and drink here."

"Won't be a problem," Death promised. She paused. "Thought you were tired of taking care of things?"

"I am," snapped Maggie. "*Tired* isn't the same as *can't*. Though if this keeps up…"

She trailed off because she truly did not know what lay at the end of being tired and it was starting to scare her a little.

Death took the possum's head between her hands. Maggie put a hand in the center of his chest.

They pushed him under the water and held him for the space of a dozen heartbeats, then brought him to the surface.

"Again," said Death.

They dunked him again.

"Three times the charm," said Death, and they pushed him under the final time.

The body seemed to melt away under Maggie's hands. One moment it was a solid, hairy weight, then it wasn't. For a moment she thought it was sinking and her heart sank with it, because fishing a dead god out of the pond was going to be a bitch of a way to spend an hour.

But he did not sink. Instead he simply unmade himself, skin from flesh and flesh from bone, unraveling like one of her flies coming untied, and there was nothing left but a shadow on the surface of the water.

Maggie let out a breath and scrubbed her hands together. They felt oily.

She was freezing and her boots were full of water and something slimy wiggled past her shin. She sighed. It seemed, as it had for a long time, that witchcraft—or whatever this was—was all mud and death and need.

She was so damn tired.

She thought perhaps she'd cry, and then she thought that wouldn't much help, so she didn't.

Death reached out and took her granddaughter's hand.

"Look," said Death quietly.

Around the pond, the fat trumpets of the pitcher plants began to glow from inside, as if they had swallowed a thousand fireflies. The light cast green shadows across the surface of the water and turned the sundews into strings of cut glass beads. It cut itself along the leaves of the staggerbush and threaded between the fly-traps' teeth.

Whatever was left of the possum god glowed like foxfire.

Hand in hand, they came ashore by pitcher plant light.

Death stood at the foot of the steps. Maggie went up them, holding the railing, moving slow.

There were black stains on the steps where the god had oozed. She was going to have to scrub them down, pour bleach on them, maybe even strip the wood. The bindweed, that nasty little plant they called "Devil's Guts," was already several feet long and headed toward the mint patch. The stink of dying possum was coming up from under the steps and that was going to need to be scraped down with a shovel and then powdered with lime.

At least she could wait until tomorrow to take an axe to the Devil's rocking chair, though it might be sensible to drag it off the porch first.

The notion of all the work to be done made her head throb and her shoulders climb toward her ears.

"Go to bed, granddaughter," said Death kindly. "Take your rest. The world can go on without you for a little while."

"Work to be done," Maggie muttered. She held onto the railing to stop from swaying.

"Yes," said Death, "but not by you. Not tonight. I will make you this little bargain, granddaughter, in recognition of a kindness. I will give you a little time. Go to sleep. Things left undone will be no worse for it."

Death makes bargains rarely, and unlike the Devil, hers are not negotiable. Maggie nodded and went inside.

She fell straight down on the bed and was asleep without taking off her boots. She did not say goodbye to the being that wore her grandmother's face, but in the morning, a quilt had been pulled up over her shoulder.

The next evening, as the sun set, Maggie sat in her rocking chair and tied flies. Her shoulders were slowly, slowly easing. The pliers only shook a little in her hand.

She had dumped bleach over the steps, and the smell from under the porch had gone of its own accord. The bindweed...well, the black husks had definitely been bindweed, but something had trod upon it and turned it into ash. It was a kindness she hadn't expected.

Her whiskey bottle was also full, with something rather better than moonshine, although she suspected that a certain cloven-hooved gentleman might have been responsible for that.

The space on the porch where the other rocking chair had been ached like a sore tooth and caught her eye whenever she glanced over. She sighed. Still, the wood would keep the fire going for a couple of days, when winter came.

The throats of the pitcher plants still glowed, just a little. Easy enough to blame on tired eyes. Maggie wrapped thread around the puff of feather and the shining metal hook, and watched the glow from the corner of her eyes.

A young possum trundled out of the thicket, and Maggie looked up.

"Don't start," she said warningly. "I'll get the broom."

The possum sat down on the edge of the pond. It was an awkward, ungainly little creature, with big dark eyes and wicked kinked whiskers. It was halfway hideous and halfway sweet, which gave it something in common with witches.

Slowly, slowly, the moon rose and the green light died away. The frogs chanted together in the dark.

The possum stood up, stretched, and nodded once to Maggie Grey. Then it shuffled into the undergrowth, its long rat-tail held behind it.

I will give you a little time, Death had said.

She wondered what Death considered 'a little time.' An hour? A day? A week?

"A few weeks," she said to the pond and the absent possum. "A few weeks would be good. A little time for myself. The world can get on just fine without me for a couple of weeks."

She wasn't expecting an answer. The whip-poor-wills called to each other over the pond, and maybe that was answer enough.

Maggie poured two fingers of the Devil's whiskey, with hands that did not shake, and raised the glass in a toast to the absent world.

SHE GAVE HER HEART, HE TOOK HER MARROW

Sam Fleming

CHANCERY HISSED AT THE SUDDEN pain of a splinter in her palm. She took a deep breath filled with the scent of dust and woodsap, and exhaled the hurt as steam to dissipate in the cold air.

"See? She's *people*," Hedron said. "*People* are a distraction. They always spoil everything, given a chance. You mustn't give them one." He bared his tiny, needle-sharp teeth, a distant storm glimmering behind his moonstone eyes.

"Kay's not *people*," Chancery said. "How do you know she's coming, anyway? You promised you'd stay away from the harbour." She put the dropped log on the stack at the back of the shed and pulled the splinter out with her teeth. It tasted of resin and woodlice.

Hedron took her hand and kissed it better. Spores cried like fading ghostly mice as they died.

"I promised I wouldn't go inside the fence and I haven't," he said. "One of ours was wandering along the road by the compound, and Kay was talking to the site manager just inside the gate."

He perched on the tree stump Chancery used as a platform for splitting the logs and ran fingers like knobbly twigs around the brim of his hat.

Chancery didn't like his hat. It was too big and sagged over his head in a floppy, shapeless mass of purple felt attracting dust, cobwebs, fluff, and stray hairs. Once a week or so, he went away for a few hours and came back with it clean. It stayed clean for a day or two at the most. He'd warned her not to touch. She wouldn't have tried anyway; looking at it made her bones restless and itchy.

He rubbed his fingertips together, sniffing them. They squeaked like soaped glass. A twist of hair fell from the hat and he herded it back with a cupped hand. "She brought chocolate." He offered no explanation as to how he knew this, but all *their* people had his eyes and ears. He told them what to do.

"Will she visit?"

"Would the Oilers care about cocoa content?"

"No."

"Then she'll be here tomorrow."

It had been a year since Kay's last visit, a year since the fight. Chancery couldn't manage the monthly trade with the Oilers without Hedron telling her what to say, and they didn't matter much. They were just *people*, interchangeable.

Kay wasn't.

Chancery's vision swum with panic. What if she said the wrong thing?

"She's not worth getting in a state over," Hedron said. "Think of all the things you could do with that chocolate." He stretched out his long, spider-thin legs and leaned back, lacing his hands behind his head. Dust spilled from his hat and returned as if it were sheep separated from a flock.

Chancery imagined bitter chocolate mousse with honeyed damsons, soufflé, and drowned cherries. She concentrated on the shape of the flavour and all the things that could slot into it, a jigsaw for her tongue, until her breathing settled and her heart stopped racing.

She placed the last three logs. "You just don't like her."

"She wants to ruin things, take you away. Of course I don't like her."

"Don't be stupid. Why would she want that?"

"Not because she loves you, no matter what she says." He kicked some of the bark that had fallen from the logs as Chancery split them.

She shook her head. "I'll make tea. We'll try the biscuits I made this morning."

Hedron slouched to his feet, hat brushing the shed roof, and stuffed his hands back inside his smock. "I'm going to check the goats."

"Fine." No point arguing if he was in a sulk.

Hedron had brought her to the farm after he found her. It was self-sufficient in all the ways that mattered, and the farmhouse kitchen alone was the size of the flat she had shared with Annabel; they hadn't been able to afford anything bigger. Back then, hardly anyone could.

Now, no one else wanted it.

It had happened suddenly. One day, everything was fine; the next,

Annabel said she was leaving.

Annabel was the only one who had seen past the lack of eye contact, the silences that could last for days, the finicky obsessions and pedantry; the disability that wasn't enough to get Chancery support in a world where everyone was expected to pull their weight. The wasted talent. She was the only person since Chancery's mother died to make her feel safe and loved; the only one not to have been *people*.

She might as well have stabbed Chancery in the heart with a boning knife.

The world sublimated; standing at the kitchen window, Chancery could see everything trembling, crumbling around the edges. Furniture, grass, trees, birds, work tops, next door's dog, all shivering into fragments.

Everything was ruined.

She hadn't known what to do.

She tried hugging her. "I can come with you."

"No," Annabel said, disentangling herself. "I love you, but I don't have the energy to go on like this, looking after you, keeping you safe. I'm not helping you by letting you rely on me so much. It's best for us both if I leave."

She didn't even kiss Chancery goodbye, just turned and walked out the door.

Chancery knew she had to stop her. This was absolute, a searing, hot-cold certainty. It sliced Chancery in two and poured acid on the cut.

Chancery stumbled after her, tripped on the doorstep, and fell on her face, smashing her nose against flagstones. The pain was white, explosive, awful but irrelevant. All that mattered was, if Annabel got away, she would become just like everyone else. She would become *people*.

Chancery couldn't talk to people. She did her best to avoid them.

Out on the street, people were having seizures, vomiting, screaming, thrashing on the ground. Chancery climbed to her feet, shuddering at the noise slicing against her skin, and tried to help Annabel, but what could she do? Nothing she said made any difference. It was as if Annabel could no longer hear her.

After a while, people stopped screaming and the world turned quiet. Eventually, over the course of several days, they all began to walk. They went to the beach, flocking to the sea in skeins and drifts like slow-motion, ground-trapped starlings.

When Annabel went, Chancery went with her, following the silent masses to the ocean. It was a rare day of heat, the sun blazing, the sea both sparkling and smooth, as if covered in partially crumpled foil. It rolled in an easy, steep swell, fat breakers crashing in spumes of froth like whisked egg whites. About a mile out, the frequent sea fog they called the Haar was a thick, impenetrable wall of white; an endless roulade of candyfloss cloud across the horizon.

People milled on the beach before aiming for the wall. Once in the water, they floundered in the surf, drowning, unable to swim, unable to stop. Bodies bobbed on the waves, a grotesquery of marker buoys, and lay puffed and bloated on the beach. Crows squabbled with seagulls over a surplus of glistening, crimson ribbons of flesh. The stink of rotting meat and seaweed coated Chancery's tongue like a mouthful of rancid fruit drenched in iodine and soy.

"Wait!" Chancery grabbed Annabel, clung to her. She pulled away, drawn to something out at sea, just like the other people, oblivious to the corpses. Chancery started after her, but she was already lost.

Chancery collapsed, bones baking. She had visions of them caramelising, could almost smell the roasting marrow. She squeezed fistfuls of sand until it hurt.

When she saw Hedron, he was blurry: a shape, a shadow in a heat haze. He wandered over, taller than any of the people, and she couldn't tell whether they made room or he passed right through them.

Prickling tendrils burst from high up inside her nose and shot through her brain, a snort of sour fizz with a chilli heat. "Hello," he said. "Aren't you going with them?"

She tried to answer but couldn't.

He bent down, cupped her face with hard, spindly fingers, and blew gently on her parted lips. The coolness of his breath on the moistness of her mouth penetrated to her bones, replacing the marrow-deep fire with a detached calm.

She looked up, and he was pulling his hat firmly onto his head. It was covered in a layer of granular soot.

She sat, arms almost too weak to push against the soft sand. "She said I couldn't. I lost her. I didn't know what to do. Then you came." She looked at her hands, thinking there should be some sign she nearly roasted from the inside. "You made me better."

"You wouldn't have been able to speak to me if I hadn't, and you're the only one who tried."

She turned to watch people falling like skittles in the surging waves. "All those *people*," she said. "They're dying."

"I know. I don't know why."

"They're going into the sea."

"What's wrong with the sea?"

"They drown."

More prickling, ticklish rather than painful this time.

"All right. We'll keep some of them. They can help me keep you safe."

Chancery picked up a dead crab and made its legs waggle, then frowned at the opaque horizon. It was so quiet. So peaceful. Her limbs relaxed outwards, as if she were a trussed chicken and someone had cut the string. "Do we have to?"

Hardly anyone escaped, Hedron had said at the time, pleased with himself. Bones still lay in bleached white drifts of fragments on the beach, barely recognisable after five years of winter storms. The Haar remained, never straying further than around three miles out, no matter the weather, although sometimes it came all the way in. Chancery knew that was when people were trying to reach the island and Hedron didn't want them to.

Armed coastal patrols kept Britain in internationally ratified quarantine. Only the Oilers were allowed to land. Their Aberdeen Harbour compound was the one place still accessible. Three years after the Walk they'd surrounded the docks with an electric fence and doused everything in chemicals before resuming work there. Maybe they really needed the oil.

Although she'd never been inside, Chancery bartered with them, with Hedron's help. Gourmet meats and preserves, jewellery she'd found—things they couldn't afford where they lived—for rifle ammunition, flour, and spices. She'd asked Hedron not to infect them and he'd agreed, as long as they kept bringing her things, didn't leave their compound, and she didn't tell them about him.

He wanted her to be happy. Cooking made her happy.

She gave them jars with lids sucked tight and Tupperware containing gold and gemstones swimming in bleach, which they had her drop into plastic bags she wasn't allowed to touch. They weren't to know the real reason they were safe.

The first few visits, they'd tried to catch her. Once, she barely escaped. She begged Hedron not to send his people to spit and shed through the fence, nor to activate the spores coating the piers and their vehicles, in case it disturbed the status quo and even more *people* came. He eventually relented, although the ones responsible had walked, and he made them stay near the compound as a warning, until they starved to death.

After that, the Oilers settled for trading. Hedron said they thought they were keeping an eye on her, as if she needed it with him around.

That was how she'd met Kay, and Kay was the only one who'd been outside since.

Chancery hadn't needed Hedron to talk to Kay. Kay wasn't *people*.

The kettle rattled, spitting water onto the hotplate. Chancery dragged herself away from one of her treasured recipe books and filled the cracked brown teapot before snuggling it under a cosy.

She retreated to the living room with biscuits and tea. Curled up in front of the fire with a notebook and pen, she made a list. Lists kept her calm. Hedron had taught her that. They were recipes for getting through the day.

After a while she opened her eyes to see Hedron peering at her notebook. The fire had died away to embers. She threw twigs and logs into the hearth to get it going again.

Skook nosed his way around the door, pink tongue lolling and his face all wet. Hedron had got Skook for her after the Oilers tried to catch her. He was an enormous dog, the biggest she'd ever seen. He had fluffy fur the colour of autumn leaves and looked like a cross between a lion and a bear. Hedron said he was a Himalayan mastiff. Even down on all fours, his head reached her chest, and Chancery loved him to bits. She had never been to see the Oilers without him since he arrived. He helped Hedron keep her safe.

"How were the goats?"

"Fine. I've got a couple of our people out by the barn." Hedron didn't say what they were doing because they both knew. They would be walking. That's what they did.

"I'll be careful." They'd learned the hard way it was almost impossible for Hedron to stop her walking when she was close to one of their people and he and his hat were elsewhere. "Are you staying for dinner?"

"I ate not long ago." He yawned, mouth impossibly huge above his pointy chin, teeth glinting in the firelight.

Chancery didn't ask what he'd had. Or who. She put the guard in front of the fire and returned to the kitchen.

She fetched rabbits and pheasants from the snares in the greyness of pre-dawn, the Haar thick and moist across the fields and forests. The rest of the morning was spent on *mise-en-place*, because Kay was coming and Chancery wanted it to be perfect. She always wanted it to be perfect, but didn't mind getting it wrong so much when there was no one around to see.

Hedron visited after lunch.

"Are you going to clean your hat?" she asked. It was making her bones itch and her toes curl. He fingered the brim and sniffed his fingers.

"Not today," he said. "You mustn't stray far without me, Chancery."

"Okay."

She frowned as he left. He wasn't normally quite so protective.

She was reading, clean and a little damp from an early bath, when Skook went mad and an engine rumbled into the yard, the sound burbling in her gullet. Her heart kicked against her ribcage.

Someone banged on the door. "Chance? Have you got hold of that carnivorous pony?"

Chancery knew Kay meant Skook, even though Skook was a dog. "Yes!"

Then she heard a much deeper voice, a voice that pattered on her skin like the first pebbles of an oncoming landslide. She grabbed the boning knife from the rack.

Kay was swaddled in a heavy fleece with the Chevroil logo on the breast, a fur-lined trapper hat, mitts, and thick cargo-trousers. She trailed a scent of soft-hard peony, orange blossom, sandalwood, and vanilla; by comparison, Chancery's honeysuckle soap smelled of cheap chemicals. Her deep brown eyes, candied rose petal lips, and complexion of smooth, dark, rich honey were so perfectly beautiful Chancery's gut twisted in a tight knot of hopeless inadequacy.

Worse, behind Kay was a man. A *people*. Hedron would be so angry.

Sick anxiety clogged Chancery's throat.

"My god, you've gotten thin." Kay pulled off her hat, hair falling in glossy waves. "Hi, Skook. Remember me?"

He growled, hackles raised.

"Evidently not. Oh, Chance. It's so good to see you."

Kay embraced her. She returned it, stiffly, not ready for the intimacy but not wanting to offend. She could smell the man. Bacon, baked beans, and black pudding. All Oilers were the same; she couldn't tell them apart.

Except Kay.

"What's this?" Kay plucked the knife from her hand. Chancery couldn't reply, but her fingers ached to snatch it back. Kay put the knife on the table.

"It's all right, Rob. Chance's shy," Kay said over her shoulder. "You must know Rob, Chance. He told me your sausages are the best." She paused, her face an undecipherable combination of smile curves and frown lines. "I'll have to see more of you or one day you'll forget me, too. Rob, would you mind helping me with my stuff? I brought coffee and I'd better get it before Chance makes me some unspeakable concoction from twigs and rabbit droppings."

"I said I'd drop you off, that's all. I thought this place was close to the beach." Rob's gravelly voice made the words clipped and fierce.

"We're only a mile inland. You can practically smell the sea," Kay told him in a harsh whisper. "Think of Sara. She's your *niece*. You've got plenty of time. Man up."

Kay turned back, expression tight and stiff. "This won't take long," she said.

They went out again. Chancery stood by the stove, shaking. She tried to calm herself by listing all the recipes she knew for raspberries. Skook growled and she shushed him.

They fetched five boxes, piling them on the floor. Kay took Rob outside and there was muffled conversation, then the jeep left with a throaty gurgle. Chancery stared at the pyramid of cardboard invading her space.

When Kay returned, she took off her jacket and her boots, dumping them on the floor by the sink instead of putting them where they were supposed to go.

"Right!" She grabbed the knife and plunged it through the tape sealing the first box. Chancery swallowed her instinctive protest. Skook pressed against her.

Kay rummaged and made piles of bubble wrap. "Teabags," she said, brandishing a box. "Coffee. Chocolate. Ammunition and clothes... Must be in another box. Preserved lemons, hickory chips, almond flour, parmesan, canned cherries, olive oil, dried pasta—"

Chancery's legs folded under her. The cold seeped into her buttocks, grocery items and packaging accumulating around her, long-lost scents worming into her head. She rocked, clutching herself so she wouldn't dissolve into the strangeness.

"Oh god. I'm sorry." Kay put the jar she was holding back in the box. "You're getting worse. You shouldn't be out here alone." She kept her voice soft, glancing at the dog. "I'll tidy this up and we can go through and have a drink, like normal people."

Kay's 'tidying' comprised throwing everything back in the box and kicking the bubble wrap under the table. She dumped the knife in the sink and grabbed a bottle of French wine with one hand and Chancery with the other. "Come on."

"They caught a few two weeks ago." Kay had drunk half the bottle. Chancery had barely touched her glass. Skook was asleep on the hearthrug. "Took them to Porton Down. Everyone thought they'd be dead by now. No one knows why they're not. I heard one of them was pregnant. They must be breeding. Can you imagine? They say the further inland you go the less time it takes before you Walk, no matter how careful you are. It's why the scientists got infected, despite all the precautions. Even the ones who didn't go near the Walkers."

That's what *people* called Hedron's people. To Chancery they were all just different sorts of people. She had to avoid them unless someone was around to look after her. Her mum, then Annabel, now Hedron.

"Oh," Chancery said.

"I heard that's why they went into the sea at first. To get away from it. Now the only one who can stay here is you. It's so sad."

That was the way Chancery and Hedron liked it. "Are you hungry?"

There was a pause. "I could eat."

Kay sat at the kitchen table while Chancery finished and plated up. Her unbroken attention made Chancery's hands tremble as she positioned vegetables in a delicate garden salad and finished with a warm dressing of rosehip vinegar and hazelnut oil. She put the plate in front of Kay and poured her a glass of oak leaf wine. Kay speared a carrot and sucked it off her fork with a loud slurp that made Chancery flinch.

"How do you make a carrot taste so good?" she asked.

Chancery served rabbit loin braised in a broth of dried leaves and mushrooms, accompanied by its own sautéed, sliced heart, and roasted venison marrow on a bed of succulent moss. Kay went into raptures over the loin and the heart, slurping and sucking on every piece, but didn't touch the rest.

"I get paid a lot—and I mean *a lot*—and I couldn't afford to eat somewhere serving food like this," she said.

For dessert, Chancery offered a honeyed apple tart with damson liqueur.

"You're too talented to waste out here," Kay said. "Chance—"
She hesitated. "We're closing the depot. The profit margins are thin and the company's worried." Her fingers alternated like legs on the tabletop.

"No Oiler has walked recently." Hedron would have mentioned it.

"I want you to come home with me. Please. There might not be a next time."

Chancery cleared the table.

"Talk to me," Kay said.

"I need to get the dishes done."

"Leave those. They're not important."

This was clearly wrong. Chancery ignored it.

"Dammit, Chance!" Kay's outburst shocked Chancery into tears, and she dropped the glass she was holding. It shattered. "When we met, you were about ten kilos heavier and I could talk to you. You didn't make much sense, but you'd talk. You're eating plants and twigs. You look like you'd snap in a breeze. You reacted to Rob like a child reacts to a stranger, and I can barely get a word out of you. You're only twenty-five. You're wasting away."

Her chair scraped, grating on Chancery's spine, and a moment later Chancery recoiled at the touch of hands on her shoulders.

"I don't want to upset you, but you can't stay here by yourself."

"I'm not by myself." She had to force the words out between choked sobs.

"Skook's a dog. You need someone to take care of you. You need people."

"I don't! I've got Hedron."

Kay's hands stiffened. "Hedron? Oh, Chance. He's not real."

Fresh tears stung Chancery's eyes. Her gut burned and her skin turned cold as fresh fish. "You said he was as real as anything."

She'd fought so long with Hedron, pleading to be allowed to tell Kay about him, so she would understand why it was safe to visit. Kay was the closest thing to Annabel Chancery had found.

"Real to you. He helped you cope with being the only survivor. But when they close the depot you'll be alone out here."

Broken glass glittered in the sink and found its way into Chancery's heart. "I need to get the dishes done."

Kay blew a sigh, then patted Chancery's shoulders, making her shudder. "We'll talk again tomorrow. I'm really tired. I'm going to bed."

"Your room's freshly made," Chancery said, and wondered if there was a way to make the last ten minutes not have happened.

❤

Chancery was woken by the door opening. The room was black, save for the bright rectangle of moonlight on the window frame. She listened so hard the soft pad of footsteps stroked her eardrums.

The bed heaved when Kay climbed under the duvet. She slid her hand around Chancery's waist, then up to nestle between her breasts. Lips pressed against her spine, pliant and moist, a patch of heat that blew cold when the kiss moved on. Chancery felt herself flush warm and tingly, even as her skin prickled in the draught. She tangled her fingers around Kay's hand and brought it to her lips so she could kiss her fingertips.

She breathed deep, and Kay's scent was thick and dense. She kissed Kay's palm, pushing her tongue against it to taste her skin.

Kay's breathing slowed and her arm became slack. Chancery kissed her hand once more, then put it back against her chest, holding it tight.

She slid out of bed quietly, so as not to wake Kay. It was early, still dark. She had chores to do.

"Why do you think she brought all this if she wants you to go with her?" Hedron asked when she entered the kitchen. He was hunched over the pile, all elbows and knees and furious angles. Chancery gaped at him. She had never seen his hat so filthy. Looking at it made her bones quiver and burn. It made her want to run.

"You need to sort your hat, Hedron."

"Answer the question."

Chancery shrugged. "I don't know."

"To show you what you're missing." He jabbed an accusing finger at the pile. "Olive oil and Belgian chocolate. Saffron, Chancery. She doesn't think lichen and leaf broth can compete with white truffle and cinnamon."

Chancery cracked the lid on a pot of *pimenton dulce* and sniffed. The heady aroma's physical presence conjured a forgotten happy memory: Annabel making a mess of spaghetti carbonara with chorizo in their tiny kitchen, laughing as the sun turned her hair to spun gold.

No one since Annabel had kissed her until Kay did.

Chancery hugged herself, remembering the feel of someone else's skin.

"You and Skook could come, too."

"You know what would happen." He held out his arms like a scarecrow and pirouetted. "All those people. This is our home and you belong here, with us, where we can keep you safe. She doesn't love you like we do."

All those *people*. How many more would walk if she did?

Part of her wanted to. Part of her wanted to because they all would.

❖

"You shouldn't have bothered putting the stuff away," Kay said around a mouthful of toast piled with fish and egg. She poured more coffee and tapped her satellite phone. "They've moved the departure date. I have to take you back tomorrow."

"I can't."

"What?"

"All those people. I can't."

Kay rummaged in her bag. "I have something for you." She produced an envelope. Chancery took it and read the letter inside. "It's an offer of a place in the kitchen at the Sanctuary in Bergen," she said, as if Chancery were too stupid and damaged to understand it. "It's an amazing opportunity." Chancery felt faint. The restaurant's recipe book was one of her favourites. "You'd have to go through quarantine, but that only takes a week. I know you're scared of being amongst people again, but you'd adapt. I think you'd blossom."

Outside, Hedron was talking to the chickens. The volcano smouldering on his head made Chancery nauseous, itchy, and restless. She shivered.

"I belong here," she whispered.

"Don't you get it, Chance? Do you know how selfish you're being?"

Skook ambled over. She rubbed his ears and he licked her arm.

"You've been out here for five years and you haven't Walked. You're the only one. You could help people come back."

Chancery put her arms around Skook's neck and pressed her face against him, her chest tight and painful. There was a long silence.

"Do you understand me?"

"Yes." Skook's fur grew damp under her cheek.

An engine rumbled into the yard and brakes squealed painfully.

"I have to go to work. I'll leave you to think about it. Please. All those people need you. *I* need you."

Kay jammed her feet into her boots, right there at the table, and left.

There were a lot more of Hedron's people around that day than usual, wandering like ghosts in the Haar. Mindful of Hedron's caution, Chancery didn't stray far from the house. Even so, she nearly ran into one, coming close enough for her to see the oozing cracks in his blackened lips and smell his off-sweet, cheese and pear-drops scent. He reached for her, eyes glistening in a face scalloped by emaciation and scaly with flaking skin, his hands shiny and dried to red, worse than her own. His song filled her head with his aching desire to hold and be held, but he didn't touch her. She wondered if he'd been told not to.

She wondered if he'd ever not been people.

At lunchtime, the temperature dropped and the sky darkened. She went out, opened the door to the barn, and put out leftover rabbit, venison, cheese, and bread.

"It's going to snow," Hedron said. She could barely see him in the gloom.

"I know." She pulled her jacket tighter, shaking. Her bones itched, hot and cold at the same time.

"This looks good."

"There are a lot of them about today."

"You're safe enough. I'm not far. You should go inside, though. You're cold."

"I'm going. I don't feel too good. What about you?"

"I've got things to do. But Chancery?" He waited until she was looking right at him. "Don't worry. Okay? No matter what happens. I'll be close."

"Okay."

She headed back to the house. When she reached the tiny road between the house and the farm she looked back and stuffed her knuckles in her mouth at the sight of him. His head was hidden beneath a seething, roiling mass of grey like storm clouds made of corpse skin. Her marrow fizzed and her skin prickled and stung. Her eyes smarted as if she were chopping onions.

"Go inside," he called, and his voice was sterner than she had ever heard it. It frightened and reassured her, both at the same time.

The snow came, fat flakes drifting until the wind picked up and sent wild flurries careening through the sky. Chancery settled down by the range, listing her supplies and flicking through recipe books. She wanted to be overflowing with so many ideas she didn't know what to try first. The ideas were there, spinning and whirling like the snow, but she couldn't tame them because Kay's scalding anger and betrayal kept forcing their way to the front of her thoughts.

Kay didn't believe in Hedron; hadn't asked why Chancery was so thin when she cooked so much. How could Chancery convince her? *Hedron looks after me. He loves me. He looks after you, too, when you visit, because I asked him to.*

That would just make Kay angry again. She should have asked Hedron what to say.

When did Kay start turning into *people?*

She was still worrying at it when an engine coughed, popping in her chest. Flustered, she tried to focus on making some dinner because it was that or run away and hide. She'd got as far as jointing the pheasant when Skook began barking out in the yard. She went to the door. He was bouncing around in the headlights, saliva flying from his teeth.

"Come!"

With a shake of his head, he ran over and pushed her back inside. She closed the door. He stood on his hind paws at the sink to stare out the window.

"Chance? It's freezing!"

"Skook, sit." He lowered his hindquarters until they barely touched the floor, growling. "Okay."

Kay came in, stamping to get the snow off. "My god, that weather. Did you know there are Walkers out there?"

"Where else would they be?"

"This many, though?"

Chancery shrugged.

"Hi, Skook." Kay reached to pet him and he snapped at her, teeth missing her hand by a careful inch. "If he's aggressive like that back home, they'll have him destroyed."

Chancery's fingers tightened around his scruff.

"I'm sure he'll be all right," Kay said, then, "We have to leave tonight."

Chancery shook her head. She had no idea what to say other than,

"I can't."

"Chance, Rob Walked. You have to come."

Hedron hadn't said anything about that.

"I can't." It was hopelessly inadequate.

Kay was silent for a moment. There were no lines or curves on her face. "Fine. It's okay. Really. I just need to get something from the jeep."

An icy gust barrelled into the kitchen when Kay went out. Chancery rubbed Skook's ears, tense.

The door opened again, snow shredding the air. Skook barked, deep and angry, and there was a tremendous crack. In the confines of the kitchen, the gunshot was deafening, stunning, a sledgehammer to the head. Chancery's ears sang against silencing numbness as she stared at Skook lying on the floor with metallic crimson matting his fur.

Someone grabbed her. She heard hollow burbling, water gurgling in distant pipes.

She was hoisted into the air. She screamed. She kicked. She pummelled with her fists and when someone tried to pin her she scratched and bit. She was released and tried to run but was grabbed again and bundled to the floor. Sharp pain lanced through her leg and she cried out. Someone knelt on her shins and someone else held her hands way above her head, making her shoulders hurt. The sound of sticky tearing preceded constriction around her wrists and ankles. Fire licked her bones.

Something like a wasp sting jabbed into her arm, then she was drowning in liquid dark, Hedron's name tangled around her tongue.

Chancery was sick. It wasn't helped by the sinuous rise and fall of the boat underneath her. She assumed it was a boat—it smelled like one.

"I'm sorry."

Chancery turned towards the wall, not wanting to see her.

"The world needs you. It's selfish to stay where you were."

Chancery's bones were baking. It wouldn't be long now. There had been no sign of Hedron since she woke up.

"I'm sorry about Skook, I really am."

She didn't sound sorry, but Chancery didn't know what sorry sounded like. Never had.

"We'll reach Zeebrugge in a couple of days. There's a team waiting to examine you. They're not going to hurt you. They just want to take a few samples, keep you in for a few days."

"They'll kill me," Chancery said.

"Don't be silly. They just want you to help them find a way to fight the disease, that's all." She paused, then said, "Try and get some rest. Shall I bring you something to eat?" She must have realised the offer was insulting. "No. All right then."

Chancery pulled the thin blanket to her chest and squeezed it between her fingers so tightly the tendons ached. Nerves fired randomly in her legs, making her knees jerk and twitch.

Not long now.

"I did this for my daughter. Sara. She's very ill. The medical bills—" A broken, halting sob. "A cure for the Walk is worth a lot of money. I took the job for the life insurance, the Walk policy, but after I met you I couldn't... I hope one day you'll understand."

The door shut. Chancery tried to go back to sleep, knowing this wasn't a nightmare, hoping it was. A minute passed, two, and then a sound that had been familiar until five years ago: the heavy, regular, fast thump of a helicopter.

She scrambled out of bed, fell on the floor. Her right leg wouldn't support her weight. She hobbled to the door. It was locked. There was no window.

"Hedron," she whispered. "Where are you? You said it'd be okay."

She sat in the corner, on the floor, waiting, fidgeting, rocking, burning up inside. The hands of the clock, high on the wall, swung from nine-twenty to almost ten, then voices murmured on the other side of the door. The lock clunked and a figure entered the room. It was covered in blue material, and had a square of clear plastic over its face. Another two figures, similarly clad, remained outside in the corridor.

Chancery stared. She couldn't breathe.

"Don't be afraid." His voice, thickly accented, was muffled. "My name is Doctor Marcello Martino. I need to take a blood sample, just to be sure everything is A-OK, yes? Miss Korsten tells me you survived five years without Walking. You are a very special young lady, and we will take very good care of you."

He carried a kidney dish. A blood collection kit, five tubes and a needle, rolled around in it.

She squealed.

Then she saw Hedron. He winked at her. "Don't worry," he said. "List all the things you can do with apples."

People wearing crew uniforms grabbed the two figures in the corridor. They ripped the hoods off the suits as the men inside screamed. Martino turned to see what the commotion was and someone ripped his suit, too.

Hedron bared his teeth and his eyes spat lightning. He removed his hat. It was a dark, irregular ball made of dust, cobwebs, lint, stray hair, soil, dirt, skin flakes, fish scales, leaf litter, and fly shit. It oozed hunger. His hair sprang up in a thick, woolly mass of green and white, rippling like an anemone covered in cobwebs.

He clapped his hands against his hat.

Dust exploded.

Chancery's eyes streamed, nausea making her stiff. Vertigo gnawed at her temples. Her marrow was on fire, her heart pounding so hard her ribcage shook. The doctor and his men doubled over, pink-tinged vomit splattering on the floor and filling the room with a sharp, bilious stench. Hedron grasped his hat in both hands and squeezed, wringing it like a dishcloth.

"Hedron—"

"It's okay. Stay there. Close your eyes."

"I don't feel well."

"I know. Don't worry. Do as I say."

She could not disobey that voice. She wrapped her arms over her head, quaking with fever. Minutes stretched the shivers into spasms. Screams echoed from the corridor, punctuated by dull slaps, wet meaty thuds, and occasional gunshots.

When everything fell silent, Hedron came and sat beside her. His hat was back on his head and it was spotless.

"It's okay," he said.

"I'm sick." Her teeth chattered.

"I know."

"Am I going to walk?"

He curled down to kiss her head. His voice surged inside her, a song without melody. "Ssh. Don't worry. I'm here. You're safe. Tell me all the recipes you know for liver."

Hours later, Hedron helped her limp onto the deck of the platform supply vessel, his hat sooty. The sky was darkening, snow drifting like ash. The control house sat five floors above the bow, bristling with antennae and radar arrays. The helicopter perched at the stern of the long, flat cargo deck, where the crew meandered in Brownian motion. They were a mile offshore. Black smoke from the harbour curled upwards against flat, grey clouds. The sea rolled in a smooth, glassy swell the colour of an approaching storm.

"What happened to Kay?" she asked.

Hedron pointed to one of the people on the deck. Chancery supposed she ought to feel sad.

But then, Kay *had* spoiled things. Just like Hedron said she would.

"Do you know how to drive a boat?"

He indicated the crew. "They do."

Chancery nodded. "I'm going to be okay amn't I, Hedron?"

"Of course," he said. "You've got me. I'd do anything to keep you safe." He gazed towards the horizon, beyond the foggy swirls of Haar, and showed his teeth. "Anything."

AFTERWORD

Jason Sizemore

Apex Magazine, Editor-in-Chief

BUILDING ANY "BEST OF" ANTHOLOGY is always a dicey proposition. Critical analysis of any literary endeavor is so subjective as to make the phrase "Best of" meaningless. Therefore, a majority of this collection leans on the selections of that most fantastic and awesome of creatures: our readers.

As a whole, I think our readers did a fine job. Lesley Conner and I supplemented your literary experience with pieces we feel go far in defining the Apex brand of fiction as we see it: strange, beautiful, shocking, surreal.

I consider being the editor-in-chief of *Apex Magazine* one of the greatest jobs in the world. Genre fiction is both a telescope to the future and a microscope of our past. In general, reading is thought to make a person smarter. With science fiction, fantasy, and horror, you step into worlds filled with jackalope wives, people changed into chocolate, and floating masses of intelligent toys in our oceans. You confront your fears of the multo and an apocalypse filled with advertising bots. Reading genre fiction, you discover that the real world can be both a much worse and much better place. Thanks to *Apex Magazine*, I am now a pessimist *and* an optimist.

As the book comes to a close, I hope you'll become a permanent reader of *Apex Magazine.* You've experienced the tip of the iceberg. You've sipped a spoonful of a delicious stew. Every month we publish new content online at Apex-Magazine.com. Go there. Read. Enjoy.

December 1st, 2015
Lexington, Kentucky

Acknowledgements

JASON SIZEMORE

There's this perception that anyone can build a website, throw up a story or two, and call themselves a zine. Certainly, there's some truth to it. But if you want to do it right, it takes a small army of editors, designers, website developers, and one stubborn publisher to bring it all together. *Apex Magazine* is no exception.

Over the years, I've had a lot of help. I'm grateful for every person who has gifted Apex with their time and skills. Unfortunately, that list would compromise several pages. For brevity's sake, I will acknowledge the most current incarnation of the *Apex Magazine* production army.

I wish to thank my two generals: Lesley Conner (managing editor) and Bianca Spriggs (poetry editor). I also want to acknowledge the contributions of Lisa Shininger (podcast producer), Greg Fazekas (web admin), and Hannah Ruth Krieger (associate editor). Andrea Johnson and Russell Dickerson are regular contributors via their insightful interviews.

And finally, our hardworking slush team deserves accolades. Thank you to Andrea Johnson, Carolyn Charron, Rebecca Hurley, Beth Sutherland, Rodney Carlstrom, Dawn Griffin, Eileen Maksym, Gabrielle Harbowy, Jessica Nelson, Joshua P'ng, Joshua Colwell, Kendall Pletcher, Lindsay Anderson, Lia Mitchell, Lisa Cox, Lisa Bolekaja, Mike Baldwin, Reese Menezes, Amanda Parker, Beverly McPherson, Eliyanna Kaiser, Kelle Dhein, Lauren Smith, Tacoma Tomilson, Zachary Tringali, and Tae Thompson.

LESLEY CONNER

I didn't grow up dreaming of one day being an editor. It wasn't a career that was anywhere near my radar, because honestly what an editor actually did and how a person became one was a mystery wrapped in assumptions tied up with misconceptions, and none of them fit with what I wanted for my life. That all changed when I offered to help Jason Sizemore out with Apex. What started as "helping out" five to ten hours a week has transformed into what I hope will be my career for the rest of my life.

I'd like to thank Jason for taking a chance on me. When I started, I had no idea what I was getting into or what I was doing. He has been endlessly patient, answering endless questions, and in the end I think we've become one hell of a good team.

I'd also like to thank the rest of the Apex Magazine team: our slush readers, Andrea Johnson, Russell Dickerson, Bianca Spriggs, Hannah Ruth Krieger, and Steph Jacob. Despite all of my emails and spreadsheets, they remain enthusiastic and pumped for each new issue of the magazine. It is amazing to work with a group of individuals who are just as excited as I am to be creating Apex Magazine every month.

And finally, I want to acknowledge our authors. Every month I have to swallow back the squeeing fangirl inside of me and be professional in my role as managing editor, so I'm going to let it out here:

Holy mother of all things bookish and wordy! Look at the names in the table of contents!! Can you even believe that I get to work with amazing writers just like this EVERY SINGLE DAY and I get to call it my job?!?! So cool!

swoons in overflowing happiness

Contributor Bios

An Australian living in Seattle, **LIZ ARGALL** plays roller derby with the Rat City Rollergirls, writes, draws comics, and spends a lot of time with dirt under her fingernails. Her work can be found in places like *Apex Magazine*, *Strange Horizons*, and *This is How You Die: Stories of the Inscrutable, Infallible, Inescapable Machine of Death*. She recently cracked the Escape Artists Trifecta: audio versions of her stories in *Pseudopod*, *Podcastle*, and *Escape Pod*. Liz writes love letters, songs, and poems to inanimate objects and two of her short stories have become plays that are regularly performed. She creates the webcomic *Things Without Arms and Without Legs* and her website is lizargall.com.

PETER M. BALL is the author of the novellas *Horn*, *Bleed*, and The Flotsam trilogy from Apocalypse Ink. His short stories have been published in *Apex Magazine*, *Shimmer*, and *Daily Science Fiction*. He convenes the biennial GenreCon writing conference in Brisbane, Australia. Find him online at www.petermball.com and @petermball.

KATHARINE E.K. DUCKETT is a writer living in Brooklyn who collects canes, bookmarks, and unusual earrings. Her fiction has appeared in *Apex*, *Interzone*, and *Wilde Stories 2015: The Year's Best Gay Speculative Fiction*, and her nonfiction has appeared on *The Toast* and *Tor.com*. In her day job, she talks about how much she loves the novellas and novels of Tor.com Publishing.

AMAL EL-MOHTAR is an author, editor, and critic: her short fiction has received the Locus Award and been nominated for the Nebula Award, while her poetry has won the Rhysling Award three times. She is the author of *The Honey Month*, a collection of poetry and prose written to the taste of twenty-eight different kinds of honey, and her fiction has appeared most recently in *Lightspeed*, *Strange Horizons*, and *Uncanny*

Magazine. She contributes reviews to NPR Books and the LA Times; edits *Goblin Fruit*, a quarterly journal of fantastical poetry; is a founding member of the Banjo Apocalypse Crinoline Troubadours, a contributor to *Down and Safe: A Blake's 7 Podcast*, and divides her time and heart between Ottawa and Glasgow. Find her online at amalelmohtar.com and on Twitter @tithenai.

CHIKODILI EMELUMADU is a Nigerian writer whose corporeal self resides in London. Her work can be found in *Eclectica, Luna Station Quarterly, Omenana, One Throne,* and *Sub-q* magazines, and is forthcoming in *African Monsters,* an anthology published by Fox Spirit Books. "Candy Girl" was nominated for the 2014 Shirley Jackson award. She is working on her first novel which is determined to kill her.

SAM FLEMING'S work has appeared in *Black Static, Fish* from Dagan Books, and *Looking Landwards* from NewCon Press. She lives in northeast Scotland with an artistic spouse and the correct number of bicycles, that being both entirely too many and not quite enough. Find her at ravenbait.com.

KEFFY R. M. KEHRLI is a science fiction and fantasy writer currently living on Long Island in New York. When he's not writing, he's busy working on his PhD, doing science, or editing *GlitterShip* (www.glittership.com). His own fiction has previously appeared in publications such as *Uncanny Magazine, Apex Magazine, Lightspeed Magazine,* and *Clockwork Phoenix 5,* among others.

New York Times and USA Today bestselling author **ALETHEA KONTIS** is a princess, a fairy godmother, and a geek. She's known for screwing up the alphabet, scolding vampire hunters, and ranting about fairy tales on YouTube. Her published works include: *The Wonderland Alphabet* (with Janet K. Lee), *Diary of a Mad Scientist Garden Gnome* (with Janet K. Lee), the AlphaOops series (with Bob Kolar), the Books of Arilland fairy tale series, and *The Dark-Hunter Companion* (with Sherrilyn Kenyon). Her short fiction, essays, and poetry have appeared in a myriad of anthologies and magazines. You can find Princess Alethea on all the social media and at her website: www.aletheakontis.com.

RICH LARSON was born in West Africa, has studied in Rhode Island, and worked in Spain, and at 23 now writes from Edmonton, Alberta. His short work has been nominated for the Theodore Sturgeon and appears in multiple Year's Best anthologies, as well as in magazines such as *Asimov's*, *Analog*, *Clarkesworld*, *F&SF*, *Interzone*, *Strange Horizons*, *Lightspeed*, and *Apex*. Find him at richwlarson.tumblr.com.

KEN LIU (http://kenliu.name) is an author and translator of speculative fiction, as well as a lawyer and programmer. A winner of the Nebula, Hugo, and World Fantasy Awards, he has been published in *The Magazine of Fantasy & Science Fiction*, *Asimov's*, *Analog*, *Clarkesworld*, *Lightspeed*, and *Strange Horizons*, among other places. He also translated the Hugo-winning novel, *The Three-Body Problem*, by Liu Cixin, which is the first translated novel to win that award. Ken's debut novel, *The Grace of Kings*, the first in a silkpunk epic fantasy series, was published by Saga Press in April 2015. Saga will also publish a collection of his short stories, *The Paper Menagerie and Other Stories*, in March 2016. He lives with his family near Boston, Massachusetts.

SAMUEL MARZIOLI was born and raised and that's all you need to know about that. His work has appeared or is forthcoming in various publications, including *Intergalactic Medicine Show*, *Shock Totem*, *Urban Fantasy Magazine*, *Darkfuse #2* (2014), and *Selfies From the End of the World* (2015). For more information about his work, please visit his website at marzioli.blogspot.com.

RUSSELL NICHOLS is a speculative fiction writer and endangered journalist. He writes about race, class, and other human myths. Raised in Richmond, CA, he now lives on the road, out of a backpack with his fairy tale freak of a wife (current location: Mexico). Look for him at russellnichols.com.

SARAH PINSKER is the author of the novelette "In Joy, Knowing the Abyss Behind," winner of the 2014 Sturgeon Award and 2013 Nebula Award finalist and "A Stretch of Highway Two Lanes Wide," 2014 Nebula Award finalist. Her fiction has appeared in *Asimov's*, *Strange Horizons*, *Fantasy & Science Fiction*, *Uncanny*, *Apex*, and *Lightspeed*, and in anthologies including *Long Hidden* and *Accessing the Future*. She is also a singer/songwriter and toured nationally behind three albums on various independent labels. A fourth is forthcoming. She lives with her wife and dog in Baltimore, Maryland.

Find her online at sarahpinsker.com and on Twitter @sarahpinsker.

LETTIE PRELL likes to explore the edge where humans and their technology are increasingly merging. Her science fiction stories have appeared in *Analog Science Fiction and Fact*, *Apex Magazine*, and its *Book of Apex* anthology, and elsewhere. Her work has also been featured on the *StarShipSofa* podcast. She is an active member of SFWA.

RACHEL SWIRSKY holds an MFA in fiction from the Iowa Writers Workshop, and is a graduate of Clarion West. Her short fiction has been nominated for the Hugo, the Locus, the World Fantasy, and the Sturgeon Awards. She's twice won the Nebula Award, including in 2013 for the short story included in this volume. Her second collection, *How the World Became Quiet*, is available from Subterranean Press.

IAN TREGILLIS is the son of a bearded mountebank and a discredited tarot card reader. He is the author of the Milkweed Triptych (*Bitter Seeds*, *The Coldest War*, and *Necessary Evil*), *Something More Than Night*, and the Alchemy Wars trilogy (*The Mechanical*, *The Rising*). In addition to *Apex Magazine*, his short fiction has appeared in venues including *Tor.com*, *Fantasy and Science Fiction*, and *Popular Science*. He lives in New Mexico, where he consorts with writers, scientists, and other disreputable types.

BRIAN TRENT'S science-fiction and dark fantasy appears in numerous publications, including *Analog*, *Fantasy & Science Fiction*, *Nature*, *Galaxy's Edge*, *COSMOS*, *Escape Pod*, *Pseudopod*, *AE*, *Daily Science Fiction*, *The Mammoth Book of Dieselpunk*, and several Year's Best anthologies. His story "A Matter of Shapespace" was voted by *Apex Magazine* readers as their 2013 Story of the Year, and he is a 2013 winner in the Writers of the Future contest. Trent lives in New England, where in addition to screenwriting, he divides his time between hiking, traveling, and researching. His website is www.briantrent.com.

GENEVIEVE VALENTINE is an author and critic. Her first novel, *Mechanique: A Tale of the Circus Tresaulti*, won the 2012 Crawford Award; her second, *The Girls at the Kingfisher Club*, was an NPR, Washington Post, and Chicago Tribune best book of the year. Her short fiction has appeared at *Tor.com, Clarkesworld, the Journal of Mythic Arts, New Haven Review*, and others; her nonfiction and criticism has appeared at *The Dissolve, The AV Club, LA Review of Books*, and the *New York Times*.

URSULA VERNON is the author of the Hugo-award winning comic *Digger*, as well as multiple children's book series. She writes for adults under the name T. Kingfisher. Her work has won the Nebula, Mythopoeic, Cóyotl, and WSFA Awards. She lives in North Carolina. You can find more of her short stories and novels at Tkingfisher.com.

MARIE VIBBERT is an IT professional from Cleveland, Ohio. She is a member of the Cleveland science fiction writing workshop, The Cajun Sushi Hamsters, attended Clarion in 2013, and joined SFWA in 2014. She has ridden 16% of the roller coasters in the United States and played for the Cleveland Fusion women's tackle football team.

Adrian Borda currently resides in Romania, and has had gallery showings in various places across Europe. Many of his pieces are also in personal collections, and he offers other pieces and prints on his websites. Find more of his wonderfully surreal pieces on his DeviantArt page at borda.deviantart.com, and on his website at www.adrianborda.com.

Lesley Conner is a writer/editor, managing editor of Apex Publications and *Apex Magazine*, and a Girl Scout leader. When she isn't handling her editorial or Girl Scout leader responsibilities, she's researching fascinating historical figures, rare demons, and new ways to dispose of bodies, interweaving the three into strange and horrifying tales. Her short fiction can be found in *Mountain Dead, Dark Tales of Terror, A Hacked-Up Holiday Massacre*, as well as other places. Her first novel *The Weight of Chains* was published by Sinister Grin Press in September, 2015. *Best of Apex Magazine: Volume 1* marks her debut experience in anthology editing. She lives in Maryland with her husband and two daughters, and is currently working on a new novel. To find out all her secrets, you can follow her on Twitter at @LesleyConner.

Jason Sizemore is a writer/editor/publisher, owner of Apex Publications and *Apex Magazine,* and occasional software developer. He's a three-time Hugo Award nominee and one-time Stoker Award loser. His collection *Irredeemable* was published by Seventh Star Press in 2014. In 2015, Apex Book Company published *For Exposure: The Life and Times of a Small Press Publisher.* For more information, visit him on the web at jason-sizemore.com.

APEX MAGAZINE

ISSUE 79

DECEMBER 2015

WINNERS OF OUR
CHRISTMAS INVASION
FLASH FICTION CHALLENGE!

FEATURING STORIES BY
NICK MAMATAS
LAIRD BARRON
SAM FLEMING
JES RAUSCH
TROY TANG

EDITED BY JASON SIZEMORE
COVER ART BY IREK KONIOR

APEX-MAGAZINE.COM

Apex Magazine is a monthly digital e-zine of professional-level science fiction, fantasy, and horror short fiction.

Subscriptions of nicely formatted DRM-free eBook editions of the magazine are available. Alternatively, most content can be found at Apex-Magazine.com.

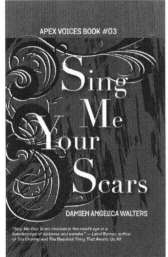

APEX PUBLICATIONS NEWSLETTER

Why sign up?

Newsletter-only promotions. Book release announcements. Event invitations. And much, much more!

If you choose to sign up for the Apex Publications newsletter, we will send you an email confirmation to insure that you in fact requested the newsletter and to avoid unwanted emails. Your email address is always kept confidential, and we will only use it to send you newsletters or special announcements. You may unsubscribe at any time, and details on how to unsubscribe are included in every newsletter email.

Visit
HTTP://WWW.APEXBOOKCOMPANY.COM/PAGES/NEWSLETTER